DEDICATION

To my readers who have given me the opportunity to live my dream.

To my wife, Linda, who reads everything I write and gives me her honest feedback, even when I don't want to hear it. Her patience as I sit before my computer, for hours on end, is nothing short of miraculous.

To my children and grandchildren, John, Michael, Kristina, Liam, Katie, and Kiera, who inspire me to look to the future.

To my parents, John and Angie who showed me the wisdom to learn from the past.

To my editor, Rick, and my critique group, Greece Writers, who worked so hard to make my books *legible*. Thank you for your tireless efforts.

To everyone who has faced life's tragedies and challenges, you are the true heroes. May we never have a time when we live without our imaginary worlds and the people who populate them. May my books give you an escape when you need it the most.

The Red Fist of Rome

Book 1 of The Red Fist Chronicles

by John Caligiuri

also by John Caligiuri:

THE RED FIST CHRONICLES

The Red Fist of Rome

Last Roman's Prayer

COCYTUS SERIES

Planet of the Damned

Sanctuary in Hell

Deal with the Devil

Face One's Demons

NOVAROMA SERIES

Perdition's Angel

Ancient Enemies (coming soon)

COPYRIGHT PAGE

This is a work of fiction. The characters and events portrayed in this novel are fictitious. Any similarity to individuals living or dead is unintended by the author.

ISBN: 9780991558216 (PRINT)

ISBN: 9780991558223 (EBOOK)

PROLOGUE

Greetings, Reader:

My name is Mara. I am here to recount the events of another place and time. My alternate world is not a fanciful one; it is very akin to your own. But for a twist of a knife and a simple misstep, the chronicles of our worlds could be the same. In this story, the history you know took a turn and followed a different path into their future.

The people you will meet in the following chapters did not choose to enter their dire circumstances, but they resolved not to cower from them.

An honor-bound dreamer, Lucius Bernius, whose misfortunes propel him forward in life will be your guide. Immerse yourself in this watershed era, altered as it may be from the past you've been taught.

CHAPTER I

HOMECOMING

The sun blazed without mercy. Lucius felt like he was being cooked alive in his plumed armor. The legionaries marching behind him maintained their pace, so with sheer force of will, he held his hand back from wiping the sweat on his brow.

It wouldn't be right to show discomfort in front of them. *They're just as hot and maybe more tired than I am from having to lug all of their own equipment. No wonder the Germanic tribes call us mules.*

Even in the year 451, the Roman army still trusted their own legs for transportation and combat. However, near as Lucius had seen, every Gaul and German who could swing a sword rode horseback. He grimaced and glared up at the sun, then at his fellow soldiers. *Sometimes that's not such a bad idea.*

Lucius Bernius looked the part of the ideal Roman noble: Tall for a provincial Italian with thick, wavy jet-black hair cropped short in the traditional Roman military style. He bore a crooked nose from a youthful brawl and a hard, lean body. Although he hailed from a family of noble patricians, they were dirt poor. Despite this, Lucius had achieved the rank of tribune without mentors or powerful connections. He did well in his lessons but always felt like a dullard next to his best friend, Marcus, who trudged along at his side.

Marcus stood at a similar height, but the resemblance ended there. He'd a thin, boyish face and lank brown hair that always rested in as much disarray as his uniform. Where Lucius was a tribune for the new infantry legion, Marcus held a similar rank with the engineer auxiliaries.

Lucius grimaced again as he twisted to study the troops following him. The rank of tribune officially put the men in this legion's cohort under his command although for all practical purposes, most ignored the fact. He squared his shoulders and eyed the aged legate on horseback, The leader of the column, Legate Albinus, was an old veteran at the end of his career. Any orders he wanted to convey, he gave to the centurions, an equally seasoned crew who had served with the legate for many campaigns.

The legionaries themselves actually had more in common with the two young tribunes than the other officers as they were all in their first year of military service. When one of the tribunes gave a command, the soldiers obeyed. When the centurions gave a similar order, they jumped to comply.

Lucius shrugged. The column was not yet a real legion, so how could one expect anything else? All of them marched to Gaul as replacement forces to be integrated into the legions already stationed there.

The legate and centurions were *evocati*, old veterans who had stayed on beyond the normal legion retirement age to serve as nursemaids, herding the recruits to their assignments.

Lucius smiled as he recalled enrolling in the military on the same day as Marcus just a year earlier. He'd joined with the fanciful notion of becoming an invincible warrior like the Roman conquerors of legend. Being the son of patrician nobility didn't dissuade his instructors from disabusing him of those notions. They told Lucius he would start in the infantry, and his job was to keep his men alive. As for the invincible Roman legions, Lucius learned that the largest portions of them now consisted of men recruited from the Germanic tribes. The famous Roman legions were not much more than an army of mercenaries. Oftentimes, the foreign soldiers were asked to confront their own people.

Lucius lowered his head. It's not a sustainable situation. Those warriors are learning our Roman discipline and tactics and leaving with them. It's poor strategy—they could murder us with our own tactics one day.

Shaking off the thought, Lucius turned to Marcus. "At least we'll be sleeping in our own beds tonight." The column was camping near Mediolanum, and the two young officers had been granted permission to leave for one week and visit the Bernius estate.

Marcus beamed at the thought and stared down the road at the landmarks they passed. "A few more hours and we'll be close. I hope your parents prepared a feast. After eating that swill the army calls food for the last year, I can't wait for a real meal."

Lucius laughed, recalling that Marcus never turned up his nose at the fare provided. In fact, the man always amazed him with how skinny he remained despite his eating habits.

They crested a low hill, and Lucius smiled again. A rider stood at ease by a small stream, holding the reins of two saddled horses. The man's face was too distant to recognize, but the scarlet silk cape bellowing in the gentle summer breeze meant it could only have been one person: Takumi Saegusa. Lucius poked his friend in the ribs and pointed.

Marcus replied with a teasing voice, "Thank God your father sent a servant to pick us up. I was wondering how we were going to get from the camp to your family's estate."

Lucius grinned back. "Are you going to call him that to his face?"

Marcus rolled his eyes in feigned terror. "No. I've been in the army for about a year now, and I have yet to see a swordsman come close to his skill."

The banter continued as they approached the motionless rider. Takumi sat in silence astride his mount, watching the marching army. Neither his posture nor his expression changed despite the legionaries' barbs and catcalls at him and his foreign looks.

Lucius had grown up with Takumi as a tutor and a friend and knew how to read Takumi's stony countenance. For instance, the tiny, bemused crinkling around the older man's eyes would be uproarious laughter in the expressive Romans. The hoots from the soldiers turned into silence when the two approaching tribunes bowed their heads to the man on horseback, and he returned the nod with a casual grace.

"Tribune Bernius and Tribune Carloman, congratulations. It appears military life agrees with you. Your performance at the academy brought honor to your parents."

Lucius bowed his head again. "We had a very stern task master before we left for Rome. Although I must say, the instructors were not overly pleased with the unorthodox fencing style you taught me. They spent much time on my reeducation on proper Roman fighting techniques."

Takumi snorted. "They have no vision. The style you Romans use is fine enough when you are bunched together like scales on a fish, but when you stand alone, it is far too limited. Innovate. Adapt to your opponent's weaknesses. Learn everything and use what is most effective for the situation."

A smiling Marcus stepped closer. "Always the teacher. Have you heard anything about my parents and brothers?"

Takumi nodded. "Your father has resettled on your properties along the Rhone River, near where it meets the Durance in a town called Avenio. He says they're all well. Please mount. We have a couple hours' ride ahead. Lucius, your mother is driving the servants to distraction preparing the place for your visit."

The two young men needed no more coaxing. They scrambled onto the horses, waved a quick salute to Legate Albinus, and followed their mentor across the field. The column commander shouted after them, his voice hoarse after herding children for ten days straight. "One week or you will be flogged!"

The three men rode on toward home, thoughts of his family rose. Lucius' face lost its smile. "How is Father?"

Takumi looked back with pained eyes. "He continues to weaken. I fear he will be joining his ancestors very soon. I believe he waits to see you one more time before making his final journey."

Lucius' eyes burned with tears he would not shed, and the bright sun dimmed around him. In the last few years, the Germanic raiding parties plaguing the northern Italian provinces had ruined his father's lands. Even in good times, agriculture demanded backbreaking work with thin profits, none of which helped the elder Bernius in his advanced age. The raids destroyed most everything he'd had in the end, including his health. Lucius could only imagine what occurred while he'd been away.

Takumi reached into his tunic and handed Marcus a sealed scroll. Marcus opened the letter with eagerness, but his face soon turned grim. Takumi studied Marcus' face and lowered his head. "It is not hard to surmise the contents of that message. It is the only topic discussed in the region around Mediolanum.

"I could not say more when we were near your troops, but the Visigoth tribes fleeing into Gaul carry many rumors. They claim the Huns are led by a demon named Attila, and he's driven them from their own lands. They believe Roman territory will be his next target. They say this Attila is invincible and cannot be beaten."

Marcus slipped the scroll into his saddlebag and lifted his chin. "My father says he was approached by some Gauls who aligned themselves with Attila soon after the family settled into our Avenio estate. Those men told him he must pay them for protection from the Huns, and he told them he would 'consider' their magnanimous offer." Marcus smiled at Lucius. "Their names reached the Roman provincial magistrate the next day."

The information roused Lucius from his personal concerns. "Just forty years ago, these Visigoth barbarians sacked Rome, and now they're being driven off by an even worse terror?"

Marcus gave a silent nod of affirmation. The conversation turned to discussions of local politics and the weather for the next few hours, interrupted on occasion by Marcus bringing up the affairs of Lucius' family.

* * *

Evening had fallen when they reached the iron-studded oak gate of the Bernius villa. Torches blazed along the walls to greet them. Lucius grinned when he saw his mother, Angela, and his two sisters, Julia and Octavia, waving to him from the wall.

He thought it strange that the elder of the two sisters, Julia, appeared the most excited, then realized with shock that she was no longer a child. The petite Julia was almost a twin of their mother except the former had long, raven-black hair curled about her shoulders, and the latter's was snowy white and piled in a tight weave atop of her head.

Something about Julia's demure smile caught Lucius' attention. It struck him then that, as a child, she'd harbored a crush on Marcus, and it appeared now that she was of age, those feelings hadn't dissipated. His lips tightened as his thoughts raced.

We could never work out the dowry. Our father is destitute, and the Carloman family is among the wealthiest in the empire. If the fates weren't so cruel, it would be a match I'd celebrate. Marcus is like a brother to me, and Julia has matured a great deal since her childhood.

The gate swung open, and the tribunes rode inside. Lucius had barely touched the ground when his mother and younger sisters crushed him in a group hug. His father, Verius, walked out of the house and paused with his hand on the door frame. Lucius looked up and frowned. Verius moved with a steady stride, but in the flickering torchlight, he looked so much older than when Lucius left a year earlier.

Many of the years on that careworn face slipped away as Verius broke into a broad grin, and Lucius let out the breath he'd held. They hugged. Verius' grip remained firm, despite how frail his arms now seemed.

Any lingering fears Lucius had disappeared as he joined his family in a magnificent feast. The fare was simpler than what had been served in Lucius' youth, but the roasted pigeons cooked in olive oil and garlic tasted perfect. Toasts to good health flowed with the wine, and even the stoic Takumi told jokes. Eventually, though, the conversation drifted to the country's troubled borders.

Verius swirled the wine in his cup and spoke in a bitter voice. "The Visigoths are marauding all over the northern Italian provinces. It's becoming a way of life. A cow disappears here, a sheep there."

Lucius leaned forward, frowning. "Aren't the legions doing their jobs?"

"The legions try to keep up, but they can't be everywhere at once, and the raiding parties are small." Verius slammed the cup on the low table, and wine sloshed out. "These looters grow bolder every day. I'll tell you, if it weren't for Imperator Aetius, we'd be overrun."

Lucius' eyes lit with fire and he curled his fists. "I've never met the general, but I've heard many accounts of his exploits. The Germanic tribes truly fear that man. He has never lost a battle to them."

Verius nodded and looked both young tribunes in the eye. "The sad truth is, he is alone. The fools at the imperial court in Ravenna and the worthless senators in Rome care more about their personal entertainments than the good of the empire. I fear the nation is adrift with too few looking to our welfare."

Lucius stared into his cup. "It's true. The year I've spent in Rome has been a shock. Young nobles who should be picking up the sword and shield are more interested in debauchery and feasting. The army is a path that fewer and fewer of the patricians follow."

After a few moments of tense silence, Marcus stood and grinned. "Excuse me, Lucius. If we could trap those prattling fools in a room for one of your impassioned speeches on the glory of Rome, they would fall all over themselves to reach the recruiters." He put his cup down and met Julia's eyes, and his smile turned warmer. "Now if you'll excuse me, I have more delicate topics to discuss." He stood and clasped Julia's hand. "Will you walk with me?"

Julia blushed and rose, moving to his side. "I've been waiting this entire evening for you to ask."

Verius' mood brightened as he watched Julia leave the dining room arm in arm with Marcus. With a hint of a playful smile, he piped up. "Now where is that daughter of mine getting to?"

Julia scowled at him but didn't slow her pace as she made her escape.

Once she left, Verius turned his twinkling eyes on his son. "So did you make any interesting acquaintances while in Rome?"

Lucius' face warmed. "Ah, no, Father. The girls I met there seem either too flippant or were spinning webs. I found no one I could talk to like you and Mother do."

Angela interrupted with a quiet laugh. "Now don't you worry, Lucius. That girl is out there. You'll meet her when you least expect it. You just make sure you hang onto her when you do find her."

The heat rose higher in his cheeks. "I'm going to bed now. This is my first real leave in over six months, and I intend to sleep until noon." Lucius beat a hasty retreat.

* * *

The next few days sped by, and Lucius saw very little of Marcus or Julia. On the fifth night, before the family bedded down for the night, a servant rushed in—a retired legionary named Silvio. "Tribunes, there's some savage at the gate who claims to have an important message for you from your legion."

Lucius exchanged a worried glance with Marcus. Communications delivered so late at night never boded well.

"Please admit him," Verius said in a controlled voice.

The whole family, and most of the servants, walked out to the courtyard. Takumi wore his long and short swords at his hips and preceded the family through the door. Outside, Lucius stared wide-eyed at the stranger.

When Silvio had called the man a savage, he'd only scratched the surface in describing him. In the torchlight beside a lathered horse stood a towering warrior with broad shoulders. The bare-chested man had his head shaved except for a thick mane of black hair in the middle. He wore an axe with a long handle on his back and a knife with a wide blade on his left hip. The man stood balanced and at the ready, calmly regarding the group as they approached him.

Takumi signaled the family to stay back and advanced alone. He bowed and stated in an even voice, "You have a message for the tribunes? I will take it."

"I was requested to deliver the instructions to the tribunes, and that is what I will do," came the response in precise but accented Latin.

Lucius noted Takumi's spine stiffen and stepped up himself before the war of wills could escalate any further. "I am Tribune Bernius. I will take the message."

Without shifting his eyes from the Bernius family protector, the messenger handed Lucius the scroll. "I am Satewa, a Mohawk of the Turtle Clan. I serve General Aetius as a centurion for his scouts. You are to return to your legion immediately."

Aghast, Lucius scowled. "Legate Albinus gave us a full week's leave."

Satewa's face remained impassive. "All leaves have been cancelled. It appears the Huns under Attila have invaded Gaul. The general intends to intercept them before they reach Aurelianum. You and your recruits are now legions in his Gallic army. All the other legions in Gaul are holed up in citadels or dead."

"But we're not a real legion. We're replacement troops for the frontier guards," Marcus sputtered as he approached and read the scroll.

For the first time since his arrival, Satewa smiled. "If I know my friend Flavius, you will be a real legion by the time we reach Aurelianum."

Lucius felt the wine from the evening's dinner sour in his stomach as he broke the seal and scanned the scrawled note from his legate. The written words confirmed what Satewa said, so Lucius lowered the note. "You will stay with us tonight, and we'll depart at first light." Satewa frowned, but the tribune raised his hand. "Your mount needs the rest, even if you do not. Besides, we'll make much better time in the light than stumbling around in the dark. On horseback, we won't have any trouble catching up to the column."

"I will keep an eye on this savage. He will take his repose with me," Takumi interjected, though his sharp tone sounded more like a command than an offer. He cast a steady eye at the messenger. "The accommodations are comfortable, but it is separate from the family residence. Silvio, take care of this man's horse, and have four ready to ride by morning."

"Four horses?" Lucius asked in confusion.

"Yes. I am coming with you. When you were a babe, I vowed to protect the Bernius family, and I will. If any member of this family is going to be in danger, it is you. Besides, in my travels from distant Nippon, I have never met an invincible barbarian. I would like to see what one looks like."

Lucius flinched inwardly. "Takumi, I'm not some helpless child who requires a nanny."

Takumi made a quick bow. "I have heard of this Attila. I helped you take your first steps as a baby, and I will not sit back in idle comfort when you take your first steps as a man."

Satewa nodded his head with the slightest softening of his expression and looked at Takumi, who was a full head shorter. "I think we are going to get along just fine." The giant turned and hefted his bedroll from the saddle. "You say you are from a distant land. My home is also far away. Tell me, in your travels, have you ever heard of the Mohawk people?"

Takumi tilted his head up as though pondering the question. "I do not recall ever hearing that name. I know I would have remembered seeing another such as you. I traveled here along the Silk Road, which traverses the lands of Cathay and the Mongols. I have been told there is a great land south of there called India that Alexander the Great once visited. Perhaps your people are from there."

Satewa sighed, and for a moment, the giant didn't look so large. "No. I have met Indians in Rome, but they look nothing like my people. Besides, my village, Caughnawaga, lies far to the west. These Indians you speak of come from the east. I can find no reference to my people anywhere. When you mentioned a land I'd not heard of, I had a spark of hope."

"Come, my friend, and we will share a flask of wine. I, too, will never see the land of my ancestors again. Although I love the people in this house as my family, I do long to see my homeland one more time."

The two men walked off, and everyone else headed inside. Lucius re-read the orders, trying to process it all. He was going to war. Lucius whispered a quick prayer that he would have the courage to face it.

Marcus and Julia walked away to the garden, and a small smile creased Lucius' face. His friend had his arm wrapped around her, quieting her sobs. "I'm going to bed," he declared, but no one heard him except old Silvio and the rider's lathered horse.

CHAPTER II

A JOURNEY BEGINS

The next day dawned with a pleasant, cloudless sky. Takumi and Satewa were already in the saddle, waiting. Relief washed over Lucius when he noticed that he hadn't arrived last. Marcus was nowhere in sight and neither was his family. Lucius turned a questioning eye toward Takumi.

Takumi smiled warmly. "They are conducting some business with Tribune Carloman. I expect they will all be out shortly."

A few minutes later, Lucius stared in disbelief. There, embracing, were Julia and Marcus with his parents beaming behind them. His younger sister giggled through her tears.

Marcus reluctantly released his hold on Julia and grasped Lucius' shoulders, keeping an eye on the former even as he regarded the latter. "Soon, my friend, we will be true brothers. Your parents have consented to our engagement."

Julia slid back into Marcus' arms, her eyes still damp. "Lucius, make sure nothing happens to my Marcus. Don't let those Hun butchers get anywhere near him."

Angela wept openly. "Lucius, please be careful. I've heard terrible things about these wild men. People say they worship demons and can't be killed."

Verius hugged his son with a steely grip and whispered, "Come back safely."

Lucius could find no words that would not betray his emotions, so he just hugged each of them fiercely and mounted the horse.

Before they rode off, Marcus shot a look over his shoulder, jumped from his horse, and rushed to Julia, handing her a purse. "I don't think I'll be able to return your father's horse soon, so I should buy it."

Julia wrapped her arms around him, sobbing. Marcus gave her a final reluctant hug and disengaged. "Please come back to me," she called as he swung onto his mount.

The four men took to the road as the coolness of the early morning evaporated into the steamy humidity of midsummer in the open land around Mediolanum. The time passed in short order, though.

The conversation started with what the men knew of the Huns, which was next to nothing. Satewa reported that Attila had swept aside all the Germanic tribes who opposed him, but the more ominous fact lay in how many of those tribes bent a knee to him and joined the Hun Empire. The tribunes' hearts sank at the thought of it.

Lucius felt his despondent mood fade when Satewa asked if they would like to hear about the land of his birth and his journey to Rome. After assessing the current situation, Lucius nodded. "I think it would be good to speak of other things than what lies ahead of us."

A distant look filled Satewa's eyes as he leaned back and drew in a deep breath. "The beginning of my story differs little from that of other conquered people. The village I am from was part of a people who called themselves Mohawks. When I was a young boy, my village fell victim to an attack by a war party belonging to our mortal enemies, the Algonquin. I was taken as a slave, and the next few years passed in a blurry nightmare."

Satewa's grim continence brightened. "I guess I didn't make a very good slave. The Algonquin chief who owned me gave me as a gift to the strangest man I had ever seen. He went by the name of Ingolfur and called his tribe the Vikings. His face bore an enormous beard the color of fire, but most fearsome were his eyes. They were the color of ice—devil eyes. It was the first time I had seen weapons of iron, and in the water by their village, they had long, evil dragon ships."

Marcus leaned closer with curiosity in his wide eyes. "I've never heard of such a tribe. Are they Germanic?"

Satewa rolled his shoulders. "I do not believe so. They are a young, savage race who lives in the far north. They are impressive sailors but keep themselves apart from the tribes to the south of them."

Marcus let out a low whistle. "The world is a very large place. Please go on."

Satewa closed his eyes and shuddered. "At first, I was terrified of these people and thought of them as gods, but I learned differently. They turned out to be as stupid and cruel as the Algonquians, so I would not work for them. I endured their tortures and became stronger in spirit.

"One day, a large dragon ship arrived, and Ingolfur declared that they were leaving this land. He commanded that the slaves would travel with them to a place he called Ribe for the entertainment of his king. It was a long and bitter voyage wrought with cold. I could look for miles in every direction and see nothing but water. Those with me succumbed to despair, and one at a time, they died. I resolved that I would live and view this strange new world. When we reached Ribe at last, I was the only one of my people still alive. It was then that I gave myself the name I carry now. *Satewa* means 'alone' in my tongue."

Curiosity shot through Lucius. "What happened to you when you reached that new land?"

"I was weak as a newborn from the deprivation of that long trip. My size and strange appearance impressed the Viking king. Taught to fight, I entertained my new masters by killing other slaves." Satewa snorted, clenching his fist. "None could match me. After each victory, I would stalk from the bloody ring glaring at my audience with defiance and loathing. They grew to fear me and kept me chained like a rabid animal.

"For three years, I grew in strength and skill. One day, Vandal traders arrived in port, and the Viking king thought it a good opportunity to be rid of me. He gifted me to their king, Genseric. I didn't care, for I no longer feared the Vikings."

Lucius grimaced at the mention of the Vandal King. "He's a wolf we need to beware. In one year, he snatched all of Rome's African provinces. I do not think his appetite is yet sated."

Satewa grunted, nodding in agreement. "I absorbed your Latin and their Germanic speech, but no one discovered this. I played the part of the clumsy, stupid savage, and they kept me at court. I listened as he sowed seeds of suspicion and envy between his neighboring states and pushed them to fight each other. They grew weaker as he became wealthier and stronger, and he eluded the Huns' yoke through his cunning.

"I was there about a year. During that time, I learned much, but I felt my soul slipping away. I could hardly recall my home. I decided to end my life as a warrior should."

"That is an honorable decision. Had I been a thrall to such a master, I would also choose to join my ancestors," Takumi added in a slow, deliberate manner. "I was more fortunate to arrive in this land."

Satewa's eyes lit with fire. "While they laughed at me for being a giant, clumsy clown, I sprang like a wolf. I snapped the necks of two guards before they realized I had moved. The other guards closed in on me, and I thought that would be my end as they knocked me down. But I awoke still in the land of the living.

"King Genseric rubbed his chin and stared at me before speaking in his native tongue to his men. 'I've seen this before among the simpletons. They're moronic and slow until, for no reason, they snap, and this happens. I can't keep him around, but instead of just killing him, I'll gift him to the Roman general, Flavius Aetius. He's far too shrewd to defeat and too ethical to bribe. Perhaps our witless savage here will go berserk with the general and snap his neck. That would solve a lot of my problems.'"

Satewa leaned back in his saddle, rolled his neck, and nodded toward his companions. "I feigned unconsciousness but heard everything. At that moment, I thought, 'A great leader who is both clever and honorable. Perhaps Aireskori, the god of war, is smiling on me. I must meet this man.'

"They chained me and shoved me into a cart, and I endured another long trip. It was the year 437, as you Romans count them, when the Vandal emissaries presented me to General Aetius. The Roman camp was wild with celebration as they had won their victory over the Visigoths at Toulouse.

"The general was squinting at papers by a flickering lamp in his tent when I entered. The Vandal ambassador was eloquent in his false praise. Aetius listened stone-faced and then dismissed them with his own pleasantries, but I heard nothing of their conversation. I had prayed for a sign, and there it was.

"Behind Aetius was a glowing eagle. Tears dripped down my face as I stared at the sign from my gods over the general's head. It was *Wanasi*, the Eagle. That was the name of my father."

He arched his eyebrows at the men riding with him. "You may laugh. The eagle was just the legion's standard, shining in the torchlight. But I knew better. My father's name means eagle, and there it was glowing at me. It was my father telling me that this was to be my home."

Satewa straightened with confidence. "My father was right. When the Vandal emissary departed, Aetius looked long at me without speaking. It was as if he were examining my soul. He then asked me, 'So why did that snake, Genseric, send you to me?' It was as if he could pull the words out of my mouth.

"Even though I had played the mindless fool for almost two years, I answered with the limited Latin I knew. 'The Vandal King wants me to kill you.'

"'And what is it *you* want to do?' he responded in a mild voice.

"The question shocked me. Not since I was captured as a boy had anyone bothered to ask what I wanted, but the answer had burned in my soul for many years. 'I want to face my enemies unshackled. I want to love a woman freely. I want to live as a man!'

"Aetius pulled out his belt knife and severed my bonds, then dropped the blade at my feet. 'You speak the words of a true man. Your honesty has given you your freedom. Join me of your own volition or depart. It is your choice.' I was stunned again."

With reverence, Satewa pulled out a knife from his belt. He continued to gaze upon it as he resumed his story and the men around him listened. "Aetius spoke to me for but a minute and knew me as well as I knew myself. I picked up the knife—this knife—accepting his gift. I followed him to his camp desk and said, 'Perhaps our paths follow the same trail.'

"I gave him my vow of friendship. In the fourteen years I've been with him, it is an oath I have never regretted. He made me one of his war chiefs, and I now command his scouts. I've found it to be a job for which he greatly needs me. You Romans and Gauls are too enamored with your iron toys. You don't read the wind and the earth very well."

Takumi bowed his head in respect. "It is amazing that two people from the opposite sides of the world could have very similar tales. I look forward to meeting your Flavius Aetius. A *daimyo* general who follows *Bushido* is someone to be honored."

Lucius mulled over the story throughout much of the day. He knew Takumi had also come from a distant land, but Satewa's tale amazed him. Before him stood a man who had lived among the almost mystical Vikings and had come from a land not even rumored to exist. It dawned on him how much more he needed to learn about the world.

As he continued to think about what he'd heard, Lucius felt very small and turned to Takumi. "The world is a very big place. Before I went to Rome, the furthest I'd ever been from Mediolanum was Ravenna. Now I'm heading toward a fight with the most ruthless barbarians the world has ever seen. You and Satewa are tested and honed warriors, but I've never faced a man who wanted to kill me before. What if I'm a coward? What if I see the enemy and run?"

Takumi stated with conviction, "You will do fine, young tribune. I've seen you grow from a toddler, and you have become your father's son. You are a good man, and you fill his heart with pride. Tell me and yourself why you joined the legions."

Lucius studied the then-dimming horizon with a blind eye and sighed. "I joined because my country needs me. It's weak, and the wolves are right outside its gates. We've fallen on hard times, and many no longer see the vision that is Rome. But I see it. There is much that is beautiful and noble here. If we fail as a people, the world will fall into a dark, barbaric chasm that it may not recover from for centuries."

"I think you have answered your own question," said Takumi.

Lucius smiled with silent gratitude. "I'm still scared."

Satewa nodded his head in agreement. "Some fear can be good. If it makes you think, it will help you live longer. If it freezes you, you will die quickly."

Marcus and Lucius looked at each other and pondered those words.

"It will be a few days before we catch up to the column. The legate is pushing the legionaries at a hard pace. We will camp here tonight," Satewa declared.

Marcus piped up with curiosity, "How do you know how far ahead they are?"

Satewa took on the voice of a teacher. "Ah, my young Roman, know the world around you and not just your cities of stone. Look at the birds. They are settled in their trees. The recent passage of many men would have them scattered about. Look at the spoor left by the supply train mules. They are dried out. Nature is as easy to read as the books of which your people are so fond."

Marcus loved to learn, so together with Lucius, he studied the crows, who studied him in turn. He observed the sun in the clear blue sky and the stools on the road. "How long ago did they pass by this spot?"

"About three days. Don't worry. They're moving at a steady pace but are burdened with a baggage train. We travel much faster." Satewa scanned the skyline. "At that last bridge, we crossed into the Narbonensis province. We're in true Gaul now." He pointed to a parcel of land ahead. "We'll camp in the woods by that low knoll there."

Before anyone else could speak, he turned his horse off the road and headed for the small hill. The others followed.

CHAPTER III

DESERTERS

The evening was overcast, and the group turned in early. They drew lots for the night watch, and Lucius picked up the middle one. He sat quietly, contemplating the stars, and jumped when he felt an unexpected tap on his shoulder.

Satewa had come up on him completely unaware. "We have visitors. I believe seven men approach."

Understanding, Lucius nodded and drew his sword from its sheath. Satewa moved like a shadow to rouse the others, then vanished into the darkness.

When Lucius heard the tethered horses nicker and shuffle their hooves, he decided to face the intruders head on. He slid into the dark away from the campfire's light. His throat constricted with tension, but he called out in the most commanding voice he could manage, "You men, step into the light right now."

The shadowy figures paused inside the tree line. Their disconcerted movements indicated that they were aware they'd been spotted first. One of them drew his sword and walked over. Illuminated by a full moon, Lucius flinched upon seeing that they wore the uniform of the legionaries that they marched from Rome with. He was not surprised when he counted seven of them.

The leader of the group appeared in the light of the dying fire and pointed his sword at Lucius. "We're not murderers. We're just sick of the army and are looking for food. We'll take what you have and be on our way."

They were all young and had no thought-out plan. Lucius refused to give them time to come up with one and stepped into the light.

One bandit gasped, "He's an officer!"

Lucius barked at them, using the sternest voice he could muster. "Why did you men desert your legion?"

The bandit leader lowered his blade and looked back at his comrades. Shocked and uncertain, they just stared back at him, shifting from foot to foot. A couple tried to straighten their uniforms and stand at attention.

The leader sighed and faced Lucius. "Sir, we just want to go home. The word is that this demon worshipper, Attila, has massacred all the legions in Gaul, and we're also to be fed to him. They say his Huns have never been defeated and that he eats his victims."

Lucius gathered his thoughts. From the corner of his eye, he saw Marcus and Takumi position themselves behind him. "So where will you hide when the Huns come to your village?"

The lead deserter cocked his head. "Sir?"

"What will you do when your wives are butchered, your homes are burned, and you hear the screams of your children? Do you think these Huns will be satisfied with Gaul when they have all the wealth from the Italian provinces waiting for them?" Lucius took a breath when he'd their attention. "Do you know who will be leading us? General Flavius Aetius. He's the one who is invincible. He has never lost a battle against any barbarians, and his legions are feared by every tribe."

"But, sir, these aren't Franks or Goths. These are Huns. He has never faced them before. Even the Germanic tribes flee from them."

Lucius smiled and let out a secret told to him by his father. "Did you know Imperator Aetius grew up as a boy at the royal court of these Huns, and as a youth, he bested this Attila in *every* contest?"

"I didn't know that, sir... but we can't go back. You know what they do to deserters; it's death by stoning. I don't want to have to hurt you, but we can't go back."

"You can go back if you're the escort of a tribune," came Lucius' quiet reply.

The men mumbled to each other in confusion when one legionary cried out, "I don't want to die!"

Staying calm, Lucius looked at the man with a steady gaze. "What is your name, soldier?"

"Gentilius, sir."

Lucius glanced over at Takumi. "Gentilius, a wise philosopher once told me that everyone dies, but the brave die only once; the coward will die a thousand times. Legionaries,

I will make you this vow before God: if you follow me back to the legion and follow orders, there'll be no punishment for your actions."

After a moment's pause, Gentilius nodded and looked back at his fellow deserters bunched up behind him. "Well, sir, I guess you have your escort, then. But could you answer our original question?"

Lucius drew a blank on that and tensed. "What was it?"

"Do you have any food? We're starving."

"Tribune, I have a sack of grain. I could cook gruel for them," Satewa boomed from behind the legionaries. They must not have known he was there and jumped back when they saw him step into the light.

Lucius looked over at Gentilius. "So do you think this Attila has anyone as fierce as Satewa here?"

"Tribune... I don't think that would be possible."

* * *

The next morning, Lucius half expected the deserters to be gone. Instead, he was surprised to find four more had joined them. All of them devoured the thin wheat porridge.

Satewa crouched next to the young tribune. "You did well last night. You gave them a reason to believe in themselves again. Now you must get them to believe in you."

Lucius nodded but felt no less nervous. Rome desperately needs all of its sons. I have to get these men to follow me into a deadly situation, and they have to follow orders when they get there.

The men watched him closely. Lucius patted Satewa on the knee and stood, resigning himself to another hot day. "Legionaries, fall in!"

Gentilius was the first at attention before him, holding his scutum shield and hasta spear as trained. The other deserters followed suit with varying degrees of success.

"You men all know the crime you committed and the penalty for that crime," Lucius barked.

The nervous soldiers shifted around and glanced at each other.

"I am Tribune Bernius, and my father, Verius, is a member of the Senate. You are now under my direct command. I promise you this: there will never be another word spoken of the actions you took, but you will act like Roman legionaries from this moment on. You will follow my every command or the full weight of Roman justice will fall on you. The punishment for desertion is stoning. Am I clear?"

One large fellow snapped back, "And why should we follow a pretty boy like you? There are eleven of us and four of you."

Lucius eyed him up and down. The man looked like another of the many rough barbarians who had come from the eastern provinces, but he stood half a head taller and looked about twenty pounds heavier. He didn't doubt the outcome of the match. Master Takumi hadn't only taught him the Nippon style of sword fighting but also their style of fighting with empty hands. The large legionary would need to suffer a defeat decisive enough that none would dream of challenging the tribune again.

Lucius made a deep but quiet breath. "Soldier, what's your name?"

The man spat with gleeful malice. "Vidin."

"Vidin, I'm going to give you an opportunity to back up your boasts. Let's all see how you fare against a rich pretty boy." Lucius gave his companions a sharp glare. "There'll be no interference."

A nervous Marcus stepped back. Satewa gritted his teeth and glared at the legionaries. Takumi crossed his arms and smiled.

Everyone soon cleared a circle, and the two men stripped down to their breechcloths. Lucius noted Vidin's nose was broken in a few places. From that, he deduced a simple fact: *He likes to charge straight in.*

The tribune had time for one breath before his opponent sprang. He dodged to the right and delivered a side kick to Vidin's knee and then a snap-kick to the side of his head.

Lucius hesitated and shifted to a non-lethal final strike. The dazed legionary never saw the fist that smashed in the bridge of his nose. With a nonchalant casualness, Lucius reached down to retrieve his sandals as the unconscious Vidin collapsed in the dirt on his face. *I need a soldier who will serve me, not a corpse.*

The remaining soldiers stared slack-jawed. Lucius straightened. "Legionaries, I am an officer and a man of my word. The army will not punish you while you are under my command. Gentilius, you are acting decurion. Have the unit ready to march in fifteen minutes. That includes the napping Vidin here."

Satewa approached him, chuckling. "I knew you Romans were called mules, but I didn't know some of you could kick like one. Tribune Bernius, you must teach me that trick when this is over."

Lucius returned a sheepish smile. "Lead my horse for today's travel. I will march with our new men. I must learn who they are, and they must get to know me."

Satewa slapped the tribune's back, a blow that rattled the younger man's teeth. "It would seem General Aetius has a real officer in the making here. But you will have to have Tribune Carloman lead both our horses. I am a scout, and now that we have crossed into Gaul, I should earn my keep. I'll be out ahead. Besides, I no longer believe you need a nanny."

Without another word, Satewa slipped his axe into the harness on his back and trotted off.

* * *

About an hour past midday, Lucius bemoaned his decision to walk. Despite the stifling heat, the legionaries maintained a good pace, and except for Vidin, just a few grumbled.

Lucius came to an abrupt halt when Takumi rose in his saddle. Farther down the road, Satewa loped toward them with a ground-eating stride. When Satewa caught up to them, however, his breathing didn't sound labored.

"Marauders are attacking a wagon and its escort ahead on this road. I saw a band of about thirty raiders and perhaps half that number of Romans still standing."

Lucius had no doubt about what they must do. *Those people could all be dead by the time we get there, but I have to try.* "Marcus, you and Takumi grab two other men who can fight on horseback and parallel us along that tree line. We'll come straight in along the road. When we get their attention, hit them on the flank. Gentilius, I want you to hold back with two other men and then come fast when we engage. I want those barbarians to see eight stupid Romans charging down the road at them and discover they're fighting twice that number once they hit us."

Marcus looked embarrassed and stepped up next to him. "Lucius... my brother, you know I would follow you to the Gates of Hell, but I'm an engineer, not a cavalryman. Give Takumi someone who can stay on the backside of a damn horse without falling off."

Vidin stepped up. "Sir, I have never fought on horseback. Actually, I have never fought in combat on foot before, either. But I'm a fair rider, and I can control most beasts with my hands free."

Lucius snorted to hide his misjudgment. He'd forgotten in the heat of the moment that Marcus was as poor a rider as he was himself. "Thank you, Vidin. Pick two other men who know how to ride. Marcus, hang back with the reserves. Just make sure you come up fast when we need you."

Marcus smirked. "I've been able to outrun you since we were boys. You always had stubby little legs. I *will* be there when you need me."

Lucius clasped him on the shoulders. "There are many things in this world I doubt, but you're not one of them, my brother." He turned to look at the men bunched around him. "Now let's show these barbarians how Romans fight. Double time!"

When they crested the last, low hill, Lucius was relieved to see about ten Romans still standing in a tight shield wall. Something confused him, though. Several people had crowded in behind them, a few of whom were slaves. But near them stood five armed men surrounding a well-dressed noble, none of whom lifted a hand to help in the fight.

Lucius turned to Satewa, who jogged at his side. With a gleam in his eye, the scout threw his head back and ululated a bloodcurdling scream. Lucius and the legionaries joined in fast, and their ploy had its desired effect. The fighting stopped around the wagon as both sides stared at the spectacle approaching them, and a dozen of the raiders broke off and charged up the hill.

Lucius swallowed hard. About half the men coming at him rode on horseback. He set the six men with their heavy shields and spears in the center and Satewa and himself on the sides. Then the horsemen were on them, and the fight broke into a wild melee. Lucius used every skill he'd just to stay alive. The pressure broke when Marcus and his two legionaries charged in screaming the same yell Satewa had bellowed earlier.

As the commotion wound down, Lucius made a hurried appraisal of the fight. Despite the gash on his arm, Satewa leapt on a horse behind one attacker and ripped the man's throat out. The half dozen marauders coming up the hill on foot never reached them. The mounted Romans rounded a small knoll and struck from behind, using their heavy hastas as lances.

Takumi slashed like a whirlwind. His razor-sharp blade severed the head right off the man before him. Four went down in seconds, and the other two fled back to their main group. Takumi led his small command up the hill toward their friends on foot. The three marauder horsemen still in the saddle fled for the hills when they saw the trap closing around them.

Lucius sucked in globs of air, reformed his men, and headed down the hill toward the main enemy body at a cautious tread to the hoarse cheers of the beleaguered defenders below. He lost one man in the engagement, but the fatal wound was struck on his front and not his back. His men and the deserters, even Vidin, fought well.

CHAPTER IV

CHANCE ENCOUNTERS

Dervla Conall never liked Romans much. She'd been a slave all of her life, and the pompous little bastard who owned her family was a cruel man who enjoyed the unfettered control held over her. But when the small band of Roman legionaries appeared on the hill crest, her heart leapt, and she joined in the shout they raised.

The Romans overwhelmed the barbarians who ran out to oppose them. The young man with wavy black hair and dark, fiery eyes who led them captured her attention. None of the Vandals who challenged him lived for long. If her family could survive for a few more minutes, they would be saved.

She knelt by her mother and younger brother, clutching a worn kitchen cleaver. Her father stood before them as a shield, brandishing a broken barrel stave. The tenacious Roman escort held their ground, but half of them now lay dead, and Publius Heraclius' Visigoth bodyguards didn't lift a finger to help. They stood around their employer with drawn swords and watched with little interest.

The brigand commander appraised the changing situation, counting the approaching Roman reinforcements and eyeing the wagon with its rich plunder.

A Vandal called out to his men. "Axise, you said this carriage would be easy pickings, but the cursed Romans hold a tight defense. Now more are coming!"

The one called Axise spit and raised his gore-covered sword bellowing, "We still have the numbers on our side, but we can't fight in two directions at once. Take the wagon and kill everyone except the fancy little fop!"

The Vandals surged ahead and scattered the thin line of desperate Roman defenders. Two of the Vandals turned toward the small, huddled group of slaves. The taller one with a scar running across his face leered. "They look pretty scrawny."

Dervla shivered as a blunt-faced brute laughed and raised his axe. "Ahh, but that one looks like she could be entertaining. She's my prize."

They advanced on Dervla's family with lust in their eyes. An old man now, her father was once an Attacotti warrior before being enslaved by the Romans. He met the brigands with a wild swing of a makeshift club, but a wicked axe blow severed his left arm from his body. Dervla leapt on the Vandal's back, gouging his eyes with one hand and slamming the cooking utensil against his neck with the other. The blow hit the iron collar the Vandal wore, but he roared and threw her down. Air flew from her lungs as she hit the hard-packed earth, but she clambered to her feet, holding the butcher knife before her.

Then the Roman leader appeared and, without slowing his pace, skewered the first Vandal who sprang out to meet him. His screaming men followed close behind, and any semblance of organized combat disappeared. As the brigands pushed through the Roman defenders, the Visigoth bodyguards joined the fray at last.

Distraught, Dervla stood over her father, who lay crumpled on the ground bleeding his life away. The Vandal she attacked earlier feinted with his sword as blood trickled down his cheek. She reacted to the move and swung the cleaver, but she lost track of the other barbarian. Rough hands grabbed her from behind in an iron grip. She slammed her bare foot hard against his instep. He grunted in pain but pulled the butcher knife from her hand. The other barbarian smashed her across the face and tore at the ragged clothes covering her body.

She screamed, but all of a sudden, the grip loosened. The young man with fiery eyes pulled his sword from one of her attacker and stood between her and the barbarian with the bleeding cheek and missing eye.

Dervla scrambled to her father. An ancient-looking bald man was already tying a strip of his old-fashioned toga around the stump of her father's arm. Dervla whispered a prayer to her druidic gods that her father still lived. She'd learned the use of medical herbs from her mother, and among the slaves at her master's estate, she was known as a clever healer. If the blood loss could be stopped, her father may yet live.

The old man looked over when she crawled to her father's side. His eyes roamed over her half-naked form before shouting, "Woman, get me a heated iron. If I don't cauterize the wound, this poor soul will die."

Dervla wept in anguish as she whipped her head around. There was no fire to be had, but she couldn't believe how fast the battle ended. The remaining marauders already fled toward the nearby hills. The few on horseback rode far ahead of those on foot.

The man who had just saved her wiped his sword on the tunic of the second Vandal barbarian, who now lay as dead as his friend. He must've been the leader by the way he watched the retreating Vandals with such a focused stare, and yet he looked so young. *He can't be any older than me.*

Dervla shook herself; she didn't have time to think about such things. She ran to the man with the wavy black hair. "Sir, I need fire. My father is dying."

Initially, he stared at her like all the filth of Rome did, but she would not budge until she could save her father. She didn't flinch when she met his eyes. The slave girl watched his face shift to a look of concern as she fell to her knees and beseeched him to help again. His Roman face softened with sympathy, and soon after, he began ordering his men.

Most of the other soldiers were checking the fallen Vandals and ensured they were all indeed dead. An exotic-looking foreigner and three riders with him pursued the fleeing marauders until they had ridden out of sight.

The man with the fiery eyes turned to the largest man Dervla had ever seen. "Satewa, we need a fire for the wounded. Can you get one started?"

The bronzed giant set out to search the ground for anything that would burn.

The man then turned back to Dervla with a warm comfort in his eyes. "You fought well against that Vandal warrior." He pulled his cloak off and draped it over her shoulders. "Here, my lady. Take this."

To her consternation, Dervla felt the heat rise in her cheeks as she wrapped the cloak around herself. "Thank you, sir. This is very kind of you." Small kindnesses were a rare experience for her.

"We'll get a fire going." He touched her on the arm, but on reflex, she stepped back. The man bowed his head. "Your bravery bought us the precious time to break through. I'm Tribune Lucius Bernius at your service, my lady. And your name?"

Dervla's cheeks grew even warmer. "Sir, you mistake me. I'm no lady; I am but a slave."

Lucius smiled, his look soft and honest. "I have little doubt about your station in life, but you showed me more nobility in this short time than I've seen in all of Rome's dilettantes since I arrived there. In my opinion, nobility is based on a person's actions, not their place of birth." His gaze turned thoughtful then, almost sad. "Rome is very different than where I grew up. On my father's villa, indentured workers labor side by side with the pensioned legionaries he hires. Almost all are able to purchase their manumission, their freedom. Many chose to stay on as freed men." A hint of playfulness entered his tone. "But since you insist on not being a noble, then you should answer my question when I asked you your name."

The tribune gestured to the small group of slaves crouched around the maimed man. "Tell me this: if this fight had gone the other way and I was captured and enslaved, would I be any different on the inside than when I came charging down that road? The Good Lord has given us our minds and our souls, and neither can be owned by another."

Dervla didn't know what to make of the man's passionate words. No one in Publius Heraclius' household had ever spoken to her like this, and Lucius sounded sincere. "My name is Dervla Conall and I..."

Their conversation came to an abrupt stop when the skinny old man in the toga grabbed a clay jar and hovered over to the giant bronzed man, Satewa. "I don't have all day. I need a hot fire and I need it now!"

When Lucius and Dervla looked over, Satewa already had some small kindling ignited and had added a couple large pieces of wood.

"I'll take over from here," said the old man. He poured a dollop of a thick liquid from the jar onto the edges of the fire, and the wood erupted into a roaring blaze.

Many of the Romans crossed themselves and stepped back from the strange wizardry. One of them, however, rushed in with wide-eyed wonder. "Good sir, what is that stuff?"

The old man quirked an eyebrow at the young, curious man. "Well, you appear to be a bit more intelligent than this collection of brutes who have nothing better to do than hack away at each other. This is called naphtha. It's a formula I developed in my hometown of Corinth. It will cling to anything and cannot be extinguished. Now put a few of your blades into the fire. I need them for the wounded."

"Gladly, sir. My name is Tribune Marcus Carloman. Who might you be? A scholar such as you should lead an academy."

"That is the truth, but alas, my name is Phokas. Until recently, I was one of the emperor's physicians. The men working with me were imbeciles, and I often told them so. It turned out our dim-witted emperor chose to listen to their advice over mine. I told him what I thought of that, and as a reward for my honesty, Emperor Valentinian dismissed me from the palace staff and sent me to General Aetius out here on this savage-infested frontier." Phokas glanced down at the hulking Satewa, who had crouched before the blaze. "My apologies if I have insulted any of your kin."

Satewa rocked back on his heels and chuckled. "No insult taken. Actually, that is also my assessment of the tribes who live at the edges of the Roman lands. I serve General Aetius. He's an incredible man, and I consider him my friend. I believe you'll find this assignment much more of a blessing than a curse."

Phokas eyed the savage-looking man, whose arms still wore the gore of the Vandals he'd slain. "Please bring me a heated iron when the blades are hot enough to sear flesh." The physician strode back to his patient.

The Roman soldiers observed the treatment and carried their wounded companions over next to the injured slave. Marcus followed him, holding the jar with the mysterious liquid. When he sniffed it, he gagged on the strong odor, and his brows creased in concentration as he rubbed the thick goo between his fingers.

Dervla returned her attention to her father's pale, pain-racked face and shuddered. Her mother and young brother sat close by, comforting him with gestures and words. She sprinted to her small bundle of possessions and pulled out an oilskin that held the dry moss and honey she used as a poultice and rushed back to her father's side.

* * *

Lucius stood with his arms crossed on the blood-smeared road, observing the tracks left by the Vandal raiders. By the chaotic way that they fled, he knew they would not return.

"I suppose I should thank you. These incompetents were doing their best to get me killed."

The abrupt words surprised Lucius, and he looked toward their source: a short, bald man with heavy jowls who planted himself before him with his entourage of Visigoth bodyguards.

"I am Publius Heraclius, the Head Chamberlain to Emperor Valentinian. I was on what was supposed to be a safe journey through Roman territory to Imperator Aetius' encampment. These stupid oafs let us get ambushed by those jackals you sent packing."

The tribune glanced at the Roman guards who had crowded together and could see the fury in their eyes at the chamberlain's insults. Each bore wounds of varying sizes, and not a single living officer stood among them.

The tribune looked back at the little man. "I am Tribune Lucius Bernius, and I—"

"Ahh, you are the son of Senator Verius Bernius. It is good to see there's still some in the nobility who can overcome the ineptitude of these peasants."

Lucius' rising anger finally snapped. "Sir, from what I observed, these men were doing everything humanly possible against bad odds." The tribune looked pointedly at the leader of the bodyguards. "I have never seen such courage, or such cowardice."

The mercenary's eyes flared with anger before he pushed his way past his employer and snarled. "I am Braun, nephew of Theodoric, the invincible Visigoth King. We are paid gold to play nursemaid to this 'great' Roman noble, and that we do. We will not waste our time rescuing Romans in a fight that's not ours. Is it my fault the vaulted Roman legionaries couldn't handle a ragtag gang of Vandals?" He started to lean into Lucius, but straightened out when two Roman legionaries, Gentilius and Vidin, stepped up behind their commander with arms crossed and death in their eyes.

Braun was of a similar height to Lucius, but by the scars on his arms, he'd seen a good share of fighting. Not that it made a difference. Lucius fumed. "These men fought three times their number to a standstill while you cowered by the wagon. The only ineptitude I saw here was from you. I find it obvious Roman courage and skill is far greater than the empty bravado of a tribe that flees their own lands at just the whisper of the Huns approaching."

Braun's eyes turned thunderous. "That is an insult to my honor and my people I will not bear. I grow sick of trailing after this overindulgent pig, so we are leaving." He spread his arms wide. "Will you back up those words, or will you run away like every other Roman?" The Visigoth mercenaries hooted agreement with Braun.

Lucius' passion cooled once he realized his temper had led him into this trap, and he appraised his adversary. Braun's confident eyes shone in a silent challenge. "So be it. We fight to first blood."

"Typical Roman cowardice, but I accept. Let's not give your boys an excuse to stab me in the back after I disembowel you. It is my challenge, so you choose the weapons." Braun turned to pick up a short sword and shield.

Lucius regarded the man's confident movement and balance. He was very familiar with the chosen weapons, so he recalled the training of his youth under Takumi Saegusa. The old warrior had taught him a fighting style he called *Battodo*, which focused more on cutting through the target versus the Roman style of stabbing thrusts. "Short sword and... longsword." Lucius smiled at the confusion that briefly darted across Braun's face as he drew his own spatha. "Vidin, may I borrow your gladius for a bit?"

A feral smile crossed the legionary's face. "Gladly, sir. Gut that worthless sow."

Takumi slid up to the tribune and rasped into his ear, "You young fool. How am I supposed to protect you when you go off making rash insults?" With a sigh, the swordmaster glanced over at his protégé's opponent. "Listen well. The man favors his left side, so you need to think backwards on your defense."

For the second time within a day, people cleared a circle with Lucius in the center. He groaned and breathed deep as he focused on an inner calm he learned from the routines Takumi called *kata*.

Lucius studied Braun as the man armed himself with a longsword and a wicked-looking curved dagger. The confident cheers of the Visigoths bellowed as their leader raised his weapons. One mercenary locked on Lucius and made a barely perceptible nod. Braun spun around and leapt in for a quick score.

Lucius saw the tension in his opponent's legs and moved into a ready guard position. His arm shuddered at the impact of their two swords meeting. He slid aside before Braun's dagger sliced through the air where his throat had been a second earlier. The Roman was just as quick on the counter-attack, sweeping in with his longsword, which Braun dodged.

Lucius anticipated the move and slipped inside his opponent's guard. Braun reacted too late as the tribune's short sword sliced a chunk of meat from his leg. The Romans watching howled their approval as the Visigoth fell, holding the open gash.

Lucius walked over to Vidin as the legionaries pounded his back. In a voice loud enough to carry to the fallen Visigoth leader, the tribune said, "Vidin, I'm sorry I wasn't able to give your blade more of a workout. It would appear our friend spends more time strutting than training." Lucius turned a cold glare on the other Visigoths, who tended to their leader. "I want all of you out of here. And if I ever catch sight of you again in Roman lands, I'll not be as easy on you as I was on your friend there."

The warriors glared back with hatred but also with an undercurrent of fear. Moments later, they gathered their horses and left in haste without a word.

Satewa smiled with admiration. "Well fought, young man. I would be proud to have you as a brother in my Turtle Clan. But you should have killed him when you had the chance. It can lead to no good to leave enemies like that one around alive."

One Roman guard approached Lucius and snapped a smart salute. The man was short with broad shoulders and the first hint of gray in his jet-black beard. "Decurion Cilla at your command, Tribune. Our *optio* fell when the Vandals sprang their trap. I'm the highest-ranking legionary left."

Every Roman guard's eyes studied Lucius, but he focused on the soldier in front of him. "What's the status of your men, Decurion?"

"I have ten hale enough for marching. The three who are with Phokas are badly hurt. The rest are dead. When the Vandals take a man down, they make sure he doesn't get up."

Lucius checked the sun in the sky. It was still early afternoon, but they weren't going anywhere soon, so he called out, "Takumi, set a perimeter around this wagon. Decurion Cilla, set a shelter for the wounded and empty that wagon. We'll need it to move the injured tomorrow. We can't stay here." He turned to where his own small band of men had gathered. "*Decurion* Gentilius!"

The surprised young man stepped forward and saluted with the same vigor as the senior decurion had just done. Lucius nodded to him. "Put together a burial detail for these soldiers of Rome who've fallen. Drag the barbarians away from here. Let the flies and carrion birds have their feast."

Gentilius saluted. "Yes, Tribune." He then spun around and shouted orders.

Cilla sighed. "I'm getting too old. Officers and soldiers all look like children." He took one look at Lucius, gulped, and stuttered, "No disrespect intended, sir. Your men fought very well, and I appreciate you shutting up that boasting oaf, Braun. That was some of the finest swordsmanship I've ever seen. I'm honored to serve under you."

A small grin creased Lucius' face, but then it turned grim. "Decurion, I'm afraid Rome will need all of its sons for the upcoming struggle whether we're ready or not."

Cilla met the tribune's eyes. "I meant it when I said it's a pleasure to serve under you."

Lucius smiled with gratitude and regarded the Vandal corpses being dragged away. "Cilla, you kept your head in a tight spot. Go see to your men." He patted the legionary on the shoulder and started ordering the camp. The road around the wagon soon became a flurry of activity with Lucius in the center of the whirlwind.

Satewa strode over wearing a broad smile. "Yes, I think my general has a real officer here. As I told you this morning, I'll be moving on ahead. The wounded and the wagon will slow you down, and Aetius needs me. Come along as fast as you can, and try not to get into too many more fights." The bronzed warrior gave a curt nod and trotted off to the west. Lucius stood, admiring the Roman scout loping off down the road.

Marcus walked over, still holding the jar of the mysterious liquid. "Well, my friend, how does it feel to make it through your first combat command?"

Lucius' face flushed underneath his dark tan. "You were as much a part of it as I. We were fortunate things worked out all right."

Marcus patted his friend on his shoulder. "My brother, I have no illusions. I'm an engineer. Even as children, you were always the one organizing and leading our games. I followed and sometimes had to pound some common sense into that thick head of yours. But I followed, and so do these men. You keep coming up with the plans, and I'll keep telling you how to do it better."

"I just did what had to be done. There was no one else."

"And you did it well. I saw it. The men saw it, and even that pretty slave girl you saved saw it. But as the *leader*, you have another problem to deal with."

Lucius rolled his eyes at his friend and waited for the axe to fall.

"It's a simple logistics problem. We have one wagon and a carriage here. We have to transport four wounded men and our supplies. What does that leave out?"

Lucius glanced sideways at Publius. The man lounged under a tarp while Dervla waited on him along with an elderly slave who kept looking back at her maimed husband.

"We'll need to make the wounded as comfortable as possible, so we'll lay them out in the wagon," said Lucius. "The supplies, we can pack into the carriage. There'll be room for Publius up on the driver's bench next to the teamster."

"Ah, yes. I'm sure the imperial chamberlain will regard that arrangement with great understanding. He's an *optimate*, a well-heeled, socially prominent aristocrat. Neither of us quite fit his class—your family's too poor, and mine's not Roman enough." Marcus chuckled without mirth. "I've counted the chests. His wardrobe and personal items make quite an impressive collection."

Lucius ground his teeth in aggravation. "I'll see the wounded receive proper care, and I'll be damned if I'll leave any useful supplies behind." He looked sidelong at his friend. "I suppose we'll need to find space for that precious dodecahedron you've been lugging with you since we left Rome."

"My dear, ignorant almost-brother-in-law, the dodecahedron is a very valuable tool. It's the latest in scientific measurement gauges. How else can one accurately determine the proper pilot hole for a rod without cracking the stone or wood it's being inserted into? Comparing my tools to that fat man's dinner plates is an insult."

Lucius grimaced. "All right, I'll deal with Emperor Valentinian's pet tomorrow. Look to the supplies we'll need. Satewa guessed our legion column will reach the main Roman camp today, but at our pace, we're about another three days out. I'm going to check on the wounded."

"Remember, he has the ear of the emperor, so handle it with tact," Marcus whispered.

The young tribune's shoulders sagged with a sudden weariness. *This has been a long day.* He walked over to where the four wounded men lay. Phokas stood close with a tight grip on Dervla's arm, wagging his finger in Publius' face. "Now what?" Lucius groaned and picked up his pace.

The chamberlain stood with his arms crossed and his nostrils flaring.

Once Lucius drew near, Phokas' eyes lit with fire. "General, will you drive some sanity into this overstuffed officious oaf? This girl here has a useful level of competence with medicines, although her concept of poultices is antiquated. He wants her waiting on him when I have men dying over here."

The chamberlain grunted and threw up his hands. "The injured legionaries have a competent doctor, if barely so, and a maimed slave is of no further use to me. I've had my bodyguard chased off, and it's well past my lunch time. The wench is my property, and I'll do with her as I please!"

Lucius looked sidelong at Dervla, who stood as still as a marble statue, and made his decision in a blink. "These men were injured in defense of Imperial Rome and have earned the best care the army can provide. I conscript the doctor and the girl to provide that service."

Publius purpled and his eyes narrowed to slits. "Very well, no sacrifice is too great for the defenders of Rome. I suppose the whore's worthless brother and mother can serve me just as well." He scowled down at the unconscious, one-armed man. "By the way, don't waste any medicine on the slave. He's useless to me, and I'll not be taking him with us when we depart."

Dervla turned ashen, and it was a good thing Publius didn't have eyes in the back of his head. Dervla's young brother stood there and his eyes blazed with hatred.

Incensed by the man's callousness, Lucius responded without thinking. "Actually, that's quite fortuitous, Publius. I had to leave my father's estate in rather a hurry and didn't bring a manservant with me. I claim the discarded slave as my own." He turned to Phokas and added in a flat voice, "Doctor, please render whatever service is necessary so my property will be hearty again."

His temper had still not abated when he swung his face back at the imperial chamberlain. "Also, Publius, I need to inform you that the army is commandeering your wagon and coach for vital military transport. Your baggage will be left behind so we can make the best time possible."

Publius glowered and answered in a taut voice, "So you think yourself important? Well, you little pup, I won't forget these insults. You've just made a very powerful enemy. The emperor shall learn of your swaggering display in great detail. You may be from an old family, but you'll find your dirt-poor father is a weak shield." The chamberlain turned without another word and stormed into his tent.

The boy approached Lucius. Thin as a rail, he could not have been more than twelve. His pale face flushed red, and he choked on his words. "My name's Seamus Conall. I wouldn't have expected such grace and mercy from a Roman. Thank you for my father's life. I'm in your debt."

The tribune and the slave boy regarded each other for a long second. "Your father will be cared for to the best of the good doctor's abilities. I can promise no more."

"I can ask no more." Seamus bowed and followed Publius to his tent, spitting before he entered.

Marcus walked over and draped his arm around his friend's shoulder. "That was magnificent. It was perhaps the finest feat of statecraft I've ever seen. You've just started your public life and have already made an enemy of one of the most powerful men in the empire."

Lucius rolled his eyes back at Marcus. "I couldn't help myself. Bullies make me mad. I never could stand to see anyone hurt someone else just because they're stronger." A sheepish smile crossed his face. "Do you think he'll hold a grudge?"

"Oh, I'm sure Publius will forget about the whole matter and laugh. Especially after tomorrow when he sees all of his treasures dumped in the field here."

"I won't back down."

"My dear Lucius, that's the one thing I am certain of. You are the most stubborn man I know." Marcus drew in a deep breath. "I suggest you hire someone to taste your food before you eat another meal, however."

Lucius' chuckle died in his throat when he realized his friend meant every word. "I think I need some wine."

Dervla reached over and grasped Lucius' hands. "God bless you."

They looked at each other for a long moment before she released her hold and knelt to tend to the wounded.

Marcius draped his arm over Lucius' shoulder, and the two tribunes walked off.

As they left, Lucius overheard Phokas say to the slave girl, "Yes, my dear. Even in these waning days, there're still a few virtuous men left in Rome."

CHAPTER V

AVENIO

By the afternoon of the third day after their skirmish, Lucius led his small caravan into the Roman camp outside Avenio. The bustling trade center stood buttressed against the Rhone River and was known as a commercial hub where Marcus' father held an expansive vineyard on his sprawling estate.

Their trek passed in relative peace. Several dispatch riders flew past them on the Via Domica from the direction of the army, and Marcus showed relief when he learned from the couriers that no Huns had approached his family's home.

One wounded legionary succumbed to a fever. Doctor Phokas took it hard, lamenting the limits of medical science and the inadequacy of his skills. However, he perked up a bit when the other two soldiers and the one-armed slave responded well to his treatments. On the night before they reached the Roman encampment, he told Lucius, "It appears they'll survive."

The legionaries had jelled well together even though Lucius' original group was far younger than the caravan guards. Decurion Cilla was a competent veteran of very few words, and Gentilius copied everything the older man did.

They made their arrival at the encampment inauspicious. Much traffic headed in and out, and everyone hurried from one place to the next. When they reached the east gate, Publius Heraclius, who had maintained a sullen silence for the entire trip, demanded in a loud, autocratic voice as to where he could find General Aetius.

The grizzled, gray-haired veterans posted at the gate exchanged confidential glances and made a proper but slow salute. All Roman military encampments were laid out in identical patterns with the commander close to the center point, so Lucius smirked as he noted that, while the directions the guards provided were accurate, they were for the long way around. He arched an eyebrow at the guards but held his tongue.

Publius spun on his muleskinner and three remaining slaves and ordered them to dump the legionaries' supplies while glaring a challenge at the tribune. Lucius bit back an angry retort when Marcus jabbed him hard in the ribs. "It's not a fight worth having."

The tribune nodded and waved Decurion Cilla over. "Have the men gather the equipment."

He approached Dervla next, who gave specific instructions to a legionary on the proper storage of the meager collection of medical supplies. When she turned to face Lucius, he told her, "I'll send word of your father's condition as often as I can. He will get as good of care as the army can provide."

The slave woman brushed her hair back and her eyes grew moist. "Thank you. Thank you for everything."

"Get up on the carriage, you worthless whore, or I'll have you running behind it!" Publius raged from inside his coach.

Startled, Dervla pulled her hand from Lucius' grip and jumped on the back of the coach. Only after she'd gone did the tribune wonder, *When did we grasp each other's hands?*

The imperial chamberlain huffed, and three slaves clung to the back. Soon, the carriage rattled away. Lucius sighed and faced the two guards who had observed the entire little drama with deadpan faces.

They started to salute the tribune in the same laconic manner they had given Publius until Decurion Cilla barked out, "Show proper respect for the tribune. He just had a sharp fight with a pack of barbarians and sent them scuttling with their tails between their legs."

The surprised guards snapped a salute. Cilla grunted his approval and went back to work.

Lucius made a wan smile, aware that respect was something he would have to earn. "Soldiers, I have wounded men here. Where's the hospital? And where can I find the legate in charge of the recruits who came in two days ago?"

"Sir, the hospital is in its normal place near the Praetorium. This is the *porta principali*. Follow the *via principalis*." The taller guard paused and rubbed his chin. "I can't give you precise directions for the legate. When he came in with that mob of children, he took over most of the base. Head to the Praetorium and someone should be able to direct you. But my best bet is that he's with General Aetius, and you won't find *him* there."

Marcus had walked up during the conversation, and when he spoke, his voice trembled. "Lucius, I must check on my family. Tell the legate I'll be back by morning." Without another word, he hopped on his horse and rode off at a gallop across the Via Agrippa.

Lucius sucked on his lower lip for a second and eyed his small troop. "Phokas, take your charges to the hospital and see that they receive proper care."

Phokas spat on the ground. "I'll not leave them to some half-trained army buffoons. They saved my worthless hide; I'll attend them personally. Maybe I'll even teach these backwoods doctors something about modern medicine if they have the wit to understand me." The old doctor clambered aboard the wagon, nodded to the tribune, snapped the reins, and headed off.

Once he'd seen the doctor off, Lucius faced the decurion. "Cilla, you are the senior noncom here. Find a spot for the men to camp. Feel free to throw my name around if any of the centurions give you trouble and leave word at the legate's tent where I can find you."

The decurion saluted and said to Gentilius, "You heard the commander. Let's get these misfits moving before they sprout cobwebs from standing around so long!"

The decurions left. Only Takumi remained now, and he stood holding two horses and regarded the tribune in silence.

"Takumi, you're with me. I suppose we should make our introductions to the general."

With the slightest of bows, Takumi handed him the tether of the brown gelding. Lucius smirked at his old tutor as he grabbed the reins of the most docile animal their little caravan had. As he settled in the saddle, Lucius sighed and noted the world had become a whirlwind of change. He wheeled his horse, and the two men trotted back out the camp's gate.

As Lucius rode over the stone bridge that spanned the Rhone River, the chaos of tents and banners of so many Germanic tribes surprised him. As they passed, he noted the glances of insolent disdain on the faces of the many warriors lounging along the road. On more than one occasion, a man darted across the road and provoked the horses into shying to the hoots and shouts of the bystanders.

Takumi studied the scene with unbroken focus. "These tribesmen hold Rome in great respect. They shall make wonderful allies."

Lucius held tight to the reins as his heart sank. He knew a sarcastic appraisal when he heard it.

They hitched their animals near the wide pavilion at the center of all the activity. The escorts of the Germanic kings and the aides to the Roman generals milled about outside, and the two groups made no effort to conceal their scorn for each other.

As the two men dismounted, Legate Albinus, who led the recruits from Rome, stormed out of the tent. The man stood shaking with anger when he spotted Lucius. "Well, have you enjoyed your vacation? It took you long enough to get here. And where is the *other* nobleman's son?"

The tribune swallowed the angry response that seethed inside him and replied in a tight voice, "Avenio is Marcus' home. He went to check on the safety of his family. As for our delay, we ran into a little trouble on the road and had to escort the imperial chamberlain here."

Albinus went outright rigid. "Publius is here? That's just wonderful. The German kings will take one look at him and go over to the Huns. If that fool opens his mouth, they won't even wait for Attila. They'll fight us on the spot."

"So how bad is it, sir?" the tribune asked with concern when the legate's stream of invectives slowed.

The legate glanced around before he leaned in closer and lowered his voice. "The imperator is here with a single legion. He plans to make the motley crew of a few gray beards and the gaggle of children we brought up from Rome into two new legions."

"Where is the rest of Rome's Gallic army?"

49

The legate looked hard at the ground. "They are either trapped behind city walls or dead. What you see across the river is the entire might of the Roman Empire."

The realization hit Lucius like a punch in the gut as he registered the words in full. "I'm sure Imperator Aetius has a plan."

A small smile crept across Albinus' face. "Oh, the old fox will have a plan. He could beat the devil himself even if he only had my arthritic mother for an army! Tribune, the imperator is in there trying to forge the Visigoths, Franks, and Alans into an alliance with Rome to fight the Huns. We've been marshalling here since word of the Huns' assault on Aurelianum reached us. I'll be honest with you: those tribes are more afraid of the Huns than they are of Rome. It's General Aetius alone who's making them listen. Each of them has faced the general in battle and lost. Without him here, they would've all bent a knee to Attila by now. I think it's still fifty-fifty which direction they'll point their spears once the fighting starts."

Lucius turned his head away, but he looked up again when Albinus patted him on the shoulder and sighed. "Well, lad, it's about time you learned something about diplomacy. Come on in, but keep your mouth shut. Getting hot-headed in there will do us no good. I had to walk out a minute ago myself or I would've challenged that boasting oaf, Theodoric, to a duel on the spot." With a quick glance at Takumi, he added, "You'll have to leave your man out here. Only commanders are allowed inside."

Takumi cocked his head at the legate and spoke before Lucius could protest. "That would be satisfactory. I want to observe these allies we have recruited. I haven't encountered most of these tribes before. Since my countenance is hardly Roman, perhaps they will speak more openly to a 'mercenary.'" He nodded to the two officers and strode off nonchalantly toward the nearest cluster of tents.

Albinus gave Lucius a quizzical look, but Lucius stayed quiet. Albinus shrugged and prompted him to follow. "Let's go. The lion's den awaits us."

When Lucius stepped inside, many men glanced his way before turning away. The stifling heat and the stench of so many unwashed bodies almost made him gag. Lucius stayed beside Albinus as he scanned the crowd for the renowned Flavius Aetius. However, his eyes swept past the general several times.

Once he caught sight of Satewa standing beside an unadorned Roman officer, Lucius reconsidered the latter man at last. The lean, middle-aged officer listened with great intent to a Visigoth war chief. The man looked ordinary until Lucius studied his face. A sharp mind lay behind those piercing eyes, and with a prominent Latin nose, he appeared to be a raptor ready to strike. He didn't look like the Roman gods of old. He bore no oversized muscles, just the face of a keen intellect who missed nothing.

That's him—General Flavius Aetius. It can be no one else, Lucius concluded.

His train of thought and reverie stopped short when the Visigoth who was speaking earlier bowed in mock reverence to the Roman general sitting before him. "Yes, we all acknowledge the leadership and prowess of the legendary General Aetius, but tell me why my warriors should bleed in defense of Rome when all Rome brings to this battle is a collection of old men and young boys. Where are your warriors? Or does the mighty Roman Empire have none left?"

General Aetius' eyes blazed with fury, but he remained calm as Centurion Satewa whispered in his ear. After a moment, the fire in his eyes cooled. "King Theodoric, perhaps you have a champion who would care to cross swords with Centurion Satewa here?"

Theodoric smiled as if the Roman leader had just walked into a trap. "Bah, we all know the reputation of your hench-man, and it's probably well earned. But do you have a *Roman* who can cross swords with my champion?"

General Aetius' eyes swept the tent wall where his officers were arrayed. Lucius' stomach lurched when the general's perusal stopped at him. "Why, Your Highness, I would wager that even that boy over there could best your champion."

Perspiration beaded on Lucius' forehead as all eyes turned toward him. By the gleeful smiles on the Germanic warlords' faces and the glum expressions on the Romans, they all had come to the same conclusion. The sole difference was General Aetius, whose face remained unreadable; and Satewa, who maintained a smug smile.

"Then we're in luck," said Theodoric. "I've received word that my champion has arrived in camp, and we could use a break from these overlong negotiations. However, I fear it will be a very short break. Thorismond, fetch Braun. Bring him to the yard outside."

"Father, I'm a prince, not a simple errand boy. Send someone else."

Theodoric roared in indignation, "And I am the king! You will do as I command."

Thorismond's eyes glowered and he gritted out, "Yes, Father." He stormed from the pavilion without another word.

The Visigoth King turned to Aetius and snickered. "So, perhaps the general would like to make a little wager on the prowess of his great champion. Perhaps... gold?"

General Aetius leaned back toward Satewa and spoke in a whisper that Lucius strained to hear. "I have gold solidus coins for bribes. If we lose that money, the alliance will never be formed in time." Satewa gave a curt nod, and Aetius' lips thinned. "I trust you with my life, and now I trust you with the life of the empire."

He turned back to face the king. "You know, Theodoric, I also tire of these tedious discussions. We talk while Attila swallows all of Gaul. I will take your wager. I will put up a chest of solidus on my champion if you'll agree to march with us on the morrow if my man wins."

The din in the room hushed as all eyes shifted to Theodoric. Although the Franks and the Alans were also present, the Visigoths had the largest force. Whatever they agreed to, the other tribes would follow.

Theodoric stared at Lucius with a dumbfounded and uncertain look. General Aetius raised his hand, and slaves brought out a large iron-bound strongbox. The servants lifted the lid, and a treasure of Roman coins glittered in the flickering torch light. The enclosure echoed with dozens of gasps.

Theodoric's eyes gleamed. "Agreed!"

The pavilion soon emptied as the tribal leaders elbowed their way out to the open field, arguing over how the wealth should be divided.

Legate Albinus scowled at Lucius. "I thought I told you to stay out of trouble. Now look at the mess we're in."

General Aetius, Imperator of Rome's Gallic Legions, approached them, and for a second time, his intense eyes regarded Lucius. "May Saint Michael the Archangel protect and guide you. Don't fail me." He patted the tribune on the shoulder and walked outside. A groaning Legate Albinus followed.

Afterwards, only Satewa remained in the pavilion. "Ho, my young friend. I advised my blood brother well. I have never seen such swordsmanship as you displayed last week. I spent several of my younger years dueling for the entertainment of the Vikings. There's not one of these tribesmen who can stand against you." A sheepish smirk crossed his face. "Now don't feel pressured, but the fate of your country rests on what you do in that ring." He draped his thick corded arm over the tribune's shoulder and led him out. "Come, your audience awaits you."

Lucius staggered out on shaky legs. The responsibility and the expectations that Rome's greatest general had just laid on him felt like a giant stone on his shoulders. Emotions roared through his body, and part of him wanted to run to a corner and cry. But another part of him recalled the general's calm confidence. *How can I even think of failing him?*

The sun blinded the tribune as he left the gloomy interior. When his eyes adjusted, Lucius gaped internally. The enormous throng of warriors surrounding the field grew by the minute. As he followed Satewa through the packed crowd, he noticed a silent presence walking at his side and made a wry grin. "So you want to see the show?"

"What in the world have you gone and done?" Takumi hissed. "How can I protect you when you go picking fights with every barbarian you run into?"

"Master Takumi, I swear I did nothing. One second, I'm listening to a debate; in the next, the whole course of the war rests on my shoulders. I still don't know what happened."

They broke into the open area, and Satewa turned to address Takumi. "It is simple. My general needs the Germanic tribes to help in this fight with the Huns. Negotiations and bribes would have taken far too much time. When I arrived in camp, I made a full report. It included the young tribune's exploits on the road here." The giant centurion shrugged his shoulders. "Aetius weighed the risks and tossed the dice. If it makes you feel any better, I have never seen my blood brother lose a gamble."

Takumi gave Satewa a hard glare. "This boy is like my own son. You have no right to risk his life like this."

Lucius grasped his shoulder. "Master, I have the greatest teacher in the world. I will not shame him."

Takumi clamped his mouth shut, but his eyes glistened. "I... I am very proud of you. You were an admirable student, and you have become a great man."

Lucius squeezed the older man's shoulder again and stepped into the ring. He stripped off his tunic and started the stretching exercises his old swordmaster had taught him to loosen his body and focus his mind.

Many hoots and chortles rose from the Visigoths in the crowd. They exchanged bets with joyful exuberance. Those choosing to back Lucius received very good odds.

Lucius looked around with unease when the crowd noise subsided. Then the concern shifted to a grim smile. Standing across the makeshift arena with his left leg bandaged was the Visigoth bodyguard he'd dueled just a few days earlier.

* * *

Braun's blood drained from his face once he saw the Roman who Thorismond said would be easy meat even on a bad leg. There would be no first blood this time; he hadn't come close to matching this man with two good legs. Glaring with pure vitriol, he turned to Thorismond and snarled, "That innocent-looking boy over there had me on the ground in three strokes, and that was after he fought a pitched battle against a band of Vandals, and I was fresh."

Thorismond paled. "Father's been outfoxed by Aetius again." The corners of his eyes tightened and he whispered, "Our people need a real king to lead them. That fool makes a mockery of our tribe's greatness."

"You know I'm with you," Braun grated.

"Our time will come." Thorismond whipped around and stormed over to his father, who studied him with lowered brows.

* * *

Lucius observed the Visigoth prince as he gave Braun a startled look before striding over to the king. Theodoric's face purpled with fury as he absorbed what his son was telling him. Without thinking it through, the tribune locked eyes with Braun and stepped into the arena.

He declared with a loud bravado he didn't feel, "It is known that the Visigoths are a fearsome tribe with great warriors, so their champion must be quite remarkable. However, the man is obviously lame. I will gladly battle him when he is hale again, but I ask the noble king to choose another to test the greatness of Rome. It answers nothing for me to kill a cripple."

Braun glared with even more hatred and limped over to where the Visigoth King and his son exchanged heated words. Soon after, he joined their conversation.

Theodoric glowered at the young tribune, who stood at ease in the middle of the enclosed area. The Visigoth King pasted a smile on his face, raised his open hands above his head, and stepped into the temporary arena shouting, "Friends! Although the contest would have been entertaining, we should waste no more time. This Attila and his vassals are sweeping through Rome's lands, and soon, he may set his eyes on our homes. I say we unite and destroy this marauder once and for all."

The gathered crowd murmured in confusion.

A disdainful Theodoric sneered at Lucius and raised his hands again. "With the leadership of General Aetius and the valor of the Franks, Alans, and Goths, the godless Huns will be vanquished and their plunder will be ours."

The crowd erupted in hoarse cheers.

Theodoric strode over to Flavius Aetius with a smile that belied the anger in his eyes. Lucius could hear Theodoric just enough when he said, "So you duped me. How long were you plotting that little trick?" The Visigoth King raised the general's arm for all to see and shouted to the crowd, "The great strategist can even bring his legions of little boys if he can get them away from their wet nurses!"

The tribesmen roared with appreciative laughter. Theodoric gave General Aetius a cruel smile and stalked back across the field, brushing Lucius with his shoulder as he passed.

As the warriors drifted away, Lucius felt weak in the knees. All he did was stand there, and the world changed. With his *spatha* still in hand, he turned and walked back to Satewa and Takumi. He didn't walk far as dozens of ecstatic countrymen swarmed to him, knocking the wind out of him, pounding him on the back, and congratulating him. Almost all the hair on the men had gone gray.

Satewa made a subtle nod and smiled. "You did well."

Beside him, Takumi sighed. "After all that shouting and posturing, it appears we actually need to prepare for a war."

CHAPTER VI

NEW COMMAND

Legate Albinus strolled back across the bridge with Lucius. Takumi followed with the horses in tow. "Lucius, when your friend Marcus decides to grace us with his presence, tell him he's been assigned to the engineering team with the artillery auxiliaries. I'm putting you in charge of the First Legion's Seventh Cohort. I am woefully short of centurions, and the Seventh needs a commander."

Lucius groaned. The Seventh Cohort in any legion is always the most inept.

"By the way, it's also undersized. We had a lot of desertions during our trek from Rome."

"Can I at least keep the twenty odd legionaries who came into camp with me?" the tribune asked, growing hopeful.

Albinus looked sidelong at him. "Certainly. It saves me the problem of assigning them to another unit. So where did you find twenty legionaries?"

At that moment, the two Roman officers had to leap to the side of the bridge. No sooner had they done that, a very ornate carriage careened across at a reckless speed. As the coach passed, a very red-faced imperial chamberlain glared at Lucius and yelled at the driver to go faster. Three pale slaves clung to the baggage rack on the back. One slave's long blonde hair whipped in the wind, and she looked back at him with a worried glance.

Lucius saw her concern turn into a warm smile as he climbed to his feet. A foolish grin of his own broke onto his face, and then the carriage was gone. The dust that had risen from the wheels drifted to the ground.

Albinus brushed off the grime from where he landed. "Thank God we'll be on the road tomorrow. That jackal, Publius, will foul the air around here. I'm just glad Aetius has to deal with him and not me. There are few people who can get on his bad side and survive."

57

"I... I... I better get going and see to my men," Lucius stammered as the blood drained from his face.

"Lad, what's the matter?"

Although hesitant, Lucius relayed the details of his confrontation with the imperial chamberlain.

To his surprise, Albinus nodded in approval. "Your statecraft is incredible. I can't believe someone as young as you can get into so much trouble in such a short amount of time." The legate then gave Lucius a hard look. "Try to stay out of sight until we get going. You may be safer facing Attila than Publius. At least the knife won't be in the back." The legate departed to his command tent.

It took Lucius an hour to find his men. He gave them a wry grin when they spotted him and trotted over. "Cilla, today is your lucky day. You and your men have been assigned to me. You are now part of the Seventh Cohort, First Gallic Legion."

"The Seventh Cohort? But that's reserved for the newest and most inexperienced legionaries and commanders..." Cilla's face flushed and snapped his mouth shut.

"Unfortunately, Decurion, your assessment's quite accurate. In actuality, the situation is even worse. I'm the only senior officer and we're very short of centurions," Lucius responded in a flat voice.

It took a few moments more, but Cilla soon nodded with some focus in his eyes. He straightened to attention and faced the tribune. "Sir, I've served with good officers and bad ones. You're levelheaded, and you care about your men. I'm proud to serve under you."

"That's good because I'll need to rely on you to open your mouth if you think my instincts are going to get us all killed. Now send a rider to the Carloman estate. Have him tell Marcus we depart at dawn and that he's with the artillery engineers. The rest of you, follow me. Let's find our cohort."

The encampment was a total bedlam, but they had little trouble finding the Seventh Cohort. Lucius' heart sank as he observed them. "They're the most unorganized group here." But he shook his lamentations away and roared orders. "Seventh Cohort, assemble!"

As the legionaries aligned themselves in a semblance of order, Lucius' apprehension grew. The Vandal King was not far off in his description of the Roman troops. Although he'd marched from Rome with these men, he'd never assessed them as a fighting force. He pursed his lips as he thought of the hardened Germanic warriors who surrounded the makeshift arena just a short while ago. His own little private army stood not far behind him. *I defeated a large band of Vandals with a small group of such boys.*

The centurions stood at rigid attention. They were five of the oldest men in uniform the tribune had seen. They held themselves straight as spear shafts but appraised him with cautious eyes. Lucius sighed and resigned himself. "Centurions, what's the status of the cohort?"

The centurions looked back and forth at each other, and at last, one spoke up. "Centurion Vivarius, sir. We have a mess here. The cohort should be at six hundred men, and we have about five hundred unorganized boys who've never seen combat. As far as officers go, you have what you see before you and nothing else."

The tribune held the centurion's eyes for a long minute as he mulled over the situation. "Decurion Cilla, Master Takumi, please step forward." As the two joined the officers, Lucius continued, "Takumi, you're not a Roman soldier, but if you're willing, find ten men who can ride and form our cavalry auxiliary."

A thoughtful look passed over Takumi's face. "It would be an honor to serve the Bernius family in such a role. I will accept under the sole condition that, if I learn of any danger approaching your father's estate, I have permission to depart at once."

"Agreed."

"Then I accept, Tribune Bernius. I already have my first three riders selected. They fought well against the Vandals."

Lucius then faced the veteran soldier. "Cilla, today is still your lucky day. You are now Centurion Cilla, and you'll command the First Century. Your men and my escort are the only battle-tested legionaries, so they'll be the core of your command."

Cilla turned pale. "Sir, I'm no officer. You're jumping me two ranks."

"*Centurion*, you kept your head and held your men together against overwhelming odds. You can do this." Lucius leaned close and whispered in his ear, "I need you to do this. Look around you. There's no one else."

Cilla looked warily at the old centurions before nodding, but his shoulders remained tense.

Vivarius walked up. "It'll be good to have at least a few real soldiers in this godforsaken cohort." With a smile, he broke the tension with an honest applause. "Congratulations, Centurion Cilla."

Lucius cleared his throat. "Okay, Master Takumi. You now have the rank of optio. You have first choice for your team." To the centurions, he said, "Divide up the men as you see fit. I want the First Century at full strength. They will be the point of our spear. Choose the noncommissioned officers from the recruits who seem to be the most levelheaded. Now let's get going. We march on the Huns in the morning."

Vivarius shuddered. "So it's true. The rumor has been racing through the camp." A dozen objections flitted through the man's eyes, but the old centurion held his tongue. The gray-haired soldier saluted, stepped back, and conferred with the other centurions. Cilla and Takumi joined them not long after.

Lucius sighed again. That's one task done. Now, just a thousand more before morning.

Suddenly, a loud, reedy voice screeched behind him. Soon after, an irate Phokas stormed over to him. "They're idiots, complete idiots! Those doctors have the intelligence of a goat! Would you believe they threw me out of the hospital tent all because I tried to instruct them in the latest medical science?"

Lucius smirked at the old man's consternation and asked, "And our men? How do they fare?"

Phokas dug his heels into the ground, but his voice calmed. "Fine, fine. Those imbeciles are competent enough to handle men who have already been treated. Even your new servant is coming along well."

Upon hearing this, a thought struck the tribune. "Doctor Phokas, we're moving out come morning. If you have no assignment, I would be honored if you would travel with my cohort. We have no medical personnel at all."

The old doctor's face lit up. "Gladly! As long as you keep those other fool doctors away from me."

Lucius smiled as he checked off another item on his endless list. "Take two of the men and retrieve your wagon. Commandeer any supplies you think we might make use of."

CHAPTER VII

JUDGMENT

"The prescribed punishment is death by stoning. Or do you believe you are above Roman law, General?" Publius rocked back on his heels with a satisfied smile. "I overheard those peasant soldiers who escorted my carriage after those marauding bandits were driven off. Those oafs who followed that pretentious tribune spoke out loud that they had deserted. Now they must pay for their crime." The chamberlain pointed a fat finger at Aetius and flushed. "They thought it funny to toss my possessions away. We'll see if they're still laughing when their bodies are reduced to bloody pulps. Any one of my togas is worth more than the lot of them."

Imperator Aetius rolled his eyes imploringly at his friend Satewa and whispered, "This is the last thing I need. I'm preparing to march out for the greatest challenge of my lifetime, and I have to deal with this." In a louder voice, he grated, "Centurion, is any of this true?"

Satewa gritted his teeth. "It's true, sir. But those men accepted Tribune Lucius' promise and followed his orders. They fought with courage and defeated a Vandal band twice their size, saving the life of the emperor's chamberlain here."

"You ask a witless savage to confirm the word of a Roman nobleman?" Publius sputtered. "General, you push your authority too far."

Flavius Aetius clenched his fists. He hated wasting men, especially good men, on the vengeful whims of corpulent fools. Unfortunately, the chamberlain was the voice of the emperor, and the general couldn't defy the emperor with the fate of Rome hanging by a thread.

The three legion legates stood by a map pinned on top of a small camp table. Their occasional side glances told the general that they had paid more attention to the argument than on planning the next day's trek.

Exasperated, Aetius looked in their direction. "Albinus, put together a detachment and arrest the deserters who came in with Tribune Bernius. Assemble the rest of the First Legion on the field in front of your camp. Let's get this bloody business over with. Everyone else, for God's sake, get this army ready to move."

* * *

Seamus stood a good distance behind his master and snarled to his sister, "Typical Romans, executing men on the word of a bejeweled ass."

Dervla looked around in alarm. Seamus had spoken his words in a low voice, but he'd made no attempt to hide the disdain he felt. Thankfully, no one paid them any attention.

Dervla patted Seamus on the shoulder. "You must warn Tribune Bernius. He won't let this vile deed happen."

"Are you in love with that man, big sister? Hide any feelings you may have. You're a slave and he's a Roman noble. Nothing good will ever come of it."

"I'm not some lovelorn dreamer, *little* brother. I've been abused in ways you can't even imagine. I have no delusions about where I stand in life, but I trust him, and we owe him for saving Father. Go. I'll cover for you here."

Seamus gave his sister an annoyed frown. She was his one friend in the world, and he swore to exact vengeance someday on all the animals who had hurt her. That day was not now, however, so he turned and stalked from the audience room. The guards didn't give the mere slave boy a second glance. Once outside, he let out a great sigh. *It's good to breathe clean air away from those damn Romans.*

Around the camp, men ran in every direction. How would he find the tribune in all the chaos? Without any other options, he started trotting at an easy pace while swiveling his head in every direction.

Seamus never found Lucius, but he did find Phokas at the supply depot. The old doctor scowled at a somewhat familiar tribune, who was doling out coins to an eager legion quartermaster. Large barrels and sacks found their way onto the doctor's wagon.

Phokas fixed an impotent glare on the senior supply clerk as the silver coins vanished into a pouch on the man's belt. "Marcus, I had the situation well in hand. It's this fool's job to provide supplies. Even this donkey head would've seen reason eventually."

Marcus smiled as he closed the leather thong around his purse. "Yes, eventually, you would've won, and the grain would be half spoiled and full of weevils. Now take this to Lucius before some enterprising legionaries decide to lighten your load."

Seeing an opportunity, Seamus rushed over to them. "Good sirs. My father... can you tell me of my father? How does he fare?"

It took a moment longer before the doctor and the tribune glanced over at him. Their looks of surprise soon faded, and Phokas replied, "He's doing well, lad. I see no sign of infection, so he should live."

Marcus nodded. "In fact, with the army moving out, I've arranged for him to be sent to my father's estate along with our two wounded legionaries. He may be mending, but he would never survive the trip we're going on. He'll be well cared for there and should be hale and hearty when we return this way."

Tears welled in the young slave's eyes. "Thank you, sir. I am in your debt." Seamus felt very odd about thanking Romans a second time, but then he shook the thought away. He didn't waste another second and told them about the meeting between the imperator and the chamberlain.

Phokas pinched the bridge of his nose, groaning. "Well, that snake put the general into a tight spot. Those poor souls. Stoning is a slow and painful way to die."

Tribune Carloman gritted his teeth. "No, you don't know Lucius. My friend gave those men his oath that nothing would happen to them, and Lucius is the most honorable man I've ever known. He'll die before he lets that sentence be carried out."

CHAPTER VIII

STONING

Lucius had never felt so scared and angry in his life. One minute, he was putting his new command into order, and in the next, the ten deserters who recanted were being dragged off for punishment. Some pleaded with him to save them. Others just stared stone-faced with looks of betrayal.

He could live with neither and stood tall before the general. "Imperator Aetius, with all due respect, I cannot allow these men to be punished. I had already judged them and set the terms for their return. I cannot go back on my word. If there's any transgression here, it is mine. They have fully abided by my conditions."

The ten shackled men looked up with their first hopeful glances.

Publius crossed his arms and huffed. "The answer is clear, General. The person who should be stoned to death stands before you. He flaunted Roman law and countermanded your order."

Aetius looked over at his senior officers, but all of them stayed silent except for Satewa. "He's the hero who managed to get the entire army moving. We should be piling honors on him, not threatening him."

"Hold your tongue, savage. I heard he just stood half naked in the field while the Visigoths argued and never even lifted his sword. I would hardly call that a hero. General, you must do your duty." Publius pointed his flabby hand at Lucius. "You'll never control the emperor's army if every whiskerless boy can flout Rome's laws. I shouldn't have to remind you that the military code is very specific."

Aetius looked around the packed audience chamber with a hard gaze. In a soft voice, he spoke to the trembling Lucius. "Forgive me, son. I am as bound by my word as you are by yours." He released a curt breath. "Lectors, take the tribune out to the yard and tie him to the post. Unshackle those legionaries. They are free."

65

As cruel, callous hands took hold of him, Lucius' numb mind snapped into focus and he shook free of their grasp. "I am a tribune of Rome. I'll go of my own accord."

The chief lector chuckled with glee. "It's not often I get to ply my trade on a nobleman." The thick-necked torturer raised his club to smash Lucius for his insolence. However, his hand stopped in midswing, held by the firm grip of Flavius Aetius.

"You'll escort him with the dignity he has earned or I swear I'll have you staked to the ground next to him," roared the general.

The lector turned to his men. "Strip him."

Lucius stood stiff and silent as his clothes were torn from his body. When they had finished, he raised his head and walked out on legs that had difficulty supporting him. He didn't walk alone for long as Takumi rushed to his side.

"I resign my commission, young Bernius. I may not be able to save you, but you will not die alone. I will be honored to stand with you."

"Master Takumi, *no*," said Lucius. "This was my vow, and I will stand by it. There is no need for you to sacrifice yourself."

"You aren't the only member of the Bernius household with honor. I also made a vow. I promised your father to protect you. How can I face him having failed in that task?"

Suddenly, another man began to walk on Lucius' other side, a man he recognized as his old friend. "Marcus! Please go."

"Sorry, Lucius, but there were two tribunes by the campfire that night."

"What about Julia? You have a full life ahead of you. Don't throw it away."

"And how could I face her after this, my brother?"

The midday sun seared the marked off area that the three men and their escorts approached. Row after row of silent legionaries already surrounded it.

Satewa snarled as he walked beside Aetius. "You are wrong, my general. There is the law and there is what is right. The two aren't always the same."

Aetius followed behind the prisoner and looked at the towering centurion at his side, nodding as he listened to those words. A beaming Publius Heraclius trailed behind.

The chief lector finished tying Lucius' leg to the pillory and stepped back into the circle of soldiers, hefting a rock the size of a fist. His voice bellowed the announcement: "The sentence is stoning unto death!" He hurled the stone at the tribune, but in the next second, the stone caster himself lay unconscious.

Takumi had grabbed the projectile in midflight and sent it back the way it had come. However, many stones soon poured in from the wide circle. One hit Lucius in the back of his head, and the world went black as he hung limply in his shackles.

CHAPTER IX

A SURPRISING MORNING

A cool cloth rested on his forehead when Lucius opened his eyes. His head felt like it burned in flames.

"Stay still, young man. You took a nasty blow. You're lucky your skull is as thick as that of most other Romans."

The speaking blur soon coalesced into a person. A concerned Doctor Phokas looked right at him.

Gentle hands removed the cloth and replaced it with a fresh one. "Will he be all right, doctor?"

Lucius felt his heart skip a beat, recognizing the voice as Dervla's.

"We'll see." Phokas held his hand before Lucius' face and formed a V. "Son, how many fingers am I holding up?"

"Ah… two." Lucius squinted as more of his environment focused into a bedroom. "Where am I? Why am I still alive?"

The doctor turned to Dervla with a smile. "Yes, Dervla, he'll be fine. His eyes aren't dilated and his voice isn't slurred. Why don't you answer his questions? I'll tell the others that the blockheaded fool will survive."

Phokas gave the tribune an affectionate pat on the shoulder and climbed to his feet. Lucius watched the old man open the door and leave. Afterwards, he spied the sun rising in the distance as a cool morning breeze wafted into the room.

"He stayed by your side all night, you know," said Dervla. "He even sewed up that nasty gash on the back of your head."

Lucius turned to regard her, ignoring the nausea it caused. The morning sunlight flowed around her like an aura that highlighted her beauty. "How do you know he was here all night?"

Dervla brushed back her hair from her face. "Well, to answer your first questions, you're in the Carloman family estate. I've never seen anyone as upset and enraged as Tribune Carloman's father when they brought you here. He has allowed no one inside his gate except for Doctor Phokas and the legionaries who carried you. I thank your Christian God that Tribune Carloman wasn't seriously injured. Only his intervention stopped the nobleman from going after my master."

"Marcus and Takumi... are they all right?"

"Yes, yes. A few scrapes but nothing serious. The stoning stopped right after you went down."

"What happened?"

"The good doctor said he screamed at General Aetius, my pig of a master, and everyone else to stop the insanity. The only one who would meet his eyes was the general, who shed a few tears and said, 'It's not right that leaders must be shown the meaning of courage and honor by those who serve them.' Then the general shouted, 'Enough' and strode onto the field where your battered body hung. That big savage friend of yours ran out with your men close behind, and they brought you here. You weren't responsive until a short while ago."

Lucius sighed. Dervla's deft hands felt so warm as she leaned in and checked the dressing on his head. Though comforted by her presence, he felt numb otherwise. "That has to be about the shortest career for a military tribune in history. It looks like my father will get to make a farmer out of me yet. Ah, Dervla, I..."

He stopped short when a nervous Marcus stuck his head through the door. "Lucius, it's good to see you're awake. You have a visitor... and Dervla, Publius Heraclius is storming about outside the gate. He 'asked' for you to come right away. He's leaving for Ravenna and seems rather perturbed that my father's men won't let him enter."

Dervla's response rang with sarcasm. "I'm sure he was very polite in making that request."

"Actually, he stated his 'property' should not be used to save the life of a criminal." Marcus studied his friend. "He's not very happy you're still alive."

Dervla shuddered as she rose, and her fingertips lingered on the tribune's cheek.

Lucius impulsively grabbed her hand. "Thank you for your kindness. I won't ever forget this."

Tears rimmed her eyes. "A slave does what she is told."

"And a free woman helps others when she is under no compunction to do so. Dervla, you may have been born a slave, but your spirit is freer than many a noble I know. The scars you bear tell where you've been. They don't dictate where you're going. Hold onto that spirit. I will do what I can for you and your family."

The color rose in her cheeks as she pulled her hand from his grasp. "Just send me word of my father when you can. I worry about him." Dervla slipped away without saying another word.

Marcus tossed him a bemused smirk. "I see you haven't lost your touch with women, Lucius. They still flee from you as soon as you open your mouth."

Lucius regarded his friend as the latter walked over to his bedside. He'd a jagged gash on his left arm and a purple bruise on his forehead. "Marcus, that was a very stupid thing you did. You could've gotten killed out there. Even now, your future is in ruins. I expect that defying generals is not considered a good career move."

The two tribunes then noticed a man watching them from the doorway—none other than Flavius Aetius himself. He nodded to them and said, "That's true in most instances. But when a tribune can teach one of those pigheaded generals the importance of loyalty, friendship, and honor, those transgressions can be overlooked. Just don't make a habit of it."

A very haggard Aetius walked in and sat on the stool just vacated by Dervla Conall. "I want to thank you, Tribune Bernius. You opened my eyes yesterday. Through all of my victories and strategies in defense of Rome, I have lost sight of what I was fighting for. Emperors come and go. Some are wise and some are fools. You are the idea of Rome, not the imbecile sitting on the throne. You shamed me. You made a pledge of honor and you stood by it regardless of the consequences." The general straightened his back. "I promise you this: never again will I back down from what is right for Rome because it's politically expedient. I don't think our friend Publius and his puppet master, Valentinian, will be very happy with the results. But a man without honor is not a man. You reminded me of that yesterday."

Despite any lingering pain from his injury, Lucius listened closely as the general began to tell a story—his story.

* * *

The sound of a small child giggling wafted to Aetius from a distant room in the estate, and his mind drifted back forty years to that life-changing moment when he was six years old.

King Alaric and the Visigoths besieged Mediolanum, an impressive city-fortress with high walls and many towers. The Visigoths could not breech the walls, but neither could the small Roman garrison drive them off. Aetius remembered standing on the ramparts holding tight to the hand of his centurion father, Circei.

"Father, how can this happen? Rome is the greatest empire in the world, and we're hiding behind these walls while the barbarians destroy our crops and steal our livestock."

Circei regarded his son with a grim face. "Flavius, Rome has lost its way. We've held sway over the world for so long, we've forgotten what's important. There are too many craven people in Rome who care more about planning the next feast than thinking about the malevolent beasts who dwell but a few weeks' worth of travel from their homes, savages who would rip their throats out if given the chance. Many have forgotten that we Romans are builders. Nowadays, they care far too much for their debauchery. Flavius, look long and hard at the howling mob out there. It's our future if Romans true to our heritage don't change our country's direction."

Aetius heard horns blow and watched from the battlements. Out across the open field, the standards of five legions marched against the Visigoths. Pride filled his heart as he held his father's hand and cheered with the soldiers on the wall as the Roman general, Stilicho, drove off the Visigoths from Mediolanum at last. Young Aetius felt the thrill of the citizens when word of the great victory spread.

Circei hoisted Aetius on his shoulders. "Now there's a true Roman. Flavius, aspire to be like General Stilicho, and perhaps Rome can be saved."

Aetius giggled as he bounced on his father's shoulders while people danced through the marketplace.

In the nine years that followed, the small boy grew into a man. One day, he learned of his father's death during the Visigoths' sack of Rome, and he returned to Rome. As he rode his horse through the shattered Porto Salaria into the city, he seethed at the devastation around him. He arrived at his parents' estate, situated in the path of the Visigoth horde, and discovered that his whole family had been killed. At the age of fifteen, he became the lord of a burned-out estate and an orphan.

As he contemplated the destruction of Rome's Sallust Gardens, he pulled out his belt knife and sliced the palm of his hand. He squeezed his fingers onto the pulsing vein until his fist was red with blood and vowed, "As God is my witness, I will never let this happen to my homeland again. I will be its shield and its sword."

* * *

"The next day, I became Rome's newest army recruit," Aetius finished.

Lucius exchanged a stunned look with Marcus. After a pause, the latter turned to Aetius and asked, "Is it true that you and Attila grew up as brothers?"

The imperator snorted and sat back. "Is that what the story has become?" He loosed a rueful sigh. "I did know Attila when we were both boys. I was among a group of Roman youths who were held as treaty hostages to the Hunnic king of that time, a crafty ruler named Rua. I relished challenging the Hunnic boys in youthful combat and was soon accepted as one of their own." Aetius twisted his face into a smile of mischief and amusement. "The most ambitious and fearless of the youths at court was a wild boy named Attila. We developed a wary respect for each other."

The general breathed deep and gazed out the window at the gleam of the rising sun. "Tribune, I leave today for what may be the greatest challenge of my life, and I need every true Roman to march with me. Would you forgive me and return to your command?"

Lucius stared slack-jawed. He'd been prepared to beg the man to allow him to stay in the army and didn't register at first that he wouldn't have to. When it clicked, he sputtered, "Gladly, sir!" hoping Aetius wouldn't change his mind. Lucius tried to rise but crashed back down on the cushions with a spinning head.

Phokas burst into the room and fumed. "For God's sake, what are you doing to my patient? He needs another day of rest before he can go traipsing off. I leave here for one minute, and you have the lad jumping up to get his head lopped off by some barbarian."

"So you're the imperial physician my medical staff told me about?" The imperator chuckled with sudden understanding. "No wonder Valentinian sent you out here. I'm sure you had the palace in a complete uproar. Well, Publius hates you, so that puts you in good stead with me." He rose slowly and twisted the kinks out of his back. "No, my good sir, young Bernius will not be leaving with the main army."

Worry surged through Lucius, catching his breath.

General Aetius turned to him. "Tribune, there is a column of Franks under a nobleman named Martinel due to arrive soon. We're breaking camp and cannot wait, and the Huns already have Aurelianum under siege. We'll be strung out over a long distance on the road, so I want you and your cohort to join these Franks and cover the northern approaches to our column. I don't want to be surprised by any of Attila's raiders. I also don't want the Franks to get any ideas about gathering items from the Roman citizenry around here."

Understanding, Lucius nodded. It didn't hurt as much this time.

"I left the details with Centurion Cilla. Your cohort will be bulked up to full strength, and I'll supplement it with two centuries of Gallic horsemen. Do you have a capable cavalry commander?"

Lucius made a wry grin. "Yes. The man who was being stoned with Marcus and me, Master Takumi, is an excellent horseman and a clever tactician."

Aetius returned a wan smile. "Yes, I met him at the estate's gate. He struck me as very competent, and Satewa speaks well of him. He is quite an effective barrier to any unwanted guests." The imperator turned to leave with a weary gait. "I have much to do. Thank you again, young man. I was lost and didn't know it. You showed me the way back."

After the general left, Lucius turned to Marcus, who stared at the now empty doorway, his expression thoughtful. "I don't believe I will ever have a more curious day than today."

"If you have a day that is more 'interesting' than this, please let me know so I can be far away," Phokas snapped.

The two young men snickered at each other, and then, as if a dam holding back their emotions burst, they laughed until tears streamed down their faces.

In time, however, they calmed and recalled their current situation. Marcus patted Lucius on the arm. "Well, I must be going. I can't sleep in like you since I'm leaving within the hour."

Lucius sobered. "Be careful, my brother. Be careful."

Marcus arched his eyebrows. "'Be careful.' This is coming from the man who challenged the Visigoth's greatest swordsman and accepted death by stoning all in the same day. Lucius, I think there are very few people who would survive what you consider caution." The fellow tribune gave his friend a mock salute and strode from the room.

With a soft chortle, Doctor Phokas smiled at Lucius with fondness. "Lad, get some sleep."

CHAPTER X

MARTINEL

Lucius didn't wake again until midday, and Phokas snored in the chair by his bedside. The Franks Imperator Aetius spoke of arrived late that evening. With his injury no longer impeding him, the tribune set out to meet them.

Lucius didn't know what to make of the boisterous man who greeted him. The Frankish nobleman named Martinel had a thick thatch of reddish-blonde hair chopped off at the shoulders. He was lean and angular, and he moved with lightning quick reflexes but didn't seem to take anything seriously. As far as Lucius could tell, the man was not much older than himself.

They sat before the hearth in the great room, the fire crackling quietly nearby. Both Lucius and Martinel had their senior officers with them. Five minutes after the introductions, Doctor Phokas began snoring on a couch. No one else in the room paid him any mind.

Once again, Martinel pointed to Lucius. "So, Roman darling, how did you earn that nasty wound on your head?"

Lucius bit back his aggravation, having evaded the question for over an hour. For much of the meeting, Martinel had shown far more interest in how his head got split open than in planning the logistics for their march.

Suddenly, a light gleamed in the Frank's eyes. "It was an affair that went awry! What a fiery wench she must be. Or was it her husband?" Martinel settled back on his stool. "Now, how long must I wait before we can start killing these Huns? I have never fought one and I hear they are worthy foes."

Lucius didn't relish what he would have to say. The Frankish arrivals hadn't been what he expected. Their two forces were a similar size, and half of the Franks were a well-armed mounted force who appeared very capable. However, the rest looked like they were farmers and herders until very recently as their armament appeared almost nonexistent. He had no other options, unfortunately, so the tribune explained their role in the campaign.

"What glory lies in that? We get to tramp through fat farmlands while everyone else will test themselves." The Frank slumped in his seat with grave disappointment etched on his face.

Martinel didn't venture many suggestions during the meeting. The most useful input Lucius received came from the old centurion, Vivarius, and a gray-bearded warrior named Johannes, the captain of Martinel's foot soldiers. Lucius had his doubts about the Franks' martial organization, but they were ready to leave by morning.

The transformation in the small market town amazed him. Two days earlier, merchants and soldiers had swarmed it; now, all that remained was the small Roman garrison stationed at the bridge. The stores shuttered their doors and windows, and not a single townsman roamed the streets.

When they hit the road, Lucius was pleased but sore. The two commands remained wary of each other but meshed well enough. The Seventh Cohort marched at the core with the Frankish foot soldiers serving as a rear guard. The cavalry rode in an arc around the column. Lucius put Takumi's riders out on a wide perimeter not because they were better scouts, but so they could try to minimize poaching from the local villages by their erstwhile allies. Despite this, the occasional skewered pig and goat still showed up roasting over the campfires.

Martinel loved to boast about his exploits to the Roman officers by the evening campfire. Centurion Cilla grew irritated by the bragging one night and countered with the story of how Lucius defeated the Visigoth swordmaster, Braun. This fired up Martinel as nothing else could, and the Frank pestered Lucius for every detail. "The Visigoth warriors pale next to the Franks, but this Braun has an impressive reputation nonetheless. We must test each other."

Each evening after that, the tribune dueled with the Frankish nobleman. They used weighted wooden practice swords, but it hurt nonetheless. Lucius' head injury still ached on the first night, but he had little trouble handling his opponent. However, Martinel possessed a quick mind and proved to be a serious student of the sword. By the second night, he landed blows; and by the sixth night, they fought to a near draw.

Both men collapsed, exhausted, on the spot where they sparred. Sweat dripped from their bodies, despite the cool evening air. Lucius saluted Martinel with the practice weapon and tossed it aside.

The tired Frank laughed. "Roman, I came close that time. You have to admit it."

Lucius groaned, slumping in his place. "I know I don't need any more victories like that one. You're the fastest man I've ever fought. My whole body aches."

Martinel rose to stand, grabbed a jug of wine held by Johannes, took a long swig, and plopped down next to Lucius. "Roman, you're the most tenacious fighter I've ever encountered. You never quit." After taking another long gulp, he handed the container to the tribune. "Here. This will ease some of the pain and perhaps slow your reflexes for tomorrow."

Lucius wiped the sweat from his brow and poured the wine into his clay cup. He looked over his shoulder at the gathered officers as he took a sip. "So how did I fare in the betting...?"

He never found out. A dispatch rider walked onto the field and looked around in confusion. "Tribune Bernius?"

The grin on Lucius' face vanished and he waved the man over. The messenger gave a hesitant salute and handed Lucius a scroll from General Aetius. Lucius broke the seal and scanned the page in the fading evening light.

"What news from Aurelianum?" Vivarius asked as the senior Roman and Frankish officers crowded in.

"It appears the general arrived in time. The Huns broke off the siege and are fleeing north. He wants us to hold our position and wait for the main army."

"That's good news. The best battle is the one not fought," Takumi quipped with Johannes. The senior centurions nodded their heads in agreement.

Martinel jumped and thrust his fist in the air. "Ha! I knew this Attila was a coward. It's one thing to trample those weak tribes of the north, but the thought of facing the Franks has routed him without a drop of blood spilled."

"Sit down and shut up, you fool," Phokas snapped. "Attila is a cagey fox. The Huns have never lost a battle with him leading. He'll turn and fight at the time and place of his choosing."

Martinel glared at him, then at the other officers, before sitting down, his expression sullen. "Well, then, he'll soon learn what defeat tastes like."

Before any further arguments began, Lucius stopped them. "I suggest we turn in early. We can spend tomorrow seeing to our equipment. I expect when we rejoin the main army, there won't be many more opportunities."

The officers took the hint and drifted off until only Martinel remained. He stared into the fire and glanced furtively around the area. In time, he approached Lucius and spoke almost in a whisper. "I must confess... I've never been in an actual battle before. My brothers have had many such trials and have returned home with stories of their fearless exploits. I just hope I won't shame them."

Thoughtful, Lucius watched the fire and poured both of them some wine from the almost empty jug. *Who am I to give advice? My total combat experience consists of one fight with a band of Vandal brigands.* But he understood the man's feelings, and it compelled him to offer some sort of solace. "One cannot be brave without fear. If you fear nothing, then there's no courage required. It's a question of what you do with that fear. Will it paralyze you or drive you? All I can say is to keep your head, listen to those who are wiser, and pray the mistakes you make don't cost too many lives."

Martinel nodded his head. "You know, Roman, when we first met, I was expecting to encounter an over-civilized, pompous oaf, but you aren't. You are no older than I, but your men and officers obey you without question. Someday, we may face each other in battle. Gaul should belong to the Franks, and you Romans are in the way. But I don't believe I could ever think of you as an enemy." He lifted his eyes to look Lucius right in the face. "I don't believe your head wound was over a woman. Will you tell me that tale?"

Lucius laughed mirthlessly and told Martinel how he'd accepted death by stoning. The story would've come out at some point anyway. When he finished, he braced himself for ridicule.

Instead of being laughed at, Martinel stared at him with awe. "These legionaries you spoke of were mere peasants? They were men not of your clan?"

A glum Lucius swirled the wine in his cup and nodded his head.

Slowly, Martinel stood with a hint of awe. "You put your word of honor above your very life? Roman, I take back my words from earlier. If and when we face each other in battle, I will not lift my sword to strike you."

Confusion filled the tribune as he faced the Frank. "What else could I do?"

Takumi Saegusa returned to the fire then, and Martinel turned to him. "Will you please educate this man? The real world will destroy him!"

"Perhaps he should educate the world. He would improve it," came the even reply.

Martinel looked back and forth between the two men. "Thank God there're not many Romans like you or I would have to change my allegiance. Tomorrow evening, we duel again, and this time, I will triumph." He drained his mug of wine and stalked off.

Takumi chuckled as he sat down. "I think that young man's head would explode if he ever met your entire family."

"Master Takumi, what else could I have done? Those men took an oath to me; I couldn't cast it aside."

"Ah, my young commander, that is why it has been an honor to serve your family all of these years." Takumi stared into the fire, and his eyes grew distant. "Only your father knows my story. I would like for you to hear it, too."

"Master, I would be honored if you would share your tale with me." Lucius drew in a breath, waiting for Takumi to begin.

CHAPTER XI

JOURNEY TO THE WEST

Takumi Saegusa watched the dancing flames for a long time and began without warning.

"The story of my travels started in a land called Korea. I was a young captain from Nari in Japan. My *shogun* tried to wrest the port of Sabi away from the Chinese scum and their Silla allies. We lost that battle, and I was wounded and captured. Since I was a poor man's son, they didn't hold me for ransom. One of the Chinese generals took me as a slave, and I served as a pack mule for that oaf's possessions all the way to Changan. My own swords were part of the burden I carried.

"It was in Changan where my misfortune took a turn for the better. A civil war raged between the Qi dynasty and the followers of Liang. The military column I was a part of was attacked, and I slipped away in the confusion. I acquired my swords from a distracted guard who moved far too slowly. Then I was free.

"I laid low until nightfall and headed back toward Changan. The market was outside the city's walls, so I didn't have to figure out how to get in. The traders scrambled to move their caravans and escape the war zone. I approached the first merchant who looked prosperous. He was a small man with shifty eyes and a pointed, oily beard, but he wasn't too particular. He asked a few questions, I told him a few lies, and I was hired.

"The caravan guard captain was a bit tougher to convince. Without asking any questions, he tried to take my head off with his spatha. I saw the gleam in his eye and anticipated his move, so I parried the blow and pressed my *katana* against his throat. The man grunted, 'I guess you'll do. I want you on the left side.'

"Only then did I ask where we were going. He laughed and slapped me on the back. 'My friend, Shamir, is a silk merchant.

You are in for the journey that will take years and will test your spirit. He is from Antioch, in the land of the Romans.'

"I didn't have time to rethink my decision. The caravan left within the hour, and every step I took carried me further away from my home. On consideration, I decided I would like to see these strange new worlds. I was now *ronin*, a dishonored warrior without a lord, in the midst of a country that hated my people.

"We traveled through many wild lands. I got along well with the captain, Tarack, and he was an interesting character. He said that, in his youth, he was a Roman legionary and served under General Stilicho, but he was forced to flee when the general was accused of treason. He taught me Latin and a little Greek.

"I also learned that being a caravan guard was not a long-term career. Shamir paid the tolls and bribes necessary, but bandits always looked for a chance to get more. The guards paid the price of denying them that opportunity. By the end of the first year, I was the lieutenant in charge of the caravan's left side, and most of the men I commanded were not there at the start of the trip. Outside Bagdad, we lost Tarack in an ambush, so Shamir made me the new captain and hung the medallion of his merchant house around my neck.

"When we finally reached Antioch, Shamir posted new guards from the family's warehouse, and we celebrated until the sun rose. The next day, someone dumped a bucket of water on me to wake me, and a red-faced caravan master screamed at me to get up. I had never seen Shamir so angry. It turned out that some clever traders had smuggled silkworms to the Byzantine Empire, and those worms liked the Greek mulberry bushes just fine. However, it also meant the price of silk had plummeted. Shamir growled, 'We're moving to Rome! I've heard the prices there haven't dropped yet. We leave tomorrow by ship.'

"The next day, we loaded the precious cargo onto three galleys the merchant had hired. I didn't like the looks of the boats or the crews, and I warned Shamir of the same. He laughed it off and said I was too nervous. The wind and the weather held fine. We were a day out of the Roman port of Bari

81

when the sailors sprang their trap. They were pirates. I rallied the guards on my ship and we held together. The other two ships were not as fortunate. Shamir heaved chests overboard, screaming as the cutthroats closed in. They cut him down and tossed his dead body into the sea along with the men who served him.

"As the sun set, the pirates from the other two galleys boarded my ship and overwhelmed my small band of guards. As my last soldier fell, I jumped overboard so those cowards would not have the honor of killing me. I bobbed in the water as they laughed, raised sail, and left with their stolen treasure.

"I watched the sails disappear in the dusk and was about to surrender myself to a cold, watery grave when something bumped into me. It was one of Shamir's chests empty enough to float. I threw myself on it and kept myself warm by swearing revenge on those murderers.

"Midway through the next day, a fishing boat rescued me. The old fisherman took me right into the port of Bari. There, I saw three familiar galleys tied up at the wharf. At the dock standing before one of the crates was the pirate captain dressed in Shamir's own robes. He was showing off the silks to Verius, your father. I didn't know this land, and I didn't know its people, so I bared my blades and advanced on the business transaction. As I approached, I shouted, 'Sir, do you always purchase product soaked in the blood of innocent men?'

"Verius stopped examining the quality of the material and turned a startled eye toward me. He told me later that I appeared to be a madman emerging from the sea, what with my foreign looks and holding two drawn swords. However, he also said he saw a righteous anger blazing in my eyes. He replied to me, 'I have dealt with the house of Shamir on previous occasions and have no reason to doubt the source of their goods.'

"I then displayed the captain's medallion from under my tunic and asked, 'Would the Shamir Trading House unload cargo without their guard captain present?' Lucius, your father looked at me for a long time and said, 'No... they wouldn't.'

"The pirate captain glowered at the two of us and declared, 'Dead men tell no tales. Kill them.'

"I lunged for the leader but was knocked down by a pirate who snuck up behind me. Instead of fleeing, Verius drew his spatha and stood over me as I tried to unscramble my wits from the blow. A half dozen of those barbarians closed on us while the rest untied the ships from the wharf.

"We both would have been dead in seconds, but at that moment, the old fisherman who rescued me ran down the pier with the port's navy legionaries in tow. The galleys didn't wait for their erstwhile comrades and pushed away from the dock. With a cry of anguish, the now trapped cutthroats tried to surrender, but the legionaries' captain didn't let them speak for long and had them slaughtered on the spot. Everyone hates pirates, so no one complained.

"Your father, Verius, was a respected merchant in that port. He always paid his taxes and was generous with his bribes to the port authority. After Verius assured the officer he was all right, the officer left with his men dragging the corpses behind them.

"Although groggy, I rose to my feet and bowed deeply to him. I knew it was a rare and treasured gift to find an honorable man who would be willing to sacrifice his own life for an unknown innocent. I spoke the Latin that Tarack taught me. 'I am Takumi Saegusa, a native of faraway Nippon. Noble sir, you have saved my life, and I am honored and indebted to you forever.'"

Takumi leaned back and chuckled as he looked over at Lucius. "I must say I surprised your father with my oath, and at first, he didn't know what to make of it. After all of these years, I have learned that Verius is an excellent judge of people's character, and that day, he read my heart. 'Forever is a long time. How about if you come work for me? You have shown courage and integrity this day, and I could use such a man.'

"I bowed again and started to speak when he slapped my shoulder and said, 'Come with me. I need some wine... and a new tunic. I think I soiled myself in this one.' We headed into town, and I have been part of the Bernius family ever since."

Takumi rose and wiped a tear from his cheek, smiled at Lucius, and dumped the dregs of his wine into the fire. "Now you know. I'm going to bed."

CHAPTER XII

AURELIANUM

The next morning arrived gray and gloomy, and the smell of rain wafted in the air. Lucius stretched the aches out of his back as he exited the tent. Since they'd been ordered to stay put, he granted himself the luxury of sleeping in late. He was thinking about breakfast when Vidin jogged toward him with a grim look on his face. All interest in breakfast vanished.

"Sir, that savage friend of yours is at the gate. He said he must speak with you now. He just yelled to me, 'In the name of your Christian God, get the tribune.' Hurry!"

"Why didn't you just let him in?" exclaimed an irate Lucius.

"Sorry, sir, but the other guards are all new. I was the only one there from your old command. They didn't like the looks of Satewa and wouldn't let him in on my say so."

My old command? How long has it been? Three weeks? Nonetheless, Lucius regarded Vidin with pride; the man was turning into a model legionary. "Go gather up the centurions and the Frankish commanders, and have them meet me here. I'll go save the guards from the vicious brute prowling outside the gate."

Vidin smiled, gave a sharp salute, and trotted off.

Lucius strapped on his sandals and jogged to the gated entrance of the squared breastwork encampment. Satewa panted, and sweat dripped off his near-naked body; all he wore was a breechcloth and soft-soled leather boots. Two rattled legionaries pointed their heavy hastas at him, but their bodies sagged with relief when Lucius shouted, "Ho, Satewa. What word do you bring?"

Satewa looked hard at him and grated in a cold voice, "They're coming!"

Lucius had no doubt about who Satewa referred to, and his stomach twisted into a knot. "Come with me. I'm already gathering my commanders."

They exchanged no other words as they passed through the camp, but all the soldiers followed them with their eyes, and the morning bustle subsided into silence. Satewa's head turned as though assessing the mounded dirt walls and the number of troops. As they approached the gathered officers, Takumi bowed, Phokas nodded his head in greeting, and everyone else just stared.

Lucius arrived and found that everyone was there, even the Frankish commanders who made it a habit of showing up late. "Gentlemen, for those of you who don't know him, this is Centurion Satewa, commander of the Gallic Legion scouts and one of Imperator Aetius' most trusted advisors. Satewa, everyone is here. You may speak."

The large man replied by crouching down, smoothing out the dusty soil, and marking a spot. "You are here. Thirty thousand Huns are coming straight toward you from the south. Their vanguard will be here in a few hours. Aetius and the main army are in pursuit, but they're perhaps a half day behind."

"How wide is their front?" Vivarius asked.

"Almost all of them are on horseback and travelling in clans and tribes, so they cover a wide area—perhaps a mile. You must abandon this camp and flee."

Martinel snarled with a wolfish grin. "No Frank will run from a band of Hunnic barbarians. Their blood will flow as a river when we meet them."

The Frankish captains cringed and the Roman centurions stared at him in disbelief.

Vivarius in particular whipped his head from side to side. "You young fool! We'll be cut to ribbons in minutes. It'll be *our* blood that will soak these forsaken rocks."

Martinel's eyes blazed, but before anyone could issue a challenge, Lucius yelled. "Stop this nonsense!"

All wary eyes turned toward him. Lucius flinched but went on. "I agree with Lord Martinel." The veteran soldiers started sputtering their objections, but Lucius raised his hands. "Listen to me! Most of our men are raw recruits and are on foot. Do you seriously think we could avoid a swarm of horsemen thirty thousand strong? And when the Scourge of

Europe catches us in the open, how long do you think a single cohort of untested legionaries and a collection of Frankish farmers will last?"

The group fell silent as Lucius looked each of them in the eye. A defiant Martinel glared back, but even his face reflected doubt.

"We will stay right here. Green troops can fight better from behind thick walls, and our communications won't be a disaster. We can only hope they'll just pass us by with our main army hot on their heels. Martinel and Takumi, take your cavalry and ride. If they do stop for us... a few hundred more defenders will not matter."

Martinel rolled his shoulders and looked around, thoughtful. "I apologize for my rash words before. I must seem as a child to you. But there is another way. I will lead my riders out of here and make contact with the Huns. When they pursue us, I will lead them on a merry chase far from here."

Takumi bowed to the Frankish nobleman. "Your words are sound, but your plan will fail. The Huns are renowned for fighting on horseback, and rumors say their steeds are tireless. You will be caught and butchered, and then he will turn to Lucius. For myself, I will not leave. Choose another for your cavalry."

"My teacher, I don't think you understand. We'll probably die here," said Lucius. "Those on horseback are the only ones with a remote chance of surviving."

Takumi looked up at the early morning sun filtering through the thick, leafy trees. "Then this looks like a good place to die."

Lucius snorted in exasperation at the defiant man. "All right, then we have an hour to make this place more defensible. Commanders, to your men. I want that ditch as deep and the walls as high as we can make them. Doctor Phokas, the center of the camp is yours. Gather whatever you need. Satewa, please give my regards to the imperator. Tell him... tell him I'm sorry. Perhaps he could see that my men get a decent Christian burial."

"That is a request you will have to give to one of your horsemen. As Takumi stated, this looks like a good place to die." Satewa pulled out the hunting knife he wore on his belt, drew it across the palm of his hand, and squeezed his fist until thin droplets of blood ran across his knuckles.

Lucius nodded in understanding, took the blade, and did the same. Satewa then grasped the tribune's hand until their blood mingled. Each officer followed suit until Lucius' fist was red with blood, and he met everyone's eyes. "Now move. The devil himself will be here soon."

The officers scattered, shouting commands, and the camp exploded in a flurry of action. Martinel walked over to Lucius during the mass shuffle. "I do hope I never have to face you in battle, my friend... but I will take my cavalry out of here. This is not false bravado; my horsemen are the only seasoned fighters here. I will set up a screen so the camp is not surprised. Just don't bar all the entrances until we get back. I would hate to be trapped between those demon riders and your spiked ditch." The Frank slapped Lucius on the shoulder and walked away without another word.

A short while later, a column of a hundred Roman Gauls rode out and galloped hard toward the southeast. Behind them followed four hundred Frankish lancers who fanned out in a wide arc around the road coming up from the south. They vanished from sight in the dense forest.

The rhythmic sound of axes and shovels resounded everywhere. Men at work had less time to dwell on the fear gnawing at their bellies. Felled trees across the road would slow any rapid advance, and the thick dirt barricade would block any arrow ever made. However, while the open dale had a clear view of a hundred yards in every direction, the flat ground offered no natural defenses. Lucius studied the field along the road and played out different scenarios in his mind. None of them had a happy conclusion.

The tribune felt a presence near him and found Phokas examining the same ground. "I may have told you this before, but I'm originally from the small town of Corinth. In fact, my brother and his family still live there on a small estate. Not far from there are the ruins of the ancient city of Sparta. Our legends tell us that they fought a vast Persian army with but three hundred warriors at Thermopylae."

Lucius returned a bittersweet smile. The story of King Leonidas and his Spartans was one of his favorites as a youth. "Ah, my good doctor, but King Leonidas had a very narrow pass to defend, and after three days, they were overwhelmed."

"That is indeed true. But he bought the other Greek city-states enough time to unite and face Xerxes' Immortals. How long do you think you'll have to hold off these 'Immortal' Huns before Aetius arrives?"

Lucius sighed and was about to answer when the forest to the south erupted with screams. The tribune shouted to the *conicen*, "Blow the clarion and signal the men in!" The conicen complied, and soon, the axe men scampered in from the edge of the woods, and those in the ditch clambered over the wall. "Centurions, have your men ready their pilas. Cilla, hold the First Century in reserve."

The *pila* was a staple of the Roman army for centuries. Its soft-leaded shaft bent when it hit its target, rendering it useless to throw back.

Lucius looked back at the screen of trees, and the Frankish cavalry emerged, navigating through the felled trees. Martinel took the lead, waving his sword in the air. As their horses picked their way through the fallen trees, screams of terror burst from those at the rear of his column. The riders urged their mounts to greater speed toward the sanctuary of the walled fort. Some abandoned their animals and sprinted to the enclosure as the sound of bloodcurdling chants, blaring horns, and booming war drums poured from the forest.

Martinel halted at the lip of the ditch beside the extended gangplank as his men scrambled to safety on foot and on horseback. The Huns swarmed onto the field and butchered any Franks within reach. Arrows landed in the ground beside Martinel's steed as he rode up the gangplank just before the legionaries pulled it in. He was the last living Frank to leave the field, and he dismounted his horse and stood next to Lucius. They watched in amazement as an endless horde of chanting warriors streamed from the forest.

"Well, Roman, it looks like there are more than enough for the two of us."

Lucius smiled at the jest despite the fear twisting his stomach. "Martinel, if you could, pull together your dismounted cavalry. Place them on the eastern wall. It's our most exposed position, and if those Huns breech our perimeter, this will be a very short fight."

The Frankish nobleman flashed a nervous smile. "My dear Roman, your wish is my command."

Lucius turned and watched him walk over to where his surviving men gathered. As he did so, Vivarius jogged up. "All the men are in position, sir."

"Good. Tell the other centurions they're to launch their pilas at the next blast from our clarion."

Vivarius nodded and started to leave, but then turned around. "Sir, your plan is sound. The situation is impossible, but this will give us at least a slim chance. Now we'll see how well these unbloodied recruits can fight." Lucius returned a wan smile, and the soldier saluted him. "Sir, it appears it will be a short time, but it has been a pleasure to serve under you."

He took off before the tribune could reply, leaving the latter to eye the oncoming mass of men. There didn't appear to be a great deal of order to their advance, but they split into two distinct prongs, and a large band of archers lined up behind them.

As the first wave of arrows arched over the field, the centurions shouted, "Shields up!" The legionaries raised their *scutums*, the large semi-cylindrical shields. The incoming arrows had little impact on the legionaries, but many of the lightly armored Frankish infantrymen fell. The chants of the circling horde turned into a chorus of bellows and the Huns charged.

Lucius shouted to the conicens, and the clarions blared a piercing note. On signal, hundreds of javelins flew through the air. With the Huns packed together, their light horse shields provided little defense. This allowed the pilas to bite deep.

"Again!"

The clarions blew another note, and a second volley of pilas swarmed into the air. The lead Hunnic warriors tried to back up but were held in place by the thousands pressing from behind. The drums sounded, and with a roar of bloodlust, the horde surged again, trampling their dead and wounded comrades.

The steep ditch was wide, but the Huns dragged along logs and baled straw. The few Frankish and Roman archers available did little to dissuade them. The Huns soon clambered up the barricade and began fighting the Romans and Franks barring their path.

The defending Romans fought with a desperate determination, but their attackers surged up the wall with recklessness. The Roman reserves flew into the fray; meanwhile, the dismounted Frankish cavalry held the eastern wall well with their long swords.

With a gash on his left leg, Takumi hobbled toward Tribune Bernius, shouting and gesturing wildly at the western wall. "Lucius, the men are breaking! In another minute, they'll be routed!"

The tribune looked over and saw, to his horror, many dead Romans sprawled along the wall and several starting to abandon their positions. "The fools! Where are they going to run to? If our line gives, we're all dead!"

He shouted the war cry he learned from Satewa and ran ahead with Takumi limping at his side. Soon, Satewa and Martinel joined him in screaming the same sound. Their loud charge apparently had an effect because the Romans who had begun to flee turned to face their pursuers. However, the Huns who had crossed the wall advanced on the tribune's small band undeterred.

Numbers counted for much, but in small, tight areas, skill prevailed, and Lucius was a master. The world narrowed to the opponents before him and the thought left him as his instincts for survival took control. Takumi became a blur of motion, fighting in his two-weapon style. Martinel charged with abandon, showing great skill and courage, but soon found himself cut off and surrounded by barbarians. With a shout, he lunged at a tormentor and then collapsed from a hard blow partially blunted by his helmet.

Lucius leapt into the fray and held the attackers back until Martinel staggered to his feet and moaned, "Roman, I owe you one." A feral smile then crossed his lips as the two men turned to face their attackers shoulder to shoulder.

Lucius dispatched his last opponent as the survivors fled back over the wall. As he reached the wall, his cry of triumph stuck in his throat as he saw his certain death. A thick mass of barbarians covered the field, and they gathered for another assault. Even so, Lucius found his companions stood with him. Blood smears covered both Takumi and Martinel.

Vidin ran up next to him and gazed at the gathering horde. "Sir, tell me again how many times a brave man will die?"

The tribune replied, "Only once, legionary. Only once." At that moment, he noticed his whole band of reclaimed deserters now stood with him. He grinned and felt free of the fear clutching at him. Lucius threw back his head and screamed Satewa's war cry again. As he gasped for breath, the sound didn't stop as it had been taken up first by the men around him and then by every fighter manning the walls.

The barbarians paused and exchanged puzzled looks with each other before they moved with more caution. The Romans at the wall could do nothing but watch. Then the Huns' advance came to a halt at the blare of many horns and a parade of resplendently armored men riding onto the field. The man leading them wore a bearskin cape and a golden crown, and he cantered on a white horse right up to the edge of the ditch, fearless of any arrow launched by the men inside.

The man was of average height and build. He scanned the wall and locked onto Lucius with predatory eyes, then laughed and shouted in clear Latin, "Tell Aetius, once and for all, we'll see who's the better man. Tell him I will await him at the Rhine." Without another word, he turned his back on the defenders, twisted the reins of his horse, and trotted to the road. The horns blared again, and the endless army of warriors streamed past them on the road north.

A whole hour passed before the last Hun vanished from sight. The tribune posted as many exhausted sentries as he could muster and gathered his commanders to assess their losses. Two of the old centurions had been killed, and of the Frankish commanders, Martinel alone survived.

Vivarius gave the final tally. "We lost a third of our men. The Franks fared worse; they lost about half. Those Hunnic archers wiped out whole companies."

Martinel looked around and appeared to have aged ten years since the morning. His sword was notched and his armor rent in several places. His eyes, on the other hand, burned with questions. "So why did they leave? They had us. We were breaking all around the perimeter. Another hour and we would've been crushed."

Lucius studied the ground, thinking hard, until a conclusion hit him. "Because the Great Attila is afraid."

The officers gaped at Lucius as if he'd gone insane.

He smiled back at them. "No, gentlemen, it's true. Attila's not afraid of us; that's for sure. But why didn't he fight Aetius at Aurelianum? Why is he moving his army so fast and marshalling all of his troops for a fight on ground of his choosing? He can't afford to waste that precious hour getting rid of us. My guess is, we'll see Rome's Legions come up that same road very soon."

By midafternoon, a column of Frankish lancers rode within sight of the makeshift fort. Martinel yelped and rode out to meet them across the lowered plank gangway. After a few minutes of conferring, he returned and called to Lucius, who sat atop the wall and watched with curiosity. Some of Martinel's bravado had resurfaced and he shouted, "Roman, I go to report to Merovech, my king. I will take my riders with me, but could you take charge of my footmen until I can summon them?"

"Gladly. They fought with great courage. I will see they are as cared for as my own men."

"I can ask for nothing more. By the way, your Roman friends should be coming along soon."

The legionaries slid out planks to span the ditch, and the surviving Frankish horsemen worked their way onto the field strewn with dead Huns and felled trees.

Martinel gnawed on his lower lip as his last rider descended. "Roman, I think I will miss you. Our paths have crossed for just a brief time, but I have learned much. There are many things I held as truths that I need to reconsider. I would like to think of you as my friend."

Lucius smiled back. "It is done—as long as I don't have to duel with you anymore. I'm still sore from the beatings."

Martinel turned away laughing. "Ah, my dear Roman, you know little of Frankish pride. We must fence until I can master you."

Lucius gave an exaggerated groan and told the departing rider, "Then consider yourself victorious. I yield."

The only response was barking laughter and a waving hand as the Frankish column rode off.

Satewa leapt over the barricade and nodded to Lucius. "I, too, must take my leave. My general must learn what transpired here."

CHAPTER XIII

RED FISTS

It was late afternoon when the watchmen spotted a large cloud of dust rising from the road to the south. A short while later, ranks of young Roman legionaries trudged up the road with their heavy hastas perched on their shoulders. They stared with wide-eyed fear at the scene of the battle until their centurions hurried them along. Most of Lucius' cohort who were not aiding Doctor Phokas or being tended by him sat perched on the dirt berm, watching the parade go by.

The tribune called the men to attention as a nondescript armored officer rode up to the small fort. He recognized the plain-looking face as that of Flavius Aetius, Imperator of Rome's Gallic Legions. The general regarded the field of battle, and to the tribune, he just smiled. Lucius was not surprised to see Satewa help the general off his horse and follow him up the gangplank to where Lucius stood at rigid attention.

"So, my young tribune, why am I not surprised to see you here in the thick of this?" asked Aetius.

Lucius gave Satewa a quizzical glance for a clue as to how he should respond, but the warrior from the distant land of the Iroquois remained unreadable. Lucius didn't have any time to answer anyway.

Aetius climbed to the top of the berm and faced the legionaries marching by. "Behold, the invincible Hun!" he called out as he gestured to the dead barbarians strewn across the field. The general then lifted Lucius' arm high to catch everyone's eyes. The tribune's hand tightened into a fist with pain as the general grabbed his injured arm. "Behold, the Red Fist of Rome who vanquished them!"

The exhausted Lucius looked at his fist, and it was indeed quite red; he would have to go see Doctor Phokas for a poultice. He didn't know about the vanquished part, though. Behind him, dead legionaries lay lined up in neat rows, and the many wounded writhed in pain waiting for treatment. The

Huns could have taken his little encampment without much more effort.

The effect on the troops, however, was quite different. His own men lining the wall pumped their fists high and cheered. The shouts carried over to the legionaries on the road.

The fear slid away from their eyes as they listened to the general's declaration. As if planned, the gray-haired legates and centurions up and down the line repeated the words. "If the Hunnic horde could be defeated by a single Roman cohort, then perhaps they're not as invincible as they boast. Look at the evidence before you. The barbarians are dead, and the Roman legionaries stand tall. Aetius is invincible, and we are Rome's Red Fist!"

The tribune looked sideways at the imperator, whose face adopted a quiet satisfaction. "Sir, did you plan this? Was my cohort sent out here to be sacrificial lambs? How did you know we would even survive?"

At this, the imperator looked aghast. "Tribune, you misjudge me both in terms of cleverness and ruthlessness. I have sent many good men to certain death to achieve a greater good, but I never do so lightly. In this case, however, I actually thought I put you in a safe position. I thought for sure Attila would fight me at Aurelianum. Instead, he retreats. It must gall him." Aetius calmed then and looked the tribune square in the eyes. "When Satewa told me what happened here, I improvised. The army is untested and they're afraid. That's a very bad combination, but this will inspire them. They need to believe. It doesn't matter that those dead warriors aren't even Huns."

Lucius almost fell over in disbelief. "Excuse me, sir, those *aren't* Huns? Then who are they?"

"Those were Ostrogoths. Their King, Valamir, has bent a knee to Attila, and he is now a vassal to the Hunnic Empire. In fact, he's also a blood relative to the Visigoth royal house." The general gazed at the sky and sighed. "Sometimes, it seems I'm juggling with knives. My young tribune, I can afford very few mistakes."

"That reminds me..." Lucius pursed his lips. "Sir, this Attila left a message for you. He said he will meet you at the Rhine, and then we'll see who's the better man."

The general sighed again. "I told you that as a boy, I spent some time in the royal court of the Huns. I was the one person who could beat Attila in those youthful competitions. Even then, he had a grand view of himself and couldn't tolerate anyone besting him." Aetius rubbed his nose. "The Rhine, is it? I can't let that happen. If he reaches the Rhine, he will indeed be invincible against any force I can muster.

"Young man, you kept your head and did well today. See to your men. The army will camp here tonight so they can revel in your victory. By morning, the tale of the Red Fist of Rome will grow, and morale will be high. Every tribune will be looking to curry my favor and match your exploits." Aetius' face clouded, turning grim. "Attila is indeed strong, and our alliances hang by a thread. Tonight is going to be a very long night."

The imperator patted Lucius on the shoulder and headed back into the open dale. Horns blared, and the field came alive with activity.

* * *

Lucius slept like a rock that night and didn't awaken until someone kicked him in the side. "Wake up, you sluggard. Are you going to sleep all day?"

The tribune slit open his sleep-crusted eyes and discovered Marcus grinning down at him. "I was going to douse you with a bucket of water, but that wouldn't be appropriate for the heroic Red Fist of Rome."

Lucius turned away from Marcus. "Then go away and let the great hero get some sleep."

"I would, but the army's moving out, and fast." Marcus sobered and knelt. "I wanted to see you before we left. I knew the stories couldn't be half true, but I also knew that if there were trouble, you would be the cause."

Lucius sat up, his whole body still aching, and rolled his shoulders. "It was close, my friend. Very, very close. So how goes it with you? What's happening in the wider world?"

Marcus snorted back a short laugh. "All I've done so far is march, then some double time, and then march some more. Meanwhile, it looks like you managed to get things stirred up all by yourself. The imperator had a meeting with our allies last night, and they're now chomping at the bit to pursue Attila's horde. In fact, the Frankish King, Merovech, rode out with his warriors before dawn. Some of his captains led by that new friend of yours, Lord Martinel, tried to convince him to stay with the main army, but the king would hear nothing of it. He wanted the glory of being the first to defeat the Huns."

Lucius hid a laugh as he considered the idea of the impetuous Martinel arguing caution, but the image faded when a sudden thought occurred to him. "The general told me he needed to find a way of catching Attila before he reached the Rhine." The tribune shuddered. "He said that he would send good men to their deaths to achieve a greater good. I wonder if he planted a few ideas at that meeting. Although badly outnumbered, the Franks would definitely make the Huns stop and fight."

Marcus regarded his friend. "Lucius, no one ordered the Franks to charge out this morning. Come, my friend, I'm hungry. Let's see about breakfast."

Lucius rubbed his chin as he contemplated the power of suggestion and a few well-placed comments. It sent a chill down his spine. "I'm not very hungry right now. I need a shave." The tribune sighed, rising to stand. "C'mon, I'll join you for another round of those meals the Roman army is famous for."

Marcus half-groaned, half-laughed and asked, "I wonder if it'll be gruel or gruel?" as they left the tent. Once outside, Cilla fell in behind them with a silent nod.

As if on a signal, Doctor Phokas descended on Lucius with a long list of demands for shelters and poultices. Lucius paused and scanned the sheet. "Half these items are impossible to get." He handed the sheet to Cilla, then looked the old doctor in the eye and saw heart-rending sorrow there.

"Phokas, there's clean water here and reasonable security. Let Cilla know what you need for support and we'll try to leave it." He put his arm on the old man's shoulder. "My guess is you'll be very busy over the next few days."

The doctor's shoulders sagged, and his voice cracked as he spoke. "I've never seen anything like this before. One poor lad with his entrails hanging out threw himself between me and some raging barbarians rampaging through my hospital. Helpless men lying in my care were hacked to death." The dim embers of his tired eyes flared, looking at his hands in disgust. "Yesterday, for the first time, I learned how to kill, and I will gladly do that again. Those men were in my care. I should've been able to save all of them."

Cilla offered a sympathetic smile. "Sir, from what I heard, you worked miracles. You denied Dis Pater many a life yesterday, and it was not with your sword."

A wan smile crossed Phokas' face. "It's a good thing those Frankish priests who were aiding me know as much about fighting as they do about praying. One was even useful treating the wounded. That Father Patricius is pigheaded but has a keen mind and nimble fingers."

Cilla turned to the tribuno. "Sir, we have another problem. We lost two centurions yesterday. My optio can step into the one role. The man is no intellectual, but he can follow and give orders. He won't do anything stupid. For the other post, I don't know who to suggest. We're out of gray hairs, and the other cohort consists of children."

"Children they might be," said Lucius, "but yesterday, they showed their mettle as true Roman legionaries."

The centurion's faced went ashen. "I didn't mean you, sir. Yesterday, you also pulled off a miracle."

Lucius looked down and kicked absently at the swirling dust. "It wasn't me. It was the men. They did it all." To Takumi, he said, "Honored teacher, could I add one more to the long lists of debts I owe you? Would you take command of the leaderless century? You have commanded men before and know Roman tactics."

Without taking a breath, Takumi bowed. "It would be an honor to serve you in that role. They will be the finest soldiers in your command. But remember, it must be temporary. My pledge is to your family, and I will return to them when this is over." Without waiting for acknowledgment, he bowed again and turned to Cilla. "Now take me to my soldiers." The two hurried off with Phokas trailing behind them, shouting out his needs.

The two tribunes completed the short walk to the camp's kitchen area. When they arrived, they were greeted by a single pot and a lone cook standing over it.

Marcus cocked his head. "Vidin, they made you the cook?"

The legionary looked back with proud eyes under a blood-soaked bandage wrapped around his head. "If I had anything to work with, I could make a meal that would have you dancing. A Bulgur can always outcook you Italians. But, alas, this is the same slop we've been eating for two weeks—boiled wheat."

The sight of the kettle reminded Lucius that he was no longer hungry. Marcus, on the other hand, dug right in without a care. As his friend ate, Lucius turned to Vidin. "Are you all right? That looks like a nasty cut you have there."

The legionary gingerly touched the side of his head. "It's fine, sir. My cap took most of the blow. That goat of a barbarian never got a chance to take a second swing at me."

Lucius put down his bowl without drawing his gaze away. "You did well yesterday, Vidin. When the imperator called us the Red Fist of Rome, he was right. You men could stand shoulder to shoulder with even the great legions of antiquity."

"Thank you, sir. I guess those Huns aren't as invincible as we all thought."

Before he could respond, Gentilius trotted over. "Tribune, Lord Martinel is outside the berm and would like to speak with you in private."

Lucius slapped his old friend on the back. "Come on, Marcus, Martinel is a person you need to meet. You both have a lot in common—like the destruction of my self-esteem, for one."

Marcus shook his head. "I need to get back to my own unit. We're probably moving already, but I suppose a minute to meet this amazing Frank won't slow up the legion too much."

As soon as the tribunes approached the Frankish nobleman, Lucius sensed something wrong. Martinel crouched with a couple dozen of his cavalry, waiting a respectful distance back. "Hello, Roman," he called out in a voice at once boisterous but strained; meanwhile, he glanced at Marcus walking next to Lucius.

Lucius was quick to say, "This is Marcus Carloman, my closest friend. When we were boys, he got me out of more tight spots than I can remember."

Martinel and Marcus grasped each other's forearms in the traditional Roman greeting. "I sure could've used such a friend last night," the Frank added in a whisper as the smile slipped away from his face. "It appears I don't know when to shut my mouth. After I reported on our battle to King Merovech, he lost all sense. He yelled that it would be the Franks who should crush the Huns and not the Romans. I tried to use logic as I had seen the size of just a small part of Attila's army, and it dwarfs the number of warriors my king has. But he would not listen. It didn't help that the Vandal King's ambassador, Helos, was plying Merovech with wine and singing the praises of Frankish valor and the boundless treasures piled in the Huns' camp. When I protested too much, he called me a Roman lapdog and threw me out. Those men you see behind me are all who remained loyal."

Lucius clapped him on the shoulder. "Speaking truth to power can be very unrewarding."

"Very true." A hard look crossed Martinel's face. "Roman, I like you. Someday, our people may be enemies, but I will always consider you a friend. Beware of King Genseric and his Vandals. He's an ambitious man, and his envoys visited all of the kings gathered here. He's plotting something, and I don't think that something will be to the benefit of you Romans."

Lucius recalled hearing a similar warning from Satewa and filed that thought away. "Your king will learn the wisdom of your words soon and welcome you back." The young tribune gave a small smile of assurance. "For now, if you don't mind being a Roman lapdog for a while, I'm in desperate need of a cavalry commander."

Martinel made a lopsided grin and clasped Lucius' shoulder. "You Romans seem to know nothing of horses and appear to care even less. It would be an honor to serve with you again."

Marcus slapped his forehead and piped in, "If this is a lapdog, I would hate to see what a wolf looks like. I'm off, my friend. Take care of yourself."

Like a giant centipede, the army soon wound its way forward. Two hours later, the small dale fell quiet except for the workers building shelters to Doctor Phokas' uncompromising specifications.

* * *

Two days later, word reached Lucius that the Franks had caught up with the Huns. It was a massacre, but Attila had to stop and fight.

Aetius and the main army arrived that evening, and the remnants of King Merovech's broken army took refuge behind the Roman lines. As the sun set, Aetius and Attila sat astride their horses at the head of their great armies and studied each other across the broad valley the local Gauls had named the Catalaunian Plains.

The night was as silent as death in the Roman camp. Men did what they needed to do to prepare for the next day. Lucius sat by his small campfire with Takumi as a quiet companion when a very pale Martinel sat down. "Roman, there is serious treachery afoot. A few days ago, I told you the Vandals are trying to cause mischief. Tonight, I know it."

Lucius looked up, startled at the abrupt declaration, then nodded for the Frank to continue.

"You were right about my king forgiving me, but it cost the lives of a lot of very good men to achieve." Martinel cleared his throat. "I am here at my king's command. He said to find the highest ranking Roman I trust and deliver this message for General Aetius." He handed a sealed scroll across to Lucius.

"I'm honored you trust me, but what is this all about?"

Martinel stifled a chuckle. "Don't feel too honored. You are the *only* Roman I know. But I do trust you." He settled on a log by the fire. "There is more going on here than a poor soldier like me can understand. In essence, the Germanic tribes will be fighting on both sides of this upcoming battle. It seems the Vandals want the Romans and the Huns to bleed each other to death tomorrow and then turn on whoever is the victor.

"My king heard the envoy through and then threw him out declaring, 'I took an oath and I will stand by it.' King Theodoric did the same, but there were many in both courts who agreed with the Vandal plan. I have been told King Theodoric's son, Prince Thorismond, spoke passionately for it. He's been sending messages to his cousin, King Valamir of the Ostrogoths, across the valley. Of the Alans, I can say nothing. King Sangiban has kept his own counsel, but he is nothing more than a vassal to the Vandal's King Genseric."

"And why are you the bearer for such critical news?" Takumi asked in a flat, even voice.

"Because, my wary friend, everyone at court is spying on everyone else. They ignore me because they all saw me thrown out on my ears by the king. But that is why Merovech says he can trust me. I was the only one who argued with him that night."

Lucius rose and held the scroll like it was a venomous snake. "Will you still serve as my cavalry commander tomorrow?"

Martinel stood up and put his hands on the Roman's shoulders. "For tomorrow, our paths run together. You need never fear any deceit from me. Under the eyes of God, I vow I'll never commit any act to cause you harm even if it means my own death."

Lucius then grabbed the Frank's shoulders. "Then I better deliver a message."

Lucius learned that was easier said than done. His rank and station did little to move the general's bodyguards. After shouting for a time, Satewa stuck his head outside the command tent, grinned at Lucius, and dragged him inside.

General Aetius looked up from the roughly drawn map he studied. The man seemed to have aged many years in the last few days. Aetius took the scroll from him, broke the seal, and read the message. "This confirms what my spies have told me."

He handed the scroll to the legates standing next to him and slid two markers to the center of the map. "I'll take the left flank facing Attila's German vassals. Theodoric will have the right flank facing the Huns themselves. I don't want to give his men any thoughts of switching sides in case they happen to run into a stray cousin or two. I can't trust Sangiban. He and his Alans will hold the center with Merovech and what's left of his Franks behind him. The old fool will have nowhere to go but straight ahead."

The general studied the map a bit more and moved a few other markers. "On paper, this should work. Attila was always headstrong and a risk taker. He'll attack at sunrise with everything he has, but the question is, will the men stand?" Aetius sighed and hailed Lucius. "Tribune Bernius, I put much stock in what you and your cohort did a few days ago. If the rest of the army can fight as well, there's a real chance we may actually win tomorrow."

Lucius froze where he stood and said nothing. He could not even envision the great Flavius Aetius ever losing a battle, or that the odds were more against them than with them.

General Aetius gave him a bitter grin. "Yes, young tribune. We are badly outmatched. Our numbers are about the same, but most of our troops are untested. Attila's warriors are the scourge of Europe and have never been defeated."

"Sir, there's always a first time for everything. The men believe you're the one who's invincible."

The imperator frowned and summoned the legates. "I want the Second and Third Legions on the front line. Albinus, your legion is in reserve. I have a little surprise for Attila. I'm going to use our siege weapons in the open field. Every catapult and ballista must be ready to fire by first light. I'll show him that those weapons can be used for more than just tearing down fortress walls. Now, gentlemen, go prepare your legions. The kings will be here soon, and they'll all want to have their say. It will be a very long meeting."

The commanders saluted and left. Albinus grabbed Lucius when he left the tent and pulled him along. As they walked outside, the legate leaned close and asked, "Tribune Bernius, tell me. Your cohort has been bloodied. How did the legionaries fare?"

Lucius thought back on the desperate struggle a few days earlier. "Sir, given any rational thought, there's no reason why I'm alive today." Yet, despite their own losses, they had survived and stood unbroken. With that image in his thoughts, he answered at last, "Tomorrow, Attila will meet Imperator Flavius Aetius and three Roman legions. I don't think the Huns will be happy with the encounter."

CHAPTER XIV

CATALAUNIAN PLAINS

The next day broke gray and drizzly. At the first sign of dawn, Attila flung the might of his horde at the Romans and their allies. Lucius sat out of sight of the conflict but could hear the terrible screams as if they were right next to him. One by one, the First Legion's cohorts were called up.

By midday, showers arrived and turned into a soaking rain. A panicked dispatch rider raced up to Legate Albinus. "Sir, Imperator Aetius implores you to move everyone you have left to the right flank. The Visigoths are caving. If they break, the army is doomed. For God's sake, hurry!"

The legate looked around. Only three uncommitted cohorts remained. "Bernius, take the point. Lord Martinel, take the cavalry and screen us. We'll be moving fast and won't be ready for any surprises."

Lucius bellowed for his centurions. Soon, his men jogged by his side through a cesspool of mud that used to be a well-worn trail. Several hundred mounted lancers passed by them with Martinel at the lead. He smiled at Lucius as his warhorse splashed through the muck and sprayed water on the lumbering foot soldiers.

With the din of battle roaring ahead of him, Lucius balked at the chaos as he reached the crest of a low rise at the edge of the battlefield. Roman cavalry already engaged in heated combat with the Huns, who routed the Visigoths across the wide field. Carnage abounded, and he quailed at the thought of charging headlong into that hell.

Lucius regarded his men, many of whom looked toward him with expectation. *What am I to do? They trust me to make the right decisions.* Self-doubt racked him, and he caught the eyes of Vidin and Gentilius beside him. They looked back at him with pride and confidence. *My God, they believe in me, and as God is my witness, I believe in them.* The fear gave way to some courage.

"Shields up. Pilas at the ready. Forward!" The order given, Lucius led his men into the nightmare. They became the point of the Roman spear, and their arrival on the scene drew the Huns like a magnet.

Lucius shouted, "Loose!" and six hundred javelins smashed into the oncoming Huns. The Huns' advance didn't slow.

"Draw swords!"

The barbarians slammed into the Roman shield wall and threw themselves at the legionaries with the reckless abandon of those who believe themselves invincible.

The tight line broke in several places, and Lucius found himself alone. A swarthy Hun swung a broad war axe, and his first blow cleaved Lucius' shield. Stunned, he felt the second blow shatter the shield and send him sprawling. Lucius lay dazed, waiting in helpless fear for the bite of the axe.

However, it never came. When the focus returned to his eyes, Vidin's hand reached out to pull him back up. "Sir, you're going to have to take more care. You won't always have me to look after you."

Lucius staggered as he rose and studied the battle. The Huns that broke through lay dead, and the Roman ranks had closed. "Thanks, Vidin. Now let's show them how Romans fight. Forward!"

The tribune's men responded. They had faced certain death already and didn't shrink from the onslaught, turning into an iron island in a field of blood. The cavalry and the Visigoths snapped at the Hunnic warriors and ran behind the Roman troops when pressed, but they soon ground to a halt. The Huns lived up to their fierce reputation.

Lucius cast his eyes about the chaotic melee, searching for a means to break the stalemate. Across the field, Martinel waved his sword in a frantic motion screaming, "Your king is dead! Avenge your king!"

Lucius gaped at his friend and didn't understand what the Frank was yelling about until he spotted Prince Thorismond and Braun standing over the prostrate form of the Visigoth King. At first, they glared at Martinel, but then they took up the call: "Theodoric is dead! The Huns have slain him!" Soon, clarions blared, and the almost defeated Visigoth warriors turned on the Huns with a wild ferocity.

The Roman cohorts pushed like a methodical machine. By late afternoon, Lucius reached the ridge of the opposite hill. When no more enemies opposed him, he let out a hoarse cheer and pumped his sword in the air. His legionaries and the Visigoth warriors echoed the shout. They routed the Huns' flank, and for the first time in his life, Attila retreated. The battlefield belonged to Aetius.

* * *

That evening, Lucius sat by his campfire with his centurions, satisfied. "Come morning, we will crush the remnants of Attila's horde. The Huns are huddled in their encampment awaiting death. The Scourge of Europe will be no more."

Lucius glanced around at his small gathering, and every face shared the same opinion except one. "Lord Martinel, why so glum? We've just achieved a tremendous victory."

Martinel looked fish-eyed at Lucius and then at the small circle of Roman men. Nothing about his stony face changed when he gestured to the tribune. "I need to speak with you privately."

Catching the gravity in Martinel's tone, Lucius gestured to his soldiers. "Centurions, tomorrow could be another long day. Look to your men."

All the centurions shuffled to their feet and walked away grumbling. Takumi stayed planted on his stool. Lucius glared at him but received an unreadable face in return.

Lucius sighed. "So what's the big secret?"

Martinel nodded to Takumi and spit out one word: "Murder!" Lucius cocked an eyebrow. "Thousands perished today. That's what happens in war. I would hardly call it murder."

"Yes, that's war. Unless it's a knife in the back by your own son."

Lucius stared at him, stiff and slack-jawed. "What are you talking about?"

"When the cavalry rode onto the field, I looked for King Theodoric so we could coordinate our attack. I saw Thorismond and that henchman of his, Braun, slide their knives in the old man's back. There was no mistaking it; I was looking right at them. That's when I started bellowing about the king being dead. Those two were quick to cover the crime with their own shouts."

He swirled the wine in his wooden cup and then tossed it down his throat. "With you Romans arriving and all that shouting, it put some spine back in the Visigoths and the battle turned. A tremendous victory, to be sure, but it was still murder."

Lucius' mind spun. "You said yesterday that Thorismond spoke strongly about breaking the alliance, but Theodoric wouldn't budge. It sounds like Prince Thorismond wants to start making decisions for himself."

Martinel spat into the fire. "This is starting to look like a three-corner fight between you Romans, the Huns, and the Goths, and I'd rather not see my Franks caught in the middle."

"I will not name you unless I must, but this information must reach the imperator. He must be told tonight. Takumi, pull together an escort."

Martinel poured himself more wine. "If you don't mind, I'll stay here tonight. Getting my throat slit by a Goth assassin while I sleep would not be pleasant."

Lucius nodded to that and added, "Takumi, have extra guards posted so we don't have any unexpected visitors slipping over the wall." Above them, the night sky had cleared and showed a gibbous moon.

Two hours later, the mud-splattered tribune was shown into the headquarters. The imperator and the three legates had settled around a candle-lit map talking in quiet voices. Satewa stood beside Flavius Aetius and looked with concern when Lucius entered. "Ah, Storm Crow, what strange tidings do you bring this time?"

Lucius swallowed the lump in his throat as the eyes of the senior commanders turned in his direction. He squared his shoulders and repeated what Martinel told him about the murder. As promised, he didn't give a name to his source.

When he finished, Albinus eyed him with suspicion. "Do you believe this Frank?"

"We know Thorismond has been communicating with his cousin, Valamir, and we know his ambitions have no bounds. It's not hard to believe this story." A thoughtful Aetius furrowed his brow and plucked his lower lip. "In finally defeating the Huns tomorrow, the Ostrogoths would no longer be Attila's vassals. They would be free to unite with the Visigoths. Their combined might would crush what's left of our army, and the road to Rome would be thrown wide open."

Aetius sat down heavily on a camp stool and pounded the coarse plank table. "I must convince Thorismond that he needs to hurry back to his city and claim the throne before one of his brothers does. His ambition will drive him to believe me."

"But Imperator, we won't have enough men to finish off the Huns without the Visigoths," Albinus sputtered. "The Alans fled during the battle and haven't returned."

A bitter Aetius looked long at the markers now scattered about the map. "It's our only choice."

The next day, Thorismond rode out with his warriors trailing behind him.

* * *

Attila waited three days for the Romans to spring some nasty trap. It never came. With food running out, he slipped out of his camp with his horde, leaving behind the loot they pilfered in their rampage across Gaul.

On the fourth day, the Romans stood as the sole army left, and the legions claimed the riches left behind. Aetius and Satewa strolled through the ransacked encampment with a few of the most precious treasures. "Satewa, look. We have some very interesting messages from an old friend of yours."

The scout centurion took the offered scrolls with a quizzical look on his face, but it turned grave as he read the documents. "I should have guessed King Genseric was behind this move by the Huns. I would not be surprised if the Goths also have a set of very similar letters. It would appear he has given up hope that I'll be successful in murdering you."

Aetius chuckled at the reminder of their first meeting. "My friend, he's the biggest threat to Rome right now. Without Attila, the Huns will disintegrate into squabbling tribes. The Goths will be a dangerous foe, but Thorismond does not have the leadership skills of his father, and he will need time to consolidate his power. It's Genseric and his Vandal army I fear the most. He's sitting in Carthage with a large fleet of captured Roman ships. He can strike anywhere he wants."

Satewa growled and answered through gritted teeth. "The greatest danger to Rome is that imbecile, Emperor Valentinian. If he spent as much money on rebuilding the navy as he does on his palace in Ravenna, Rome could recapture its African provinces. If he thought as much about the empire as he did about himself, you wouldn't be out here cobbling together alliances with one enemy to fight another."

Aetius sighed at the thought of imperial politics. Anyone who comes close to challenging the emperor will find themselves quite dead.

As if reading his thoughts, Satewa added, "You better be very careful, my general. You're far more popular with the legions than Valentinian. Look at the legionaries who fought for you here. They call themselves Aetius' Corps, and most have been with you for just a few weeks."

The imperator returned a wry grin. "I'm still too valuable a tool for the emperor. He's deathly afraid of the Huns, and Attila is the best insurance I have for staying healthy." He chortled at his own joke.

Satewa didn't smile. He just tightened his grip on the long bone handle of the knife belted to his waist and searched the camp for danger.

That afternoon, dispatch riders went out to proclaim the great victory. The next day, the Aetius Corps started a leisurely march to the Rhone River. The general decided to leave them in Gaul as a permanent force.

CHAPTER XV

OUT OF THE SHADOWS

It was late at night before Dervla could stagger away from the orgy. She sank down in a dark alcove along the wall in the ornate empty reception hall of the imperial palace. As she rubbed her bruised breasts and watched the blood trickle between her thighs, she knew she'd been lucky. The drooling bastard who grabbed her had drunk much from his cups when he knocked the wine flask from her hands and dragged her to an empty couch. She didn't know who he was, but it didn't matter; they were all the same.

In the six months since the announcement of Rome's victory over the Huns, the depravity of the emperor's celebrations grew worse. The truncated scream of terror from an unfortunate slave pierced the air. Dervla pulled the scarlet tribune's cape around her tight like a magic talisman and wept silent tears. It was the one thing in this hellish world that truly belonged to her.

Dervla leaned back on the hard stone wall. Mother hasn't been well since she became separated from Father. She needs me, but not like this.

Upon hearing sandaled feet echo across the marble floor, she hunkered back in the dark crevice. The men who made the sound paused in front of the dim alcove where Dervla hid. One wore the imperial purple of the emperor. The other she knew very well.

Publius Heraclius hissed through clenched teeth. "I tell you, Your Majesty, he's a danger to you. The people love him, and the legions will follow him anywhere. In fact, those raw recruits we sent him less than a year ago now call themselves the Aetius Corp."

Emperor Valentinian's weasel-like gaze flitted across the empty hall with a frown. "You're right, Publius. Aetius is the true danger to the empire, but I can't dispose of him while the Huns prowl our borders. The imperator is the one obstacle keeping those animals at bay."

"The Huns are nothing without Attila. Once he's dead, they'll be at each other's throats and won't pose a threat to us."

"And what makes you think Attila will conveniently meet his demise? I hear rumors he's planning another campaign against us."

"It'll take time, Your Majesty. Attila is a wary man, but I think I have spent the treasury's gold well. The assassins will see to him. In the meantime, the imperator may be untouchable for now, but his allies in the senate aren't. I suggest you start eliminating them."

Valentinian chuckled, clapping his fingertips together. "Flavius has few friends in that body of incompetents. The man is as unskilled in politics as he is unbeatable on the battlefield. Those who speak for him, like Senator Bernius, have little influence."

"Bernius! That's a dangerous family, my lord," Publius sputtered.

"Do you still hold a grudge against the Bernius whelp? I understand Tribune Lucius played a key role in the victory and accounted very well for himself against the Huns."

"Yes, he did, and he's totally loyal to Flavius Aetius."

"Then you need not fear. When we take care of this upstart general, we will deal with every little toady who follows at his heels."

"I would relish the sight. That insolent pup has tweaked his fingers in my face one too many times."

"Well, my good chamberlain, the night is waning, and I must rise before noon. I'm going to bed." Valentinian yawned and stretched. "I'll be returning to Ravenna as soon as I can get away from this infestation of small-minded bureaucrats and fawning nobles. Besides, Rome is so full of disease this time of the year."

"Good night, Your Majesty. I think all of our little problems will resolve themselves quite well."

Dervla listened, barely breathing, as the sound of the footsteps receded across the hall. A thousand thoughts swirled through her head as she digested what she'd just heard. *Lucius survived and is a hero! Of course he is. I knew that the first time I saw him. He's the best man Rome ever produced. But he's in danger and doesn't even know it.* A tear trickled down her cheek as she envisioned masked killers sneaking up on his smiling, open face. *I must find a way to warn him.*

Dervla rose with caution. No one saw her, so she forced herself to move fast. Her battered body hurt everywhere, but she kept her pace, hobbling to the squalid quarters she shared with her mother and brother.

When she opened the thin curtain that served as a door for the family's dwelling, Dervla gasped. There, sitting by her mother's bedside and talking to her, were two well-dressed men. Her brother, Seamus, hovered over their shoulders listening to everything they said. One man she recognized as Doctor Phokas; the other wore the garb of a priest. Both men turned to her when she entered.

The smile on the doctor's face vanished when he saw her. "My dear God, child, what happened to you?" Without another word, he helped her to the thin straw pallet she used for a bed.

Terror shot through Dervla's veins as Phokas pulled off the ragged remnants of the translucent gown she'd been put into for the emperor's party. The fear subsided as he covered her with the scarlet cape and probed her bruised body with gentle hands, studying her with professional eyes.

At last, he sat back disconcerted. "Well, at least you're whole. There's little I can do to ease your true wounds. That's more the providence of Father Patricius here."

The cleric was a lean man wearing a crumpled brown robe cinctured at the waist with a rope. He had long chestnut-colored hair and a thick beard, and he looked over sadly at the mention of his name. "I know you'll find little comfort in my words, but Jesus will sit in judgment of us all. Evil will languish in eternal damnation, and the good will find succor in his sweet grace."

"If your God is good, there are many who should face that judgment very soon," Seamus snarled as he curled his fists with impotence.

Phokas leaned forward. "We just arrived in Rome. The good Padre has never been to the home of the church and wanted a glimpse of Pope Leo. I told the worthy cleric I still have a few connections here and volunteered to get him a private audience." He paused and fingered the hem of the cape covering Dervla, and a small smile crossed his face. "I was also asked to bring you news of your father from a certain thick-headed tribune."

The three sets of Conall eyes locked on to him.

"Unis is hale and hearty. The old fellow has adapted well to life with a single limb. You may not know this, but Tribune Carloman is set to marry Senator Bernius' daughter, Julia, next month. Unis drove the cart with the wedding gifts from the Carloman estate to the Bernius villa. Someone should've taught the man to carry a tune. I rode with him and had the misfortune of listening to him sing off-key for a whole week. He sends his love and says he misses you terribly." The doctor's face broke into a wide smile. "In fact, he's now a freed man. Senator Bernius held the manumission ceremony for him just last week."

Dervla's mother rose with a light shining in her eyes, and her voice choked. "My husband is free?"

"That, he is. Also, the tribune will be coming to the city in a few days to address some legion affairs. He mentioned he wanted to check and see if his old cloak needed to be replaced."

Dervla felt alarmed and looked hard at the ground. *No! I don't want him to see me like this.*

"The tribune also said Senator Bernius would be coming to Rome on business after the wedding, and Unis would be coming along with him."

The old woman threw her arms around the doctor and hugged him, weeping until coughing jags racked her frail body. Father Patricius helped her lie back down and gave her a cup to drink. The coughing subsided as she sipped the foul-smelling brew.

Dervla shared a worried look with Phokas, and he gave her a sad nod. "It's the consumption. The elixir I made for her will ease the pain, but I have no cure."

Dervla squeezed back the tears that welled up. She'd come to the same conclusion sometime before, but to hear it confirmed shook her to the core. There was little druid lore or modern science could do. "Will it be soon?"

Phokas looked at the young woman and sighed. "Within the year."

Seamus' eyes darted back and forth between the doctor and his sister. After a long, tense moment, he bolted from the dingy little room. Dervla called after him, but the only response was the ragged cloth over the door flapping back into place.

Father Patricius stood and rested his hand on her shoulder. "I'll find the lad. He has a lot of anger and pain bottled up inside." With nary a sound, he disappeared out the door.

Dervla gave her mother a worried glance, though the older woman breathed easier. She went to Phokas next as she trusted him and needed to tell someone about what she'd discovered. "Sir, I overheard something just a short while ago. It has dire implications for someone I think we both care about."

Curiosity rose in the old man's eyes. "What is it, my dear? Any rumor you heard is as safe with me as I can manage." With a soft chuckle, he added, "Unless I'm tortured. I have very little tolerance for pain."

Though aware that the doctor was joking, Dervla paled at his words. "I overheard a private conversation between the emperor and the chamberlain. Tribune Bernius should not come to Rome. Heraclius hates him and means to see him dead."

The doctor stiffened and gaped at her before he spoke again. "You'd better tell me the story from the beginning."

Dervla nodded and told him every detail of the conversation she could recall. When she finished, Phokas rocked back on his heels, deep in thought. Dervla shook in silence, all while wondering what in the world they could do.

She estimated that Phokas had been with Imperator Aetius for six months now, and his glowing words about the man displayed great admiration. The doctor had said once that, if they could choose, the legions would support Aetius over the little peacock currently on the throne without a second thought.

At long last, Phokas grunted and rubbed his jaw. "There are still a few influential folks who owe me favors. In fact, my dear, I know someone you should tell that story to."

Dervla drew back with alarm. "Sir, I'm a slave. Who will believe me?"

"Oh, I think this person will because he cares little about one's station in this life. I'll have to get you a more appropriate garment, though. It may take me a few days to arrange it, but you'll be addressing Pope Leo himself."

Dervla felt her jaw drop open. "But he's the head of the Christian world. He'll eat me alive when he learns I still follow the druids. I can't just leave the imperial palace, either; I'm the property of Heraclius."

"I'll handle that fat fool. He'll be hustling you out the door as fast as he can for the request he's going to receive." Phokas patted her on her knee. "As for that antiquated cult you adhere to, if you mention it, you better be able to defend it. His Holiness spent many of his younger years in Gaul, and I understand he was quite effective at converting your kindred. He has a keen mind and can be very persuasive."

"Very well. For Lucius, I'll go. But if I get flayed alive, I'll pray to your God you're at the scourging post next to me."

Phokas closed his eyes for a short while. "Let me give you his own words from his last Christmas sermon: 'The saint, the sinner, and the unbeliever are all equal as sinners, and none is excluded in the call to happiness.' Now, does that sound like a man who would order your torture?"

After taking some moments to process those words, Dervla sighed. "No. I'll give it a shot."

The curtain opened, and she almost jumped out of her skin. However, she calmed a little when Father Patricius and her brother entered the room. The rims of Seamus' eyes were red, but the fire in them had cooled.

Phokas rose and twisted the kinks out of his back. "Well, I have much to arrange. Come, Father. The hour is late, and these good people need some rest. I dare not be wandering the palace halls come morning. If those idiots who call themselves 'imperial physicians' spot me, half the Praetorian Guard will be in pursuit." To Dervla, he added, "Expect the summons in a couple of days."

As they were about to leave, Seamus wrapped Patricius in a fierce hug and buried his head in the cleric's homespun robe.

"None of us know the time we will be called to our eternal home, lad. Use the time the Good Lord has given you to be with your mother. Show her your love, and you'll have no regrets." Patricius patted the boy on the head as Seamus released his hold.

"Come here, Seamus," his mother called and held out her hand. Seamus wiped his face on his threadbare tunic, put a brave smile on his face, and went to his mother. Dervla joined them, and the three held each other close. They didn't notice the priest and the doctor leave.

CHAPTER XVI

AUDIENCE

Three days later, Publius summoned Dervla. When she arrived, he pulled her close and leered at her.

"Well, whore, it appears you're not totally useless after all. Pope Leo is sending some missionaries to Hibernia, and one of his people recalled you from the emperor's festivities. The Pope thinks it'd be helpful for his priests to speak with some people from that dismal land before they travel there. You and your whelp of a brother are to attend them and answer any questions they may have." A derisive snicker escaped him. "And if they want to do any personal investigations after that, you'll accommodate their needs."

Dervla bowed her head so Heraclius could not see the burning fury on her face. *Someday, I will kill this pig.* Aloud, however, she kept her voice steady and meek. "I will provide whatever is required of me."

"Of course you will. Now go get yourself cleaned up. There're some logionaries waiting in my suite to escort you to the Pope's Lateran Palace. Begone!"

Dervla didn't need encouragement. Once she left the room, the anger she felt soon gave way to some mirth as she chuckled at the holes in Doctor Phokas' ruse. She'd been born in Rome and had rarely stepped foot outside it. All she knew about her people, the *Attacotti*, was what her parents told her. The village they came from, Drumanagh, was just a word to her. Nonetheless, she had a task to do, so she smoothed her features and looked up.

Dervla sprinted down to the scullery and gathered up Seamus. She didn't know why her little brother had been dragged into this madness or why legionaries were sent to get her, and it gave her a queasy feeling. Regardless, she pressed on. *The die is cast. If I've been betrayed, I'd be dead already. No one wastes time plotting against slaves.*

When they reached their dark, empty quarters, Dervla splashed some water on her face from the cracked clay basin and ran a near-toothless comb through her long, golden hair. The simple shift she already wore was the best garment she owned. The bewildered Seamus put on a mostly clean tunic, and they started to the door. Dervla paused on the way, grabbed the scarlet cloak from its peg, and wrapped it around her shoulders. Touching it and smelling it helped her hang onto her sanity over the last several months, a talisman against the evil around her.

They headed upstairs. Publius Heraclius lived in an opulent apartment suite on the second floor, and the large, polished brass doors hung open. She skidded to a halt as six fierce-looking legionaries stood.

"Miss Conall, are you ready to go?"

Those gently spoken words didn't match the intimidating decurion who spoke to them, but he did look vaguely familiar. After a moment's pause, Dervla ventured, "Gentilius?"

The decurion broke into a broad grin. "Yes, ma'am. You remember me? A lot has changed since that little encounter on the Via Augusta, hasn't it?"

She smiled back at him, and the nightmarish figures of her mind transformed into the man-boys she met after Lucius rescued them. "How does Tribune Bernius fare? I heard he survived that horrible battle with the Huns."

"Survive he did, Miss Conall," said another legionary. "There isn't a barbarian alive who can stand against our tribune. Why, he even spit in the eye of old Attila himself with nothing behind him except those of us in his Seventh Cohort."

Dervla looked at the new speaker. "Vidin? You're a decurion now, too?"

The legionary puffed out his chest. "Yes, ma'am. The tribune himself promoted me right after the battle at the Catalaunian Plains. We arrived in Rome this morning and weren't here an hour when that wild doctor stormed into his quarters. The next thing I knew, the tribune had us marching over here with a letter from the Pope himself. We didn't even have time to stow our gear. The tribune told us to wait for you no matter how long it took. He didn't want you making your way to the Lateran Palace by yourself." Vidin smiled with satisfaction. "Actually, it was kind of fun to elbow past those pompous Praetorians, and the fare they brought us here in the imperial palace is a hell of a lot better than barracks food."

Dervla and Seamus exchanged bright smiles. Seamus gave her a coy look, though, and hailed the legionaries. "Will Tribune Bernius attend this audience, too?"

Gentilius scratched his head. "I don't know. I expect he'll be tied up most of the day. General Aetius gave him some dispatches with instructions to deliver them in person. I expect he'll be free of his responsibilities by tomorrow, however."

Dervla's smile faded, but her face flushed. She had little choice in where she went and when she went there. "Thank you. I guess we should not keep His Holiness waiting."

"Good." Vidin bowed his head before he smirked at the decurion. "Gentilius, it's my turn to walk in front. I want to be the one who thumbs his nose at the Praetorians this time."

* * *

The Pope's palace stood beside the Basilica of Saint John at Lateran. The wide street that connected the imperial palace on the Palatine Hill to Lateran near the *Porta Asinaria* ran through the best part of the city. The short trip could be harrowing on a busy market day, but six legionaries wearing the insignia of the now famous Red Fist were not to be trifled with, so they made good time.

Dervla still tensed during parts of the conversation. The decurions spoke of everything from the desperate stand against the Ostrogoths to the legions chasing rumors of Attila's presence all along the Rhine for the last few months.

When they finished, she remarked, "This general had that decent man nearly stoned to death and now throws him in the path of every barbarian who wanders into the empire? Aetius seems as evil as my master."

The two decurions eyed each other, but it was Gentilius who spoke. "You misunderstand, ma'am. We were the ones who were supposed to be stoned. Tribune Bernius wouldn't allow it, so he stood in our place."

Dervla whirled on the two men. "Cowards!"

Vidin shrank back from her. "Aye, miss, that I was. The tribune showed me the meaning of true courage. I swear by the Holy Mother of God I'll never abandon him again. He's the standard I measure myself by each day. I doubt I'll ever reach it, but it's what I strive for."

Gentilius nodded in agreement. "Even when I stood behind that pile of dirt on that nameless road north of Aurelianum with thousands of barbarians screaming for my blood, I didn't dream of running. The disappointment on his face would've hurt me more than any Hun's blade."

Upon seeing the remorse in their honest eyes, her rage cooled. Dervla's thoughts wandered back to Lucius. "Why is he always in so much danger?"

Vidin bowed his head to her and chuckled. "He is a lodestone for trouble, that's for sure. It's up to those of us who love him to keep him in one piece. It's very strange, but I bless the day I deserted and found my way to his campfire."

Dervla said nothing, but in her heart, she agreed. As the image of Lucius' battered face lying in that bed back in Avenio swam before her eyes, she knew she would tell this Christian holy man everything, even about her own nonbelief, if it would help protect Lucius.

With these thoughts running through her head, she was surprised when their little parade reached the Basilica of Saint John. The basilica stood tall with its columns and marble facade, but she thought the adjacent palace should have been much grander. Though very large and three stories high, it was constructed out of ordinary red brick.

Upon reaching the main archway with its thick oak doors, Gentilius stood wondering if he should shout or hammer on the door when it flew open thanks to a little monk with an owl-like face and a quizzical look in his eye. Once he collected himself, Gentilius handed him the letter. The monk glanced over the note before he said, "Please come in, then."

"The invitation is for these two, and they are now properly delivered," Gentilius replied, whereupon he turned to Dervla and handed her a small courier's pouch. His head remained partly turned toward the cleric. "These letters are to be delivered directly to His Holiness, Pope Leo. The scrolls are for the Pope's eyes only."

Seamus' mouth popped open. "Aren't you staying?"

"No, lad. We've been gone overlong from our duties and must return. You will be safe here." With a nod to Dervla, Gentilius turned and headed back down the steps with his five compatriots trailing behind.

No sooner were they out of earshot, the monk cleared his throat. "Are you coming in, or do I have to stand in this broiling heat all day?"

Dervla hugged the satchel to her chest, and they hurried inside.

The monk pointed with a bony, ink-stained finger to the left. "Go in that room over there. His Holiness will speak with you when he's ready." He scuttled off in a huff without another word and disappeared around the corner. Dervla didn't even have time to ask for the letter back.

Seamus faced her and shrugged. "I guess we wait."

He strode nonchalantly into the room, a comfortable parlor with well-polished dark wooden walls. A long table adorned with well-carved icons along the far side sat in the center, and several comfortable-looking couches sat scattered about the room.

Dervla followed, surprised to see the room already had two occupants: a simply dressed, middle-aged priest with a thick brown beard that flowed over his chest and, to her relief, Father Patricius, who engaged in an earnest conversation with the other priest. Whenever he didn't speak, he fidgeted with a weathered hat with a broad rim.

When Dervla and Seamus entered, Patricius looked over and smiled in recognition. Before he could say anything, the other priest waved and said, "Please join us."

Dervla shrank into herself, blushing. "You misunderstand our station, Father. We're not worthy. We're but slaves."

Instead of being taken aback, the cleric let out a hearty, infectious laugh. "Then all the more reason to sit. You've been up before the sun, most likely. As for being unworthy, none of us are worthy of God's grace. We're just fortunate his all-encompassing love overlooks our limitations."

Dervla bit her lip, silently imploring Father Patricius not to mention her pagan beliefs, but he spoke before she could. "These are the two young Hibernians I told you about. I'm afraid they still follow the druidic deities I used to worship."

Dervla braced herself for a reprimand, but it didn't come. Rather than jump and hurl holy water at her, the bearded priest stayed seated and chuckled some more. "So this is the mysterious lady Doctor Phokas spoke of—the woman who spies on the emperor to protect one of our heroes from the Catalaunian Plains. I'll tell you this, Father Patricius, this is a soul we must win over to our side."

He looked over at Seamus, whose eyes were the size of saucers and seemed torn between running from the room screaming and throwing himself at the priest in defense of his sister. "Sit down, lad. I don't bite. I have a wedge of hard cheese and some dried fruit on the tray here. You look famished, so eat up."

Hunger overcame Seamus' fear, and he attacked the offered food with gusto.

The priest turned his attention back to Dervla, who collapsed into a chair with a hard back. "There's a fascinating tale here. I see a slave girl wearing the cloak of a Roman tribune and carrying a military courier's pouch. Why don't you tell me the story?"

Dervla felt drained and again looked over at Father Patricius.

"Go ahead and tell him. Doctor Phokas has already confided all he knows of your tale."

Dervla sighed. If Doctor Phokas trusted this priest, then she could, too. "Well... I was in an alcove in the imperial reception hall and—"

The bearded priest waved his hand. "No, my dear, start the story from the beginning. Tell me how you acquired that cloak."

"Excuse me, Father. As I said before, I am but a slave. Nothing in my experiences would interest you."

"Then humor me. If it's wasted time, then it's mine to waste, isn't it?"

With a deep breath, the young slave woman recalled the Vandal raiders attacking them on the Via Augusta. Once she began her tale, she found in the nameless priest an avid listener. Any and all terrors she'd seen and been part of over the last year poured out—everything. Whenever she froze at the remembrance of a new horror, he encouraged her to continue with gentle words. No cruel chastisements or pious mewling came from the priest, but tears trickled down his careworn face. At the end, the words spoken between the emperor and the chamberlain didn't even seem to interest him much.

"I will pray for your mother's recovery and the reunion of your family, child. I hope someday that I can have the strength of spirit you have shown." He stood and hugged Dervla, then nodded to Seamus, who had cleared the tray of every last morsel. "May the Blessed Mother of Jesus guard over you. Father Patricius, I must be about my duties. Would you see to our guests?"

"Yes, Your Holiness." Father Patricius fell to his knees and kissed the ring on the bearded priest's hand.

The cleric made the sign of the cross over Patricius' head and walked with deliberate steps out of the room.

Dervla watched Father Patricius' actions without comprehending. Only then did she realize it was late afternoon, and with that, it occurred to her they still hadn't been summoned for their audience. "Padre, who was that priest?"

"Why, that was Pope Leo, of course. Is he not truly a great man?"

Disbelief dispelled almost all thought from Dervla's head. "I think someone has played a cruel trick on you. Pope Leo is the patriarch of all of Christendom, and that man wasn't dressed any better than you."

"Oh, he is the Pope, all right. I had the blessed honor of celebrating Mass with him this very morning. On sacred occasions, he does look quite resplendent. However, His Holiness told me he likes to be comfortable when he's thinking, and these days, he's been doing a lot of thinking. Shall we?"

Dervla suddenly remembered the letters she held, sprang to her feet, and bolted from the room. She caught up with the Pope a short distance down the hall. "Your Holiness, I beg your forgiveness."

Leo turned with a bemused look as the slave girl prostrated herself on the floor before him. "Child, please stand. What can I do for you?"

"I have letters I was to deliver right to your hands. I didn't know who you were when we were talking or I would've done so immediately."

"Would you have spoken with me any differently if you knew who I was?"

"I'm sorry for that, too. I thought you were a priest like Father Patricius. I wouldn't have prattled about my woes to a lord of your station."

"Then my slight deception was well worth it. My 'station' in this world is to serve all who want to go home to the Lord Jesus in the next world. I'm too isolated in this prison of marble." Leo pulled out two scrolls from the pouch and examined the seals. "Well, well, they are from Flavius himself. I wonder what the good general thinks is so important? Please, stay the night. I'll have a reply for him by midmorning."

Dervla stared at the mosaic floor. "Sir... I mean, Your Holiness, my master will be angry if I don't return soon."

"Well, Publius was told you were here for my entertainment, and I'm grateful for the opportunity to speak with you. It has greatly inspired me that the human spirit can be so resilient in some. You will stay here as my guests for the night." The Pope bellowed in a loud voice, "Father Patricius."

The priest scurried up with Seamus at his heels.

"Would you be so kind as to put our two young pagan friends in the suite you and Doctor Phokas are sharing?"

"Certainly, Your Holiness, whatever you wish."

"Thank you, Patricius. Now I must be about my duties. I will see you at sunrise." Leo nodded to the three and walked down the long hall, already breaking the seal of the first letter.

The cleric's eyes crinkled as he scratched his chin under his long, flowing beard. "At least Phokas will have someone else to browbeat this evening. Come along."

Dervla had lived in the imperial palace slave quarters both in Rome and in the new capital in Ravenna, so she'd seen many resplendent apartments, just never as a guest. When they reached the third-floor landing, they turned left and walked down two doors. Father Patricius threw open the door and barged right in.

Dervla followed into an austere but well-lit room with the afternoon sun pouring in. A well-crafted wood carving of the crucified Christ hung on a side wall. Two real beds and a table squeezed between them rounded out the last of the furniture. She shuddered at the sight of the beds. Palace beds, in her mind, were where she was dragged to by vomit-covered, drunken aristocrats who kicked her to the floor when they were finished.

The room had the strong odor of tannin, and Doctor Phokas crouched over the table covered with tree bark and leaves. The old man ground something with mortar and pestle in a steady rhythm.

Father Patricius gagged as he walked in. "Phokas, what in the name of our Lord's Blessed Mother are you doing? This place stinks. You're going to get us tossed out."

Phokas choked back an irritated retort when he swung around and saw who accompanied the priest. His voice turned milder in an instant. "I see the intelligence level in the area has just risen significantly. Dervla, Seamus, how nice of you to stop by."

Intrigued, Dervla walked over to the table and observed a tall pile of scrapings from a tree along with the project the doctor labored on. "The bark works better than the leaves," she quipped.

Phokas' eyebrows shot up his forehead. "What makes you say that?"

"This is white willow. You're working on a potion to relieve fevers, but I've found the ground bark works better than the leaves."

"Interesting. I've been conducting experiments to improve the potency of the brew."

Dervla blushed and felt stupid. She'd learned one way of preparing the elixir and never considered there might be better ways of doing it, and it fired her imagination. What other things did she just accept without seeking a better alternative? She asked him, "How do you plan on testing your combinations?"

Phokas puffed out his hallow cheeks when he grunted. "Unfortunately, my best plan is to get myself drunk and see which concoction relieves the headache sooner."

Mirth danced in Dervla's heart, and she laughed. "I have a less painful idea. Women have a certain time of the month when things are more painful. I'm sure you would have no trouble getting some volunteers to test a relief for their discomfort."

"Use women... I never thought of that. An excellent idea! See, Patricius? I told you the intellect in the room just rose. Now I'm hungry. Let's wander down to the kitchen and see what we can purloin from the larder."

* * *

That night, Dervla slept fitfully. She felt comfortable enough even though she was squeezed into the same bed as her brother, but the snoring of the two older men in the other bed rattled the walls. However, she much preferred being here than being ordered around by her master.

Why can't my life be different? Here are people who respect me for who I am and listen to what I think. Outside, I'm nothing more than a piece of meat. If I were free, could I talk to Lucius whenever I wanted?

Dervla must have drifted off to sleep because she woke with a start at a new sound in the room. As her eyes adjusted to the predawn grayness, she saw Father Patricius kneeling before the wood carving reciting his prayers. Dervla studied him in silence, and when he crossed himself and started to rise, she asked, "Why did you change?"

Patricius brushed at his knees and sat down on the stool at the front of the table. "Excuse me. Change what?"

"Why are you a Christian priest now when you used to follow the druids?"

The corners of the priest's mouth curled up. "Not only was I part of the druidic culture, but I was a fairly high-ranked priest." He sighed and closed his eyes. "It was not enough for me. In nature, I saw God's work, but everything moved according to God's plan. If it were spring, the trees bloomed with new life and bore fruit. If hungry, a wolf would bring down its prey. There was no good or evil to it. They did what their nature told them to do, nothing more and nothing less.

"To truly see God, one has to see people. Of all God's creatures, we are the only ones capable of acting against our nature. We are the ones who can rise to a glorious nobility or sink to a dark depravity. We alone can choose a path of good or evil. So I saw it as the answer when God became man and showed us the path to righteousness. When I thought on this, my old ways seemed shallow and empty. That's why I changed."

Dervla gritted her teeth as she thought of Publius Heraclius, an avowed Christian. "I see little good in many who follow your faith."

"Ah, but therein lies the choice and God's judgment. A man murdering another for his money has a choice. A fire burning down a house with a family trapped inside does not."

Unsure of what to make of that, Dervla sat back. "That makes some sense, I guess. I will think on it."

CHAPTER XVII

AVENTINE HILL

Someone rapped on the door, and a hooded figure in a white robe entered the room. "Good morning," he bellowed, and the resonant voice startled Seamus from a sound sleep. The stranger pulled back his hood and revealed the face of the Pope. "I like to see the city as it awakens, and I decided to walk with you. Come to breakfast with me, and we'll be on our way."

Seamus gasped as he entered the Papal dining area along with Dervla, Father Patricius, and Doctor Phokas. Morning light filtered through the tall windows and added an aura of majesty to the room, showing the masterful craftsmanship of the dark walnut paneling and elaborate tapestries. Monks dressed in coarse brown robes whisked large portions of fresh fish, breads, and fruits onto the table. A hungry Seamus wasted no time heaping large portions onto his plate alongside the numerous guests enjoying the feast.

However, the Pope didn't. A flow of monks with ink-stained hands scurried in with messages they whispered and documents they handed to the Pope to sign. A half hour later, Pope Leo sighed at the almost untouched fish, then grabbed a warm roll and pulled up his hood. "Let's go. It doesn't appear I'll enjoy this meal much."

They soon departed, and Pope Leo sighed as he stepped out onto the street. "Another reason for being in disguise is to escape the mind-numbing administration of the bureaucracy."

Dervla and Seamus exchanged puzzled glances and shook their heads. Seamus thought about his tasks in the scullery and whispered, "It would be wonderful to have hundreds of people come and ask for my opinion and judgment every day."

As they turned down a road, a surprised Dervla pointed out, "Excuse me, Your Holiness, but this doesn't look like the way to the Palatine Hill. Aren't we going in the complete opposite direction?"

However, Pope Leo chuckled without concern. "That's good because we're going to Aventine Hill. That is where Flavius Aetius' home is, and it's where those legionaries from the Red Fist are staying."

Dervla dropped her head and moaned. "Lucius will be there, and I look hideous." She ran her hands through her hair and tried to smooth the hopeless wrinkles in her belted shift. Seamus pretended not to notice.

The manor house was an austere brick building surrounded by a stout, eight-foot stone wall topped with spikes. A familiar bronze giant wearing a large sword on his hip greeted them at the heavy wrought iron gate. He had his arm wrapped around a tall, thin woman who beamed at him.

"Satewa? What are you doing here?" Phokas asked as they entered the property.

"My Brenda, of course. You have never met my wife. She draws me like a magnet whenever I am gone too long."

The woman hugged him tight and grumbled in a husky voice, "I'm not a very strong magnet, though. He's always gone for too long. He needs to learn how to settle in one spot for a while." She looked upon the five arrivals, and recognition registered on her face. "You must be Seamus and Dervla. Tribune Bernius has spoken highly of you. He'll be glad to see you again. I serve as the housekeeper for the Aetius family and am the wife of this uncouth savage."

Her eyes drifted to the other visitors and made a tiny, startled sound when she saw the face of the man in the hooded white robe. "Your Holiness, I'm sorry I didn't recognize you. Please forgive my idle chatter and come in."

Pope Leo pulled back his hood and responded with a rumbling laugh. "Hello, Brenda. Have you saved the soul of our heathen friend here yet?"

"I work on him all the time, but he's a very stubborn man."

The centurion smiled down at his wife and stroked her long auburn hair with gentle fingers. "Your Heaven sounds like a beautiful place, but I have my paradise whenever I look into your eyes."

Brenda's cheeks reddened and she sputtered. "Come inside, everyone. The day is just dawning and it's already hot."

She disengaged herself from her husband's grasp, linked her arm with Dervla's, and walked inside, leaving the men to follow.

* * *

Lucius heard Brenda and Satewa come in and glanced at the door, then was struck dumb by another sight. Walking in next to Brenda was the most beautiful woman he'd ever met. Dervla looked exactly the same as he remembered her, perhaps even more beautiful. Her smile in particular struck him as angelic.

Oh, my God, she's looking at me, and I'm unshaven, and this tunic is stained from all my traveling. I must look grotesque. Lucius brushed the crumbs from his clothes and then looked up at her, sheepish.

"You must be Lucius Bernius, the hero of the Catalaunian Plains? I had expected someone the size of one of the statues in the Forum."

Lucius tore his gaze from Dervla to see the other visitors crowding in the doorway. The hearty, booming voice belonged to the one person he didn't recognize—a priest in a white robe with a very long, thick beard and sharp, lively eyes.

He remembered his manners and collected himself. "Yes, I am Tribune Lucius Bernius, although hardly a hero by anyone's definition. This is my best friend and soon-to-be brother-in-law, Tribune Marcus Carloman. And the disreputable-looking Frank is Lord Martinel, a man who has saved my life a half dozen times already."

Martinel offered an exaggerated bow to the newcomers. "I need to preserve this fine Roman's hide until I figure out a way to master him in a duel. Unfortunately, I suspect that will be a very long time."

"Your Holiness, would you like something to eat? There's not much in the house, but I can prepare a decent meal with a little time," Brenda said, but she bolted to the pantry without waiting for an answer.

"No, no, child. I ate before we left Lateran," the Pope called to her disappearing back.

A rigid Marcus stared at the Pope, unblinking. "Your Holiness. Lateran. Are you Pope Leo?" A smirk and a nod answered him, and all three men fell to their knees. "Forgive me, Your Holiness. I didn't recognize you."

"And what is there to forgive? I was not announced by a herald." The Pope laughed as Brenda tore through the larder. "You greeted an unknown stranger with courtesy. I couldn't have asked for more. Please rise and return to your meal."

The three men stood, but none of them made a move toward the table.

Pope Leo sighed and handed Lucius a sealed scroll. "I have a response to Imperator Aetius' letter. Also, I received word just this morning that the Byzantine Emperor, Marcian, is marching a large number of his troops to our Italian provinces. It appears his spies have uncovered Attila's plans, and he suspects the Huns are planning a surprise attack from the north to hit Rome itself. The Byzantine generals believe that, with their army coming from the east and Aetius bringing his force from the west, the scourge of Europe could be trapped by his own audacity."

The two tribunes looked at each other in worry. They knew Aetius' legions were scattered all along the Rhine looking for the Huns. It would take the imperator weeks to gather his full strength and reach Italy.

Phokas distracted them momentarily when he strode over to the table. "Well, *I'm* hungry anyway. Is that fresh bread I smell?"

Brenda poked her head from around the corner. "Yes, it is. Pour some more olive oil in the bowl. It looks empty."

Phokas sat down and watched everyone mill around. "Say, Marcus, what are you doing here? I thought you were getting married?"

"Oh, I had to leave," Marcus lamented. "When my family arrived, the Bernius house collapsed into complete chaos. The two mothers almost tied me to Lucius' horse and told me not to come back until the wedding eve. I'm afraid I'm exiled to Rome for another three days."

Martinel arched his eyebrows. "Then you can serve as my guide. The entertainments of this city are legendary among my people, and Lucius here is far too dull to be a good host."

Brenda walked back in waving a wooden spoon. "Marcus, don't you dare let Martinel corrupt you. If I catch wind of any antics, I'll give Julia a full account."

"I can't stand the wait. Three days are forever. I'm going for a walk." With his face still beet red, Marcus stormed out the door.

Lucius guffawed along with the rest until Marcus disappeared down the walkway. Afterwards, he turned and searched for Dervla and spotted her huddled in the kitchen area, holding a deep conversation with Brenda. His eyes lingered on her, but he could not think of a good reason to interrupt.

He then noticed Seamus rooted in a corner, standing in stoic silence, and looking very much alone. Lucius walked over and put his arm around the boy's shoulder. "Come on, lad. If you don't help yourself, you won't get anything to eat. That wild Frank over there will devour everything in sight."

Martinel smiled and gestured to a spot beside him. "Come sit next to me, boy. Ever since Master Takumi returned to the Bernius estate two months ago, I've been surrounded by nothing but barbarian Romans."

Lucius steered Seamus to the bench between the two men, and Pope Leo soon joined them. "So tell me about the Catalaunian Plains. I've read all the reports, but I've yet to speak with anyone who was there."

Lucius told the tale, ending with a simple statement: "It was very, very close." Martinel just nodded in grim agreement.

Lucius glanced over at Seamus, who stared down at the table with smoldering eyes. Lucius made a guess at the youth's resentment. "You know, I've been in the legion for almost a year now, but I still think the greatest act of courage I've seen was what I saw in my very first engagement. This lad's father, Unis, attacked two armored Vandals with nothing but a makeshift club to defend his family. He lost an arm in the struggle but bought us enough time to reach them."

"'No greater love has any man than to offer his life for another,'" Pope Leo intoned. "I would like to meet him someday."

Seamus' shoulders straightened and his eyes shone with a newfound pride.

Pope Leo added, "Those Vandals are the ones to watch. With that Aryan heresy they follow and their fleet ravaging the Mediterranean, the day of reckoning is coming."

Lucius nodded just as his eye caught a subtle motion at the doorway that turned out to be Marcus. He looked very pale and walked straight to the table.

"My friends, I think there's some serious trouble brewing. I ran into an old friend of my father's, and he was very disturbed. It seems the emperor and most of his household left the city during the night. They took half the Praetorians with them."

The room turned dead silent.

It didn't stay quiet for long as the Pope pushed back from the table. "I've been gone from the Lateran Palace too long. I need to get back and find what my spics have uncovered."

"I agree; something is afoot. I will escort you," said Satewa.

"Marcus, Martinel, we better round up the men. Brenda, with your permission, we'll gather on the general's grounds here." Lucius nodded to Dervla standing beside the other lady. "Dervla, you and Seamus stay here. It appears your master has chosen to leave Rome without you."

Seamus rose sharply. "I'll fetch my mother and learn what's happened within the hour." Without waiting for consent, he bolted out the door.

* * *

An hour later, Marcus returned with six disgruntled legionaries in tow, but no news arrived until midday. Seamus returned half carrying his mother. She shook from her coughing jags and her face had the drawn, pale expression of one long ill.

Dervla rushed to her. "Brenda, is there some place where my mother can lay down for a while?"

"Of course, right this way." The two women guided the old slave down the hall.

Phokas became all business and headed to the kitchen area. "I'll prepare an elixir. Brenda, do you have any honey?"

His face clouded with concern, Seamus followed the women with his eyes until they vanished into a room. He turned and faced Marcus. "It appears you Romans have been caught by surprise. The Huns have smashed your border garrisons and now rampage through the provinces south of the Alps."

Marcus' eyes lit with a horrible thought. "Julia." He turned on his heels and ran for the door.

A few minutes later, the bewildered legionaries stared as Marcus drove a roan stallion through the manor's gate at a reckless gallop.

"Three hundred miles!" he snarled. With the map of Rome's northern Italian provinces vividly etched in his mind, he knew which of the border cities held the most tactical value: Mediolanum. Determined and prepared defenders could hold the city's twenty-foot walls against even a large army, but the people he cared the most about in the world were several hours south of there. Although the Bernius estate had walls, they were meant to stop marauding thieves, not an army.

Marcus cursed to himself as he passed through the Porta Flaminia and exited the city. A steady stream of people flowed into the city through Rome's massive portals. The worried legionaries warding the city's entrance didn't give the tribune a second glance as he shuffled his horse through the oncoming wave of humanity.

CHAPTER XVIII

A DESPERATE PLAN

Senator Bernius clasped Takumi Saegusa's arms with an iron hard grip. "This will work. It must work."

That evening, Senator Bernius and Master Carloman devised a drastic plan. A hidden tunnel ran from the wine cellar to a grotto several hundred yards away. "Takumi, lead the women and children out and hide in the woods until the horde passes," the senator pleaded. "We will hold their attention here for as long as we live. Please, save my family."

Takumi watched the line of women and children climbing down the ladder to the wine cellar. *It can't end like this.*

A few days ago, the estate had been full of gaiety. The Carloman family and their retainers had arrived, and everyone prepared for Marcus and Julia's wedding. Then rumor came of trouble in the north. By the time they learned Mediolanum was under siege, they'd been cut off.

The two swordsmen who were to accompany him already worked their way down the long-unused tunnel. Takumi met the senator eye to eye. "As long as I draw breath, I will keep them safe."

Tears streaked down the senator's face. "It was a fortuitous day when those pirates brought us together. God-speed, my friend."

Takumi moved down the ladder and heard the trapdoor slam down above him. Bile rose in his throat. They had no real options left, or a means of reaching the city, and the southern path was blocked.

Many retired legionaries worked on the senator's property, and together with the Carloman bodyguards, they presented a respectable deterrent to marauding looters. Senator Bernius sent for help often, but Takumi didn't think word got through. He shook as he dropped to the stone floor and hurried into the tunnel. *This must go better than the last escape attempt.*

On the day when word of an invasion came, old Silvio the stable master and Unis the one-armed servant rode out for help. However, Silvio had been flayed alive in the very stable yard where he'd groomed the family mounts. They had seen no sign of the other man. Two days after that escape attempt, what faint hope they had of holding out crumbled. A large column of Huns arrived led by a huge man wearing the skull of a bear as a helmet. The barbarian rode around the estates' walls studying them.

Takumi worked his way to the head of the column of refugees and reached the grate that opened up into a secluded grotto. Sweat beaded his forehead as he strained his ears for the sound of movement as, once the trapdoor lifted, they would be exposed. They'd extinguished the torches behind them, leaving the tunnel blacker than night, and who knew what lay ahead. Over twenty women and children lined up behind him with just two men-at-arms to protect them.

He let loose a large breath and pushed at the iron bars. Rusted hinges that hadn't moved in a generation made a deafening screech as they swung open. Takumi dove outside and surveyed the grotto for any movement in the midnight darkness. He sensed nothing but tensed for an attack.

Turning toward the estate, Takumi listened for a clash of steel but only heard hoarse shouts in a guttural language. The fight there had ended already. As flames leapt high in the sky where the Bernius home stood, bitter tears ran down the swordmaster's face. His dearest friend, Verius Bernius, was surely dead.

He signaled the refugees to follow him. When Mistress Bernius passed, she searched his face with anxious hope. Takumi just lowered his head and shook it. As she staggered away, the quiet sob she let out felt like a knife through his heart. He could accept his own death, but the horror of his family dying at the hands of these pitiless monsters left him in agony.

One hundred yards to the edge of the woods and its promise of sanctuary, their slim chance of escape evaporated. It started with the surprised whimper of the youngest Carloman son as he fell down dead. An arrow had struck the ten-year-old boy in the back. Loud whoops followed as a band of Huns rushed them from the underbrush.

Takumi had time to yell, "Run!" before he charged into the Huns.

Lady Carloman ran to her fallen son with two men-at-arms close behind. The guards slew three Huns before they themselves died. The boy's mother threw herself at the attackers like a rabid dog and drove her long dagger through the heart of the first Hun she could reach. The children from the estate scattered in every direction like jackrabbits flying over familiar ground, and several eluded the barbarians. The women were not so lucky.

Takumi tightened his grip on the razor-sharp swords he held in both hands. Six Huns circled him like a pack of wolves. One enormous man as big as his friend, Satewa, prowled around Takumi with hard, soulless eyes.

Takumi's heart wrenched at the sight of the two dead Carloman bodyguards who had accompanied him, both of whom had been competent swordsmen. *I could not refuse the beseeching look in Verius' eyes. He needed some hope to cling to, no matter how remote.*

Behind him, Mistress Bornius wailed as she held the limp body of her youngest child. Julia and the Carloman serving girls stood over her with daggers at the ready. The Huns ignored them for the moment.

There's nothing left for me to do but to die and take as many of these butchers with me. Takumi didn't wait, and in a blink, he gutted the man before him and severed the neck of the man on his left. He hamstrung a third with a diving sweep. Then the world spun as a heavy war hammer smashed against him.

He could not move. He could not speak. But his mind screamed as he watched a Hun decapitate the elderly noblewoman who had treated him as a son. The agony in her eyes reflected the pain in his soul.

Julia leapt on the killer's back and ripped his throat open with her blade. Groping hands pulled her down hard and disarmed her. Young Julia and the servant screamed in terror as the laughing men dragged them away.

Unable to focus, Takumi could still make out the barbarian with the bear skull helmet as he examined and sheathed his own two swords and then sneer at him.

"You have cost me many good warriors. Die knowing your pretty little blades will be used to skin those lovely whores you tried to protect once we're done with them." The Hun hefted a discarded spear and drove it into Takumi's stomach, then followed his men back up the path, shouting orders.

CHAPTER XIX

ENCOUNTER ON THE ROAD

The trickle of refugees on the road had grown into a torrent. Approaching them felt like swimming against the tide, but a determined Marcus pushed on. He despaired at the thought of receiving any real information from those fleeing south. Those who paused long enough to answer him reported countless Huns swarming across the border and slaughtering everyone they caught.

Finally, though, he heard a familiar voice. "Master Marcus? Master Marcus, is that you?"

The tribune's eyes locked in on the source. Unis sat slumped atop Senator Bernius' best horse. Both the animal and the rider appeared to be beyond exhaustion.

"Good God, man, what's happened?"

The man wept and gasped for breath as he spoke. "I tried, but no one will help. The garrisons are abandoned, and the soldiers are fleeing as fast as the civilians."

"Talk to me! Julia, my family! Are they all right?"

"They were all alive when I left, but the situation is desperate. The savages have the senator's estate surrounded. Master Bernius sent a few of us who couldn't fight to seek help. The women and children were going to try to sneak out through a hidden tunnel if the situation became hopeless, but that was two days ago."

"Why are you here, then? Why haven't you brought them any help?"

Unis' eyes flashed with anger. "Oh, I found Roman troops, all right, but none would turn north. They're all being summoned to the Amalfi Coast to protect your precious emperor!"

Marcus watched the hysterical mob surge by, then pulled out a blank piece of vellum and scribbled a hurried note. "Tribune Bernius and some of our men are at the home of General Aetius. Tell him what you've told me. This note will get you past any gate wardens. Once in Rome, almost anyone should be able to direct you to the general's house. It's on the Aventine Hill. Go with haste. Forgive my harsh words; you didn't deserve them."

"I will, young man. No forgiveness is necessary. I know what fear for one's family can do to a man."

Without another word, they rode hard in opposite directions.

A few hours later, Marcus spurred his flagging horse even harder in response to a new rumor sweeping over the throng on the road: "Mediolanum has fallen!"

* * *

The next day, Unis reached the house on the Aventine Hill. His horse collapsed outside the walls of Rome, so the drained man ran the last part of the journey.

Brenda yelped when she opened the door to a frantic knock, and she grew more horrified when the haggard man in the doorway wheezed, "The Huns are at the Bernius home." Immediately after, he crumpled to the floor.

Dervla rushed to his side screaming, "Father!"

Lucius turned deathly pale at the sight—and the news.

CHAPTER XX

STABLE YARD

"Leave the rich whore alone; she might bring a ransom. Play with the other one."

"Come on, Optila, there're five of us."

"What do I care? Draw lots or something. This raid was a fiasco. I lost over thirty warriors. Those bastards fought like men possessed, and there wasn't anything in that damn house worth taking."

The Hun called Optila adjusted his bear skull helmet and walked over to where they had tied the two naked women in the bloodied stable yard. "Perhaps there's someone still alive who'll pay good Roman coin for her." With an iron grip, he twisted Julia's exposed breast. "If not, there'll be plenty of time for her to entertain the army. But I'll go first. She's too skinny to last very long."

Julia showed him a defiant glare despite the terrible pain. She bit back the tears and focused on her father's head impaled on a post and how he'd shown no fear in those eyes at his moment of death. *I'm his daughter. I'll face my fate just as bravely.*

"But she's the one who shanked Donan."

"If he couldn't fight off a woman, he got just what he deserved. Now, I must find Attila. Try to find something of value in this forsaken place."

"Optila, those fancy swords you're carrying should fetch a bit of gold. You're going to share that bounty, aren't ya?"

Optila pulled out one of the long curved blades and examined it. "They're too light for my taste, but this is very fine steel." Laughing, he put the sword away and mounted his horse. "If I hadn't come along, that little man would've sliced every one of you to pieces. No, these prizes are mine." Without another word, he rode off at a brisk pace.

Julia bit back tears. *Those are Takumi's swords.* If that beast had them, then Takumi must've died in the attack along with everyone else. Only her brother and Marcus remained. *Please, God, protect them.*

A terrified scream rang through the air, pulling her from her thoughts. One barbarian dragged the Carloman servant over to the campfire, threw her down, and held her on a bloodstained blanket.

A leering man with a greasy beard stood over the girl. "Let her go. I like them frisky when I have them."

He dropped on top of her but then squealed in pain. Blood spurted around her mouth from having bitten his ear, and she strove to rip it off. Her wild hands fumbled to gouge his eyes.

"The witch is trying to kill me! Stop her!"

The other Huns roared with laughter until she spit out the severed ear and held the bloody pulp of an eyeball in her hand. The servant tried to run, but the maimed man tripped her. Another of the Huns laughed as he threw his knife, which buried itself in the girl's back. She fell with a whimper, and the hooting barbarians surrounded her and whooped as they hacked at her twitching body. The frenzied stabbing continued until there was nothing left of the girl but a gory pulp. The maimed man crawled over to his bedroll, whimpering.

The four other Huns turned to Julia and studied her with wary glances. She returned the look with a flat stare. *Lord in Heaven, help me be as courageous as that poor woman.*

One of them finally spoke, addressing the others as he stared at her. "I don't think we dare cross Optila. He's in a pretty foul mood. This whole foray's been a complete disaster. No plunder, no women, and now old one-eye over there won't even be taking a watch tonight." Grumbling, they walked to the campfire. One retrieved a poultice and examined the injured man.

"At least there's plenty of this swill the Romans call wine." A short, flat-faced Hun hefted a jug and swallowed the contents in large gulps.

* * *

Marcus arrived during the moonlit night. He remembered the trails around the Bernius estate well and knew which tunnel Unis spoke of. *Lucius and I played there so often as boys, I could find it blindfolded.*

The last three miles he covered on foot, avoiding the swarms of Huns who patrolled around all areas. A man on horseback would be far too easy to spot. Though successful at eluding detection, Marcus' chest tightened so much he could scarcely draw breath when he approached the grotto. Before him lay the aftermath of a nightmarish conflict, but instead of faceless warriors, the lifeless bodies consisted of the people he cherished most in the world.

Dead. Everyone is dead. Marcus cried as he laid the limp form of his little brother next to his mother. His eyes swept the small glen, identifying the corpses until a small bit of hope rose. *Julia's not here.*

A bitter smile crossed his face as he approached Takumi's impaled body and noticed several dead Huns sprawled around him. "You accounted for yourself well, old friend."

"I... failed, young Carloman."

Marcus stepped back in shock. *A spear has him pinned. Takumi can't be alive.*

And yet, the old swordmaster retained a glint of life in his eyes. "Come close. My time with you is short."

The tribune knelt by the old man, looking at his mangled body. He couldn't even guess what to do to help him. Marcus held the swordmaster's head in his lap as Takumi's body shook with spasms. "Lie still. I'll help you."

"Listen... there's nothing you can do for me, but you can still help Mistress Julia. You must move quickly. Come daybreak, they'll leave and rejoin the horde. Then she'll be beyond the aid of any civilized man." Takumi's voice gurgled as his lungs filled with blood. "They're in the stable yard, and there's no more than ten still here. They took the women there. Your strikes must be sure and silent."

Marcus' voice choked. "I will, Master. I'll save Julia."

A slow, guttural sigh rolled from Takumi's lips, and he relaxed all at once as the spasms ended and the stillness of death rolled over the old man's body. Even in death, Takumi Saegusa looked like he walked the line between fierceness and peace.

Marcus gently lowered the old man's head to the ground. When Marcus rose, he drew his spatha, caged his fury, and stalked his prey.

The hidden path to the back side of the stable had seen much use by Marcus and Lucius when, as boys, they had wanted to sneak away from adults. Once he emerged, he studied the Hun's campsite for a long time. Only five remained, and they all snored, even the guard propped against a shed. Many jugs lay scattered around the yard.

Marcus restrained a smirk. They're not sleeping. They're all dead drunk.

Twenty fence posts held a head each, all that remained of the able-bodied men from the Bernius and Carloman households. However, he spotted a familiar figure tied to a post in the camp very much alive.

Blessed Mother of God, it's Julia. But I see no one else.

Rage coursed through his body, and he exerted all of his willpower not to rush to her. Marcus crept forward and slit the guard's throat. The Hun fell limp with hardly a sound. One look around told him that the disturbance had roused no one.

Only Julia caught his eye, and she stared at him in amazement. Using quick but quiet steps, Marcus met her and severed the rawhide bounds. Julia threw her arms around him, her whole body trembling against his. "Marcus, they're dead. Everyone's dead," she whispered.

Marcus rested his cloak around her bare shoulders. "Go to the tunnel in the grotto. I'll meet you there soon."

"No. There are still four of them. You'll be killed."

"Darling, I must. These men will know where to look come morning, and the sky's already starting to lighten. With them dead, it'll be days before there's any pursuit."

"Oh God, Marcus, be careful. I can't lose you, too."

Marcus studied the sleeping men. "If they're as attentive as the guard, this will be no problem." He kissed her hard on the lips and added in a choked voice, "I won't ever leave you alone again."

From there, he pushed her toward the path and crept into the campsite. Marcus was no match for Lucius in a duel, but he knew how to use a sword. A swift, killing thrust dispatched three of the Huns in short order. As he approached the fourth, Marcus stumbled over a discarded jug. It clattered on the stones, the sound splitting the air like thunder.

Many bandages covered the remaining Hun's head, but his one visible eye shot wide open, and he struggled to stand. "Quick, lads, there's a Roman among us! Men?"

His one eye opened even wider as he realized his comrades were already dead. He stumbled and took a shaky swing with his axe, but he hit nothing but air. The battle-axe soon dropped, still gripped in the Hun's severed hand. He had no time to scream as Marcus delivered the final blow.

Marcus ransacked the site for anything useful and bundled it in a sack. Before leaving, he stopped for a time before his father's severed head. "Father, I must leave you desecrated for now, but I swear by all that is holy, I'll be back to honor you and mother." His eyes glistening, he turned away and didn't look back.

After taking a few steps, a shadowed figure met him, holding a gladius at the ready. His muscles tensed but relaxed as he recognized the trembling figure in the darkness. "Julia, I thought I told you to head to the grotto?"

Julia glowered at him through her tears. "Do you think I would leave the man I love to face those monsters alone? You and Lucius weren't the only ones Master Takumi instructed."

Worry and love wrestled within him. Finally, he surrendered to her defiant glare. "Let's get some rest. We're not out of this yet."

* * *

Dawn broke as Marcus and Julia returned to the hidden tunnel entrance. They crawled inside and soon fell fast asleep, not waking until late afternoon. Marcus opened his eyes to find several pairs staring back at him.

In one fast movement, he slid his hand to the sword by his side and then released his grip on it. The lead figure looked familiar, even in the darkness. "Titus?"

"Yes, Master Carloman. It's me."

Titus was old Silvio's twelve-year-old grandson. He held an old gladius loosely in his hand, and his lips trembled as he spoke. Behind him crowded seven other children with eyes of terror. Julia opened her arms and the children rushed into them. Titus dropped the sword and collapsed at Marcus' feet.

"Titus, what happened?" asked the tribune.

The boy squared his shoulders and looked him in the eye. "It was dark, and there was a lot of screaming. Master Takumi yelled, 'run,' and we took off. The Huns chased us for a little while but gave up. I hid in a tree all night. I stayed there until the sun was high and then snuck back to the grotto. The other children must've had the same idea." The boy's eyes welled with tears before he wiped them away. "They killed everyone like they killed my grandpa. I'm the oldest, so I took charge. We were going to hide in the tunnel here. I was real scared when I saw someone inside, but I'm the oldest, so I looked. Master Carloman, I'm so sorry I didn't stay to help your mother. I just ran and never looked back."

Marcus squeezed the boy's shoulder. "You did exactly what you were supposed to do. Master Takumi told you to flee and you obeyed him." He decided there and then to take the children with them, but shared a worried look with Julia. *Two people have a fair chance of escaping notice, but how am I going to manage that with eight children?*

Julia met his eyes, her gaze calm and confident. "Marcus, you're the smartest man I know. If anyone can get us out of here, it's you."

Marcus felt crushed by her trust in him but nonetheless bent his head in thought. *Whatever I come up with will have to be quick. We should be long gone when the Huns start hunting for us.*

He glanced at the dead Huns and then Titus, and in time, a plan formed. At last, he snapped his fingers. "Julia, we need to gather some things."

A half hour later, Marcus stood back to appraise his creation and sighed. It would never pass a close inspection, and he hugged the fierce-looking Hunnic warrior at his side. "Julia, this is the best we can do. We have to go now."

Julia lifted the visor of her horned helm and kissed him. "It'll work." She lifted little Victoria into the saddle and mounted the horse behind the girl.

Marcus swallowed hard as he wrapped his thick bearskin cloak around the small child sitting before him. They had little food and would be traveling obscure back trails. *It will be many days before we can reach safety, if there's such a thing anymore.*

Five Hunnic steeds walked away from the grotto, single file, with many undersized soldiers shrouded in thick cloaks astride them. Marcus had already decided on a destination. *Mantua's the nearest city still in Roman hands. We'll make for that.*

CHAPTER XXI

VIA AEMILIA

"Vidin, I told you and your men I'm going alone. I order you to stay here," an adamant Lucius commanded.

"Sir, the boys and I swore we would never desert you again, and we aim to keep that oath."

Martinel finished tightening the cinches on the pack mules. "I took no such vow, but I'll not have it be said that a fancy Roman aristocrat would venture where a Frankish noble would not. I just wish we weren't heading into the middle of the entire Hunnic army. I'm getting sick of them."

Lucius wiped his eyes when a calloused but gentle hand came to rest on his shoulder, and he gave the newcomer an imploring look. "Father Patricius, please, no. I must go, but it's a fool's errand."

"Then we're all fools," said the priest. "We'll find your family or perish in the attempt."

A man behind them spoke up with an earnest sincerity. "I'll also need an ecclesiastic to travel with us as my confessor."

The small troop of soldiers turned at the new voice. Two men approached, dressed in the plain white robes of pilgrims. One definitely didn't look like a pilgrim with his large frame and bronzed, exotic looks, but the other sent Lucius to his knees. "Your Holiness, what are you talking about? I fear this is a one-way trip."

Pope Leo, however, smiled back without a hint of fear. "My son, I'm called the Christian Lion. It's time I try to live up to that lofty title. Besides, there are no imperial leaders. Valentinian has fled to the isle fortress of Capri, Aetius is trying to gather an army, and Marcian's Byzantine force has still not reached our borders. So it's I who must face this 'Scourge of God.' Since I've no weapons beyond my voice, I intend to tag along with you until we are close. With God's grace, we'll both succeed in our missions."

Father Patricius twisted his hands together in consternation. "Please, let me go in your stead. I can speak to this Attila in your name."

"Thank you for your courage, but I'll not have you face martyrdom while I cower in my apartments." Pope Leo bowed to the still kneeling legionaries. "I wear the garb of a pilgrim, so I won't cause a commotion among the populous. Please refrain from using my name until we're well away from the city. Now, the sun won't hold in the sky. Shall we ride?"

* * *

The small procession passed through Rome's Flaminia Gate with little notice. The guards there had focused their attention on sorting out the refugees trying to enter. The trip up the Via Cassia was just as uneventful, despite an enormous, white-robed monk leading them, holding aloft a tall cross made of wrought iron. Many refugees paused for the blessings offered by the other two friars, and some drew hope from the stone faced legionaries accompanying them.

They didn't encounter any military presence until they reached the garrison post on the Via Aemilia. To their surprise, a small contingent of legionaries still manned the gate.

On their approach, the barred door opened, and an agitated centurion stepped out waving them back. He soon noticed the tribune's rank, however, and saluted. "I strongly advise you to turn those animals of yours around and head back where you came from as fast as you can."

An exhausted Lucius wiped the dust from his face. "Thank you for your warning, Centurion, but we have business with Attila."

The centurion cocked his head. "No offense, sir, but the Huns chew up whole legions before breakfast. I don't think your little band will get very far."

Gentilius approached and gestured to his commander. "Do you know who you're talking to? This is Tribune Bernius. He shook his fist in Attila's face at Catalaunian Plains."

The centurion glanced at the insignia the riders wore and sighed. "Red Fist, eh? You folks were in the thick of it, that's for sure. Well, I won't be the one to stand in your way, but don't say you weren't warned. I just wish General Aetius would hurry with the rest of your friends. It's getting very lonely out here. You're the only unit we've seen in two days."

Pope Leo dismounted, stretched his cramped legs, and stripped off the travel-stained white robe. Underneath, he wore his most elaborate clerical garment. He limped along, sore from the long ride in the saddle. Father Patricius followed, bearing a long staff with a crucifix on top. "Ah, perhaps you can tell us where we can find Attila. Rumor has him everywhere at once, and we seem to be having some problems finding him."

The centurion's mouth hung open at the sight of the well-dressed cleric. "Father, this is no place for a priest."

The Pope straightened to his full height and his eyes turned hard. "I am Pope Leo, and I will hide behind a pilgrim's robe no longer. I ride out in the open for all to see. Let the rumor of my coming travel before me." A small smile edged onto his face, and the centurion stared at him with a slack jaw.

The centurion didn't stay that way for long, though. "Your Holiness, this is insanity. You have to go back. The Huns are ruthless pagans who take special delight in torturing priests."

"My mission will be done. God will protect me." The Pope shrugged. "And if He chooses to call me home, I will be martyred in His name."

The centurion sighed and then lifted his chin. "May God protect us all. He's in Mantua right now, along the Mincio River. I'll escort you there myself."

The collection of hardened, veteran legionaries inside the stockade had come out and gathered around the small caravan. Lucius regarded the centurion with a furrowed brow. "What are your current orders, soldier?"

The centurion looked back with flat eyes. "We've been commanded to abandon our post and head south. We were getting ready to leave when you showed up. But I don't especially like running with my tail between my legs, and neither do my men."

"What's your name, Centurion?"

"Peyago, sir."

"Well, Centurion Peyago, welcome to the Red Fist. Get your men in order. We leave now."

That night, they camped on the shore of the Mincio River, their number over a hundred strong.

Lucius let out a sigh of relief. I'll slip away tonight. The Pope has his Honor Guard, and perhaps the Huns will recognize the embassy and grant an audience. My mission is on a different path, and I'll put no one else in danger.

Despite the late hour, he walked to the tethered horses and gave the guard a curt nod. If anyone asked, he'd tell them he was just an officer on inspection.

The horses nickered suddenly, and Lucius caught a glimpse of motion in the brush nearby.

CHAPTER XXII

MINCIO RIVER

A breeze didn't cause the bush to rustle, so Lucius slid behind a thick willow and drew his spatha. The half-moon cleared the clouds drifting across the sky, and the tribune froze at what he saw. The horned helm and thick furs belonged to a Hun.

Where there's one, there's many. He rushed in to create a diversion and bellowed, "To arms! There're foes among us!"

A tall gangly savage drew a wicked-looking curved blade and leapt to face him. His arm shook at the vibration of the parried blow. The man had the advantage but, for some reason, didn't exploit it.

Then, to Lucius' utter shock, the barbarian cried out in clear Latin, "I yield, Roman. For God's sake, I yield."

He received an even greater shock when a small Hun ran from concealment, crying his name in a soprano voice he knew well. "Julia?" His spatha fell from his numb hand as the demonic savage removed his horned helm and revealed his best friend. "Marcus?"

Behind Lucius, the whole camp had come alive. The first to charge into the small dell with bared steel in hand was Father Patricius wearing just his coarse linen nightshirt, but he waved the legionaries behind him to halt. Marcus clung to a diminutive Hun, and both of them wept unabashed. Lucius pulled back from his sister and desperately stared into inky darkness as several smaller savages tentatively stepped into the torch light.

Julia choked on her emotions as her brother turned imploring eyes to her. She hugged him tight and released her anguish into his shoulder. "Oh, Lucius, they're dead. They're all dead. Mother, Father, little Octavia... Marcus' family. All murdered."

Lucius held his sister and met Marcus' gaze. His friend's eyes blazed with a fury he'd never seen before in that soft-spoken man as he spoke. "I got there too late. I couldn't even give them a proper burial."

Father Patricius picked up a little girl. "You saved these children. You did more than could be humanly expected." He studied the children gathered close by, all soaked from head to toe. "Come, little ones. Dry yourselves by the fire, and we'll see what food we can warm for you." The priest led them to the campsite.

Only then did Lucius realize his sister was also drenched and shaking from the cold—she and Marcus both. "Julia, Marcus, come by the fire and tell me what happened."

They did just that. Julia told the tale while holding Marcus' hand tight in her grasp, but she left nothing from that nightmare out no matter how much she trembled. "Mantua and all bridges across the river are held by the Huns, so Marcus inflated our water-skins into a makeshift raft, and the two of us pulled the children across the water. We had to abandon our horses and supplies on the other side." She sighed and regarded the legionaries around them. "I guess we're not very good horse thieves."

The Pope sat through the tale, stroking his beard, and then his piercing eyes met Julia's. "I wonder what the odds are that you would choose this spot on the river to cross and try to steal our animals."

Julia looked at Marcus, whose mouth hung open, and then turned again to the Pope. "Only God's gracious mercy could have put you here where we needed you."

Pope Leo nodded and gazed long at the cross he clutched in his shaking hands. "I agree. The Lord in Heaven put us in this time and place for a reason." After a moment, he breathed deep and gave the tribunes a resolute look. "At first light, take the children to safety. Father Patricius and I will go and confront this Attila."

Calmness settled over the Pope as everyone buffeted him with pleas to change his mind. Peyago in particular emerged from the crowd. "You heard this young woman's story. You'll be butchered before you get anywhere near him."

The Pope shook his head. "I am resolved to do this. God's angels will protect me."

His thoughts racing, Lucius stepped forth. "As you said, God put us in this place for a reason." Lucius eyed his friend. "Marcus will take the children south to Rome with a fist of legionaries for protection. Everyone else will be your honor guard. We will parade on the road, blaring horns and banging drums."

"Lucius, I'll not leave you to face this death by yourself." Marcus shook his head, frowning.

"My dearest friend, I charge you with a much more important task. Please protect the last family I have left in this world and love her forever."

Marcus bit his lip in agony and approached the Pope. "Your Holiness, marry us now. I want my best friend at my wedding, and I want all to know he is my brother."

The Pope looked at Julia. Her eyes welled with tears as she nodded, and the Pope stood with a bittersweet smile. "Marcus, Julia, please stand before me. And who will give away the bride?"

Lucius rose and held his sister in a tight hug. "With my whole heart, I do so proudly."

The legionaries gathered around the wet and bedraggled couple. They witnessed the most beautiful wedding any of them had ever seen.

CHAPTER XXIII

ATTILA'S CAMP

As he held the white flag of truce, Centurion Peyago glanced back over his shoulder at the line of men marching four abreast behind him. "Tribune Bernius, we couldn't find any drums, but we do have one horn."

Centurion Gentilius, who bore the standard of the Red Fist First Legion, spit to the side. "I would prefer to have a few thousand legionaries instead of a damn horn."

Satisfied with the arrangement, Lucius led them onto the Via Cassia from their place of concealment. Three rode on horseback: Pope Leo, who wore his most resplendent ecclesiastical mantle; Father Patricius in a brilliant white robe, bearing a tall, wrought iron crucifix; and Satewa, also in a white robe and carrying a dented brass horn. Marcus had left earlier with twenty of the legionaries and the refugees, taking the remaining horses.

Lucius drew in a deep breath. "Okay, Satewa, let's hear what that horn sounds like."

* * *

Optila gritted his teeth and growled. "Your Greatness, kill them before they get here. That holy man they have will put a curse on you."

Attila rolled his eyes at the towering giant kneeling before him. The leader of the Huns leaned back on the gold embossed chair his men had retrieved from the sacking of the governor's palace in Mediolanum. Around him, the camp sprawled with the chaos of thousands of the world's most feared warriors rousing themselves in the early morning light.

Attila turned his attention to the giant. "Optila, it's not that simple. I had a dream before we started this conquest. In it, I was being torn to pieces by an eagle and a lion, and while I struggled with them, my right arm was severed by an enormous spirit. I think these Christians call them angels." Attila glanced over at the three druids crouched over a gutted pig, studying its entrails, and rolled his eyes. "They tell me it's a bad omen. Such deep insights. How can I even exist without them?"

The Hunnic king turned serious again. "I understood part of it. Flavius Aetius was called the eagle when he lived amongst us, but the other part confused me. There are no lions in Italy, but what do I learn this morning? Out of nowhere, this high priest of the Jesus god appears and walks straight to me with but a handful of men. Do you know what the name of this holy man is?"

Optila gulped. "I don't know. Jesus?"

Attila laughed and then pursed his lips. "I wish that was it. No, it's Leo. In their cursed language, that means 'lion.' What kind of holy man walks around with the name of lion? I'm thinking we should return home."

"My king, we can't do that. The Roman army scatters like sheep before us. Rome itself lies ripe for the taking. It holds treasure beyond our wildest dreams."

"Great wealth? We can barely feed the army with what's been looted so far." Attila slumped and whispered, "It's been too easy. Where is Aetius with his demon legions? There's no sign of him, and rumor brings word that the Byzantines are coming with a great host. The deeper we move into this blighted land, the more it feels like a trap."

Optila's eyebrows shot up. "Where's the leader who makes the world tremble? Kings prostrate themselves before you at the simple word of your approach. Is the great Attila becoming soft and cautious?"

"Take care, Optila. Men die for speaking like that to me," Attila snarled. Rather than run with his anger, however, he sighed and let his temper cool. "You speak as a true warrior and loyal friend, but I must be a king. I promise to do nothing in haste. I'll render no decision until after I meet with this Jesus mystic. Then I'll see what the omens foretell."

"That is good. Our gods will prove stronger. If you will allow, I'd like to stand beside you and study this terror from your dreams."

Attila nodded and turned at the sound of a commotion near the edge of his camp. An off-key blare sounded from a single horn, followed by a chorus of hoots and challenges from his men.

Optila gazed at the edge of their camp. "Well, it appears you won't have to wait long. They're here."

* * *

Tribune Bernius kept his face expressionless as he marched his small band through the gauntlet of Huns lining the road. His face cracked with a small smile when Decurion Gentilius whispered in his ear: "Tell me again, how many times a brave man dies?"

As he came within sight of Attila's pavilion, Lucius ordered his men to halt. The Pope dismounted and strode ahead, accompanied by Lucius, Martinel, and the two white-clad men. They stopped three paces before the Scourge of Rome.

Lucius focused on the man lounging on a gilded throne, sipping mead from a large tankard. Their eyes locked on each other, and a flicker of recognition passed over Attila's face. Lucius had seen him once before but had hoped to never see him again.

He winced when his eyes swung to the large Hun standing at the right side of Attila. The Hun wore Master Takumi's swords which brought to mind the story Julia had relayed the previous evening. Rage consumed his thoughts as Lucius realized he stood before the murderer of his family.

* * *

Attila stared at the embassy before him in shock. The holy man was like none he'd ever confronted before, returning his fierce glare with a fearless serenity. However, he recognized the Roman officer burning with hatred. He was the Roman commander who had stared down at him from that makeshift palisade just before Flavius Aetius bested him at the Catalaunian Plains.

Attila whispered to Optila, "That insignia he wears is of Aetius' legions. How far away can the general be if one of his main warriors stands before me?"

Attila stared in regal silence but cringed inside as he regarded the other men aligned in front of him. A towering man clad all in white wore a great sword on his back. Attila learned toward Optila. "That face. It belongs to no Roman. It belongs to no race I have ever seen. It's him. It's the angel of death from my dreams."

Optila snapped his head around to Attila and hissed, "The Terror of the World is scared? If you turn tail and run from an old man and a few lackeys, what tribes will still follow us? Master, don't be a superstitious fool!"

Ahead of them, Pope Leo spread his arms wide. "Great Attila, I beseech you in the name of the one true God to return to your homes and leave us in peace."

Attila almost failed to hide his awe. "No bribe offered. No threat made. I should've hung them on a cross like their god. But that dream... is this my doom?"

Without a glance back, Optila stormed his way to the front. "Let's see whose gods are more powerful. Is there a man among you who will face me, Optila, in single combat?"

* * *

Lucius leapt forward, but Martinel gripped the tribune's arm and growled in his friend's ear. "I'll fight him. I don't like the looks of that monster, but you're so full of hate, you'll fight blindly and die."

Satewa looked at Optila and then regarded his two friends. His choice of action came quickly, and he slid his great sword out of its scabbard before stomping forth with ponderous steps.

Optila tilted his head up as though to stare down at them. "So I get my choice of sheep to slaughter." After a moment's pause, he nodded and said to Attila, "Big men never learn to fight well. They always depend on their strength and their reach. Look at that man—he's so off balance, he can barely stand." The Hun straightened his posture and roared, "I'll fight the big ugly one."

"No! Fight me!" Lucius roared. Martinel dragged him back as an eager circle of Huns formed a ring in the trampled grass before the throne.

Satewa stripped off the white robe as he watched Optila pull out Takumi's two razor-sharp blades. Martinel sidled up to him and cocked his head toward the oncoming opponent. "He'll be too quick for that great sword of yours."

Satewa agreed with the observation, dropped his weapon, and pulled out the one-handed hatchet he wore on his belt, then grabbed the gladius from Gentilius' sheath. "I'll return this to you shortly." He smashed the two weapons together and howled his horrific war cry. Satewa slid into a crouch and circled the Hun like a great raptor.

Optila spat and pointed toward the savage before him. "This is no clumsy oaf, but no matter. I'll still eat his heart tonight."

Satewa feinted twice, and his opponent parried the uncommitted blows with ease. Satewa focused on the Hun's eyes, but without any telltale signs, his opponent sprang to attack. Optila became a blur of motion, and for a brief moment, Satewa stumbled off balance. The sharp edge of the Hun's shorter blade bit his side.

Blood flowed from the gash, but the sword just grazed his ribs. Satewa slid to his left and swung the hatchet while he blocked a follow-up blow from the long sword with his gladius. As the axe sliced through the Hun's leather gauntlet and struck hard, the Mohawk warrior grunted in satisfaction.

Both men leapt back from each other, sucking in air, and warily appraised each other's wounds. The din of the screaming warriors surrounding them went ignored. Balanced on the balls of their feet, they circled for another opening.

The two giant fighters moved at the same time, countering the other's moves, and clashing blades inches apart. Satewa smirked, pushed off, and snapped the blade of his foot into his enemy's knee, a move he'd learned from watching Lucius. The stumbling Hun thrust with his long sword, but Satewa parried the awkward jab.

The Hun was a moment late in raising the shorter sword to defend himself. Satewa swept aside the lunge with his axe and moved inside the man's guard, slicing into the Hun's exposed side with his gladius. As Optila staggered back, Satewa spun and buried the hatchet in the barbarian's neck. Optila stared with shock until his eyes glazed over, and he collapsed into a heap.

Satewa split the corpse's head with a second blow from his axe and spat at the dead man. "The owner of these weapons was a far better man than you." He retrieved Takumi's two swords and reverently presented them to Lucius, who looked back at him with a burning gaze cooled by silent gratitude.

Satewa donned his white robe, and his blood soon stained a large patch of it red. He strode to the Pope and stood behind him with no change to his stoic face.

* * *

The gathered Huns stared in dumbfounded silence, Attila most of all. Optila, one of their fiercest captains, had been killed in mere seconds.

Attila's thoughts ran wild. The dream was all true. My right hand has been severed. Half of my men are sick from this blighted land, and my enemy closes a snare around my neck.

The Hunnic leader stood and steadied his voice. "Lion priest, you can tell Aetius we'll leave this pathetic country for now... but also tell him I'll be back to visit again soon. Now go. You will remain under my protection until the sun sets tomorrow."

Pope Leo bowed and, without another word, led his company from the field.

* * *

Once out of sight, the Romans scuttled back to their camp in reticence as they stared at each other. In time, word came that the Huns had mounted a retreat, but Pope Leo ordered the Romans not to pursue. Lucius didn't pay the news any mind, having remained quiet since Satewa's victory.

That night, the young tribune sat by the campfire, clutching Takumi's swords to his chest. Though he faced the fire, he didn't see it. His mind ran with thoughts and images of his father and Takumi teaching him, of his mother treating a cut on his hand, of his sisters laughing together with him in the fields. He recalled helping Silvio with the horses and sharing a warm meal prepared from a fresh harvest. The images looked so clear and bright, yet they felt faint like a fleeting dream. Neither the night air nor the distant memories warmed him, and the reality that he wouldn't have moments like those anymore left him chilled and numb. Even his chance at avenging them himself had slipped through his grasp. His one source of solace came from knowing that the family he had left now lived her life in a new home with his most trusted friend. When the battle with the Huns ended, though, where would *he* go?

In time, Martinel and Satewa came to sit beside him. The latter's wound had been treated earlier in the day. It was a while still before Lucius rubbed his eyes and looked at his friends. At long last, his head cleared enough for him to speak. "You know, I joined the legions because my father inspired me with dreams of what Rome could be." He threw a stick in the fire and watched the embers rise into the night sky. "To what end? Where was the greatness of Rome in my family's hour of need?"

Martinel sipped wine from his mug and let out a slow breath. "I think I'm the last person to speak of Roman virtue, and I didn't know your family. But I do know you. Your parents raised you to know honor and nobility. On this very night, they're sitting together in Heaven, boasting to whatever angel will listen of what their son has accomplished." Martinel reached over and squeezed Lucius' shoulder. "If you represent what Rome can be, I'll be damned if I don't pray that your people take over the whole world. It'll be a better place."

"The best way to honor your parents' memory is to strive to fulfill their dreams," Satewa added. "You are fortunate to have family to remember. I can no longer recall mine."

"You're right." Lucius couldn't argue their points. He also knew little could be done to change the past, and he would do a greater disservice to his family's memory if he stayed mute and motionless like he had in the last few hours. Moving forward, at least, felt better than standing still. With a great sigh, a weary Lucius stood and stabbed Takumi's katana into the ground and looked at his friends. "I swear on my parents' sacred memory to fulfill their dream or die in the effort."

Martinel rose with him and patted him on the back. "That's more like it."

"You're not alone," said Satewa.

The next morning, the small troop walked into Mantua. The last of the Huns had left before the sun rose.

* * *

General Aetius gingerly lowered himself from his horse and wiped the road grime from his face. It had been a long forced march from the Rhine to the Mincio River, and both he and his men were exhausted. The general glanced around at the destroyed town, but no enemies sprang from the debris or hid in the shadows.

He returned the sharp salute of the centurion, Peyago, who greeted him. "All right, soldier. What in the world happened here? The last I heard, this province was swarming with Huns, and now I can't find a single one."

The centurion answered with a sheepish grin. "Oh, the Huns were here for sure. This place wasn't ruined by the legionaries having a party. Old Attila met Pope Leo. In fact, it was almost on this very spot."

Aetius cocked his head, confused. "The Pope raised an army?"

"No, sir. His Holiness had just a handful of soldiers. Some were legionaries from my command, and a few were Red Fists under a tribune the Pope brought with him from Rome."

"A tribune, hmm? His name wasn't Lucius Bernius, was it?"

"Why, that was the very man, sir." Centurion Peyago sobered. "He would've fought the entire horde by himself if his friends hadn't restrained him. It seems the Huns murdered almost his entire family up near Mediolanum."

Aetius found himself struck numb at the news. "We came through there. The Huns stripped the area bare. Where is the tribune now?"

"He escorted the Pope back to Rome. He said his job was to protect the living, and he wasn't going to let some highwayman cut the Pope's throat after witnessing a miracle."

"I forgot to ask about that one minor point. How did Pope Leo send Attila packing without an army? Did he pay a ransom?"

"No, sir, we just walked in and they talked."

"Just talked? That's not the Attila I know."

"Well, sir, there was one fight between two giants, but it was over in seconds. The fellow who came in with the Pope—I think his name was Satewa?—was on the Hun like a dog on a bone. I never saw a big guy move so fast. And I'll tell you this—after his man hit the ground, Attila's face turned white as a ghost. Given everything I heard about him, I'd never believe it if I hadn't seen it myself. The next day, the Huns were gone."

Aetius couldn't help but chortle. "God does work in mysterious ways. Satewa isn't even Christian." He looked around at the devastation, but no bodies littered the area. "Centurion, you did a good job here. There's a place for you in my legions if you want it."

Peyago's face flushed with embarrassment. "Sir, we already joined. Tribune Bernius conscripted my command on the way here."

"Somehow, that doesn't surprise me. Be wary. That man is a magnet for trouble."

The centurion showed a proud smile. "Sir, I much prefer dying under an honorable man than living with the humiliation of serving cowards."

"Welcome, then. It appears you were one of us before you ever joined. I'll be sending my troops back to Mediolanum, but I must ride to Rome and meet with the emperor. Will you stay here and guard this town? The people will start returning soon, and they'll need order and protection."

"Thank you, sir. My men and I will do everything we can to keep the people here safe. The Huns took a lot of them captive, but many slipped away when the barbarians headed back north. They've been trickling back in small groups since then. But if you want to see the emperor, he's not in Rome."

Centurion Peyago dug his heel into the ground. "The coward fled to the island fortress of Capri."

The two men locked eyes for a second, but neither said another word.

CHAPTER XXIV

PLOTS

"Yes, Your Majesty, it's true. Attila died over a month ago."

Emperor Valentinian quirked a wary eyebrow at the chamberlain. "Who's replaced him?"

Publius Heraclius smiled wide. "That's the best part. There're five different factions fighting for the Hunnic throne. They're so busy slitting each other's throats, they can't even lift a finger to stop their vassal tribes from breaking away. The Scourge of Rome is dead, and the Huns' domination is no more."

"So how did the monster die? He seemed to have a charmed existence."

Heraclius puffed out his chest. "Sire, I spent the treasure you entrusted to me well. A slave managed to slip night flower into the tyrant's wine. He died in agony."

The emperor sighed in disbelief. "Just a year ago, we had to seek safety on the Amalfi Coast because the incompetents leading the army were being crushed by that man, and now the danger is gone."

"Yes. Wasn't it an interesting coincidence that General Aetius found a way to arrive with his legions right after the Huns left? One would think he was waiting for Attila to remove Imperial Roman authority so he could come in as the savior."

Valentinian leaned back on his cushioned throne and stroked his thin beard. "Publius, I hear a lot of truth to your words. General Aetius is a terrible threat to Imperial Rome. The legions follow him blindly and do whatever he asks."

"I agree. The man's ambition knows no bounds. He'll not be satisfied until he sits on that chair and your head rests on a pole outside Rome's gates."

The one other man in the room was Petronius Maximus, the commander of the Praetorian Guard. Breathing deep, he stepped forth. "I'll be the last person to praise General Aetius, but from a purely military perspective, he had a tough task. He came out of Gaul with three legions. The Huns easily had four times his number."

Valentinian looked around the small imperial ante-chamber. The braziers lining the room lit the antechamber well despite the lateness of the hour. A fist of guards stationed on the other side of the thick bronze doors ensured their privacy would go undisturbed. He added some more water to the wine so Maximus wouldn't fall into a drunken stupor.

Maximus straightened his posture. "Your Majesty, with the Hun threat gone, Aetius is more of a liability than an asset. When the Germanic tribes seek a treaty, they send their emissaries to him, not to Rome. The men in his legions act like they're his own private army. They call themselves the Red Fist and boast to be superior to my Praetorians. Aetius may say he fights for the ideals of Rome, but we all know he just wants to possess it."

Valentinian nodded, his expression grim. "That is the truth, but what can we do? We still need him. The Vandals have taken our African provinces and possess all the warships we had docked in Carthage."

Maximus slammed his fist on the table. "Bah, the Vandals are no concern. They'll need decades to consolidate their claim down there. Genseric has no concept on how to use a navy. His raids on our islands have been nothing more than pinprick annoyances. Give me the troops Aetius has, and I'll sweep through his ragtag Vandals and reclaim our African possessions."

Valentinian rolled his eyes at the ceiling. Maximus hadn't organized anything more demanding than a holiday parade in over twenty years. If he weren't so devoted to the influence the emperor granted him, he would've been replaced years ago. Valentinian kept the thought to himself, however, and lowered his gaze to the commander. "Maximus, that's an interesting proposition. Those are rich lands. I'll consider it once we solve our current problem. Now, Publius, what kind of plan do you have for disposing of our dear general?"

"I admit it won't be easy. Poison won't work; he has everything he eats and drinks checked. His men are also fanatically loyal. If we tried to recruit an assassin, word would reach his ears in short order." Heraclius paused and gave Valentinian a hard look. "We'll need to be bold. Summon him here for a meaningless meeting, accuse him of some trumped up charge, and stab him yourself for the crime while you have him alone."

Publius eyed both men. "His legions are sheep and will fall in line with their leader dead and disgraced."

"What about his family?" asked Maximus. "They might try to rally those loyal to Aetius and lead a revolt."

Valentinian wrung his hands. "They all must die, too. We cannot leave any loose ends here. We have to coordinate this well and without warning." Trembling, he turned to Heraclius. "Why do I have to be the one to strike the fatal blow? What if there's a struggle, and he overpowers me?"

"You're the only one who can get close enough. Even that abomination of a bodyguard he has would not block your path if you approached."

"I forgot about that savage. He'd kill me if I harmed his precious leader."

"My Praetorians can handle that brute," Maximus boasted. "I'll have ten of my best swordsmen assigned to you that day. He'll be hacked to death before he can even reach for his weapon. And if your first thrust is not true, my men will finish the job. After all, he clearly wanted to harm you and stop you from administering justice."

The chamberlain added, "I'll be sure to acquire a poisoned dagger for you, so even if your stab is not mortal, the general will die anyway."

"Good idea, Publius. And my men will ensure that every-one from that bastard's household dies at the same time."

Valentinian leaned back, tapping his fingers on the arm rest. Concerns still swirled in his head, but he allowed himself to smile. "Then let it be so. We'll look for an opportunity, but let's do it in Ravenna. Rome holds no secrets, and he has far too many friends there. This plan to protect Rome must be kept between just the three of us."

CHAPTER XXV

INTO THE SPIDER'S WEB

Lucius returned Decurion Vidin's salute as he left the inn. "I'm not sure how long our audience with the emperor will be. The general's wife and son are upstairs. Make sure no one goes up there unless you can personally vouch for them."

Vidin nodded. "Yes, sir. Wish we had more of our boys here. This whole city is crawling with Praetorians."

With a glance around the inn, Lucius sighed. "I wish we had a whole legion of Red Fists here, but we don't. Our 'courageous emperor' might think we're planning a revolt."

"That wouldn't be such a bad idea."

"Too much Roman blood is being spilled every day as it is. Let's hope that this meeting is the start of a new beginning."

"Yes, sir." Lucius could tell by Vidin's expression that the man thought that idea was absurd.

Aetius approached, smiling with a hint of mischief. "We won't be leaving for the palace for a while. Why don't you scout the palace grounds? Perhaps the slave quarters. Make sure it's secure. We'll meet you in the imperial stable yard in two hours."

Lucius' heart leapt at the thought of seeing Dervla again. Their secret meetings in the past several months had been at once too infrequent and too brief, so he welcomed any chance to spend time with her. However, he scowled at the night's darkness as thoughts of all his other concerns hounded him. "General, remember the warning I passed to you from Dervla. This *does* smell like a trap."

Flavius Aetius rolled his neck. "Lucius, our northern frontier is in chaos, and the Vandals are consolidating their hold in Africa. Even Valentinian wouldn't be so stupid as to try and kill me now." He patted the tribune on the shoulder. "Ride ahead, and take Doctor Phokas and the good Padre with you. If the emperor wants to meet me at such a late hour, that is his right. Now I want to get my family settled in their rooms.

I also need to wash the road from my throat. As I remember the place, they have very good wine."

A very grateful Lucius rode off with the doctor and Father Patricius in tow. Once they had gone a short distance, he motioned to Phokas. "What do you think?"

"What do I think about what?" Phokas deadpanned.

Lucius flushed but lowered his head to keep it hidden. "It's been weeks since I've seen her, and the messages that we've smuggled to each other have been few. Does she still think about me?"

The old doctor jerked his head, smiling, as though holding back a laugh. "Well, since I've been able to visit her on a few occasions, I can assure you that you are all she wants to discuss. Just as she is all you want to hear about when I return."

Lucius shifted in his saddle and brooded.

"What? We all know you two fell in love ages ago."

Lucius could find no words to answer in the face of the truth.

When they arrived at the palace, Phokas tensed at seeing the stable yard occupied by a large number of Praetorians at such a late hour. He wiped his palm on his tunic and regarded the tribune with a half smile. "Lucius, we must be wary. You've been unbearable since we arrived in Ravenna, but visiting the emperor's slave quarters for a tryst is a weak pretext."

The guards nodded in boredom as the three men came down the stairs to the slave pens. Their cudgels leaned haphazardly against the stucco wall. The emperor didn't mind aristocrats having a dalliance with imperial property as long as he was recompensed for any damaged goods. As such, the three travelers passed by the guards without trouble.

The three men made their way to the shabby apartment where the Conalls lived. Both sister and brother were still awake, performing their personal chores that could not be done during the long day of servitude.

* * *

When the men approached, Dervla was surprised at first to see them, but then beamed when Lucius entered. However, she stopped short at the sight of the doctor's stoic countenance. "Did something happen to my mother?"

Phokas greeted her, and his face brightened. "Her situation hasn't worsened, and your father is well. We just arrived in town and stopped by to look in on you."

Relieved, Dervla didn't hear any more of his words. She desperately ran her fingers through her hair to smooth out the tangles, then looked down at her frock, aghast. *I'm a mess. Lucius must think I'm a pig.*

"Ah... Seamus, could you take me to the kitchen? I'm famished." The doctor's eyes widened when the young man stood. "You've certainly grown a bit. Skinny as a rail, but my head only reaches your chin."

Seamus laughed, revealing a voice that edged closer to manhood. "C'mon, I think there may be some fresh bread in the ovens. With a well-bred noble in tow, I bet I could snag a loaf or two." Seamus ducked under the low archway.

Phokas and the priest followed him out. As he left, the doctor added, "Lucius, remember we have to meet up with the general in an hour."

Dervla watched them depart with her hands clasped together. Lucius alone stood before her now, and she breathed deep. "I... I heard about your family. I'm so very sorry. Father says they were the kindest people he'd ever met."

Tears welled in Lucius' eyes, no doubt in remembrance.

The sight cut Dervla like a knife. "I'm a complete fool. I just hurt the man I love." She froze with the realization that she'd spoken her inner thoughts out loud.

Lucius closed the distance in two strides and embraced her with an impassioned kiss. "I love you, too. You're the only woman I've ever loved."

Dervla returned the kiss as she clung to him with a fierce hug.

"I swear I'll get you out of here," he breathed into her ear.

Shaking her head, she sobbed into his shoulder. "Publius will never grant me my manumission. I'll never be free. He hates you. He'll see me dead first."

"Then we'll escape. We can live among the Franks. Martinel can give us sanctuary there."

"But you'll be giving up the legion. The army is your life."

Lucius stepped back and gripped her shoulders in his hands. "Marcus has already resigned his commission and returned home. He's thriving."

Dervla put on a smile. "Marcus never was a soldier. He joined because of you. His love is in building things, and he dotes on Julia now that she is with child."

"That's what I want, too."

Dervla took his calloused, scarred hands and squeezed them. "Are these the hands of a farmer? You were born to lead. Will you ever be happy doing anything else?"

"I worked my father's vineyards as a boy. I can do it again. I'm tired of fighting for a Rome that only exists in my mind. Perhaps it never existed." Lucius fell to his knees before her, still holding her hands. "Dervla, marry me. We can leave tonight and never look back."

"Yes, Lucius. Oh, yes. We must take Seamus with us."

"Of course we will. I have one small task yet tonight, then I'll tell General Aetius and we'll be gone." Lucius stood with a foolish grin on his face. "Now go pack. I'll return within an hour." He turned and bolted from the room.

Dervla picked up a ragged satchel and ruefully looked about the dilapidated apartment. *Packing will take about a minute. Hurry, Lucius. Hurry.*

* * *

Decurion Vidin looked up from his wine as a group of Praetorians barged into the inn. He turned away, disgusted that just any scum could walk into the building. *We gotta find different lodging with higher standards.*

One of his men approached the black-clad guards on wobbly, drunken legs. Alarmed, the decurion kept close watch of the situation in case a brawl broke out.

The Praetorian leader stabbed the unarmed Red Fist soldier. The legionary collapsed on the dirt floor, and blood poured from the gaping wound in his chest. The Praetorians moved through the room, killing the almost defenseless Red Fists and everyone else in the common room. The attackers never spoke a word.

Vidin drew his sword and sprang to the stairwell. It was the one access to the rooms above, where General Aetius' wife and son were, and he called to them, "My lady, assassins are here! Flee! In the name of God, flee!"

He steadied his breathing and pointed his gladius at the black-armored imperial guards approaching. His own legionaries lay dead, sprawled on the tavern floor. A few men in tunics with daggers were no match for armed soldiers in breastplates.

"Move, Red Fist, and maybe we'll spare you," said one Praetorian.

"I swore an oath never to run, and I won't run from the likes of you." Vidin drove his sword through the lead Praetorian's chest, but then the other black-armored soldiers swarmed over him. The last thing he heard as light faded from his eyes were dozens of sandaled feet charging up the staircase and screams from the rooms above.

* * *

Gaudentius, Flavius Aetius' teenaged son, leaned into the makeshift barricade he threw across the room's flimsy door. "Mother, Brenda, out the window. I'll hold until you're down."

The barrier splintered as swords hacked at the thin pine panels. Pelagia regarded her son with pride; he looked very much like Aetius himself in his youth. To Brenda, she said, "You go first. You know this city. Warn my husband. I'll find a place to hide."

Brenda looked warily at the woman and leapt from the window. Pelagia watched as Brenda landed but stumbled; her ankle twisted under her as she landed. Brenda rose and limped away just as two black-armored men ran toward her. Pelagia's breath caught as Brenda pulled herself onto the stable roof and over the tavern's low wall. She saw her friend sprint down an alleyway and escape.

"Brenda, save my husband. Please, God, save my husband," Pelagia whispered as she turned from the window. Resolute, she pulled out her dagger and moved to her son's side. "I love you, Gaudentius."

"Mom, please leave. There's still time."

Spears tore their way through the barrier gaps.

She looked down at her crippled leg. "I think I'd rather spend my last minutes with my brave son, the grown man."

Pelagia slashed at an arm that stretched too far into the room, and soon after came the squeal of pain.

Moments later, the blockade gave way. Mother and son held each other's hands as the howling killers stormed into the room.

* * *

The old watchman of the Aetius estate sat, teaching young Titus how to play dice. He'd been in the legions his whole life, he'd said, and never had a family. Titus had grown to like him in the short time he'd been at the estate. At that moment, the boy scowled as he counted the pips on the three dice.

The watchman grunted in satisfaction. "That's not such a bad throw. Now you need to—" His face twisted in alarm. "Did you just hear something?"

Titus tilted his ear and tensed at the sound of pebbles disturbing something in the path outside.

The watchman's face turned grim and whispered, "Thieves."

Staying quiet, he slid his gladius from its scabbard and moved toward the door. Titus followed, holding a small whittling knife as he imitated the old man's moves.

The watchman glanced at the boy dutifully following him, smiled warmly, and ruffled the boy's thick, curly hair. "Stay behind the door when I open it. I'm going to have a quick look around."

He unbarred the door and opened it a crack. "What the—?"

The door slammed open, smashing Titus against the wall and stunning him. He never saw the four men barge in and stab the watchman to death. The cloaked figures raced into the house and didn't notice that, instead of dropping straight down, the old man crumpled against the large door, pinning it to the wall.

"Stay back there, boy," he wheezed as blood drained from his body. Terrified, Titus remained still.

Minutes passed, and then a voice said at last, "That's everyone. This was easy money. Just a few servants, and none of them had any weapons except for this old guy here." The thug in the black cloak kicked at the lifeless watchman.

"I saw a one-armed fool who was a little trouble," said another voice. "He apparently didn't like the idea of us killing the old woman he was with. I don't know why he cared so much. The old broad looked to be at death's door anyway. No matter; they're both dead."

The first man made a quick scan of the room. "Move quickly, lads. Take anything that looks valuable. Our employer wants the city's night watch to see the problem here, so we'll leave the gate and this door open. But there's no reason we can't supplement our pay with a little extra."

Titus held his breath and stared at a small man with a broken nose lean against the wall not four feet from him directing his henchmen. The boy studied that man's face, determined to commit it to memory.

A short while later, the men left and vanished down the silent streets. Titus squeezed out from where he was trapped and knelt by the watchman with tearful eyes. The city night watch found him there when they arrived a short while later.

CHAPTER XXVI

RAVENNA PALACE

"We're over an hour late for our audience," Satewa noted as they hurried up the marble stairs to the emperor's inner sanctum.

General Aetius smirked, grunting with little mirth. "I'll find some excuse to mollify him. I just hope he's not too deep in his drink to hear me. Who would've expected that tonight, our stoic tribune here would open his eyes and realize he's in love with the girl he's been mooning over for the last three years?"

Lucius' face reddened under his dark olive skin, but he held his tongue. *They're right. I've been an idiot. I just need to find a way to steal Dervla and her brother away from Publius. Tonight, we'll be out of this cursed palace and be free.*

An eerie silence hovered in the cold halls as the general and his three lieutenants strode toward the imperial throne room. A summons to see the emperor was worrisome enough these days, but a summons in the middle of the night with a small escort permitted screamed trouble.

"Madness," muttered Martinel, who flinched a bit when the general turned to him with a questioning eyebrow raised. "Begging your pardon, General, but why are we not bringing more of our boys, or better yet, fleeing the city? You know the emperor isn't looking for a report on supply inventories in the dead of night." The Frank shook slightly. Lucius didn't need to think hard as to why.

General Aetius gave no indication of his thoughts. Instead, he turned and continued down the corridor toward the emperor's throne room against the flickering torchlight, making it seem as if he walked in and out of the shadow.

Lucius roused from his own thoughts about the beautiful Celtic woman who declared her love for him and slapped Martinel lightly on the helmet. They hurried to resume their places, flanking and keeping pace behind their commander.

Closing the gap, Satewa hissed to Martinel, "Why do you ask questions to which you already know the answer? The general is following the orders his sovereign has given, and I think he still believes he can convince the emperor he's loyal."

Martinel sighed in resignation. "Romans are all crazy. How can one convince a paranoid madman of the truth?"

The four Red Fist officers arrived at the throne room doors a few minutes after midnight with a full moon peeking through the window behind them. The two Praetorian Guards watching the entrance glared at them with open scorn.

"You've got guts, General, I'll give you that," said the guard to the left. "This courageous fool just cost me two silver pieces! I thought for sure he'd have fled like a spooked deer."

"No sense in this one," the guard on the right answered with a flat chuckle.

"Be careful who you insult. If you want a lack of sense, you need look no further than your own wine-sotted master." Satewa snarled, and in a slow, deliberate move, his hand came to rest on the long haft of his axe. The cowed guards stepped back, pushed open the heavy oaken doors, and stood aside for the men to enter.

A series of six pillars placed equidistant from one another supported the vaulted ceiling of the throne room on either side of the approach to the gilded chair with the high back. The throne itself rested near the far wall in the rear of the chamber. Besides the two heavy oak doors through which they entered, the one other break in the dark stone walls was a small, bronze door near the dais. Lucius tensed as he heard the doors behind him close. A balcony ran around the upper tier of the throne room which could be used for crowds during festive events, or for archers in case of an interior threat.

Lucius evaluated the imperial chamber with professional eyes as they advanced toward the figure on the throne: a man wearing an ermine mantle and a golden breastplate. The same man looked for all the world like a spider anxious to leap onto an insect foolish enough to entangle itself in the web. A small contingent of lackey senators gathered around Publius Heraclius near a table by the bronze rear door. The Red Fist soldiers saw no friendly faces in that group.

The emperor had with him ten imperial guards arrayed in a V formation with the throne at the apex. The Praetorians all wore huge two-handed great swords strapped to their backs and had donned helmets in the shape of demons. Although made of quality steel, the helmets' stylized nature hampered visibility. The remaining parts of the uniforms consisted of leather armor, boots, and gauntlets dyed the deepest black, which was the reason the Red Fists derisively called them cockroaches. Those tavern observations often led to massive brawls.

Lucius glanced up again, but while he spotted no sign of archers, it gave him little comfort. *Considering the martial might within a few feet of us, it's an obvious move that would be unnecessary.*

The general marched to within a half dozen paces of the emperor and bowed. "I have come as requested, Your Majesty. What is it you require at this late hour?"

The emperor glared for a long moment at General Aetius. The general stood erect and unflinching. Valentinian pointedly glanced at the assembled guards, played with the hilt of a wicked-looking dagger, then eyed Aetius. "Do you know what the role of a good general is?"

"To lead the men assigned under him well and to fulfill the objectives given to him by Rome," Aetius replied.

"Then why, pray tell, when I instructed you to destroy that traitorous town of rebels in Mantua, did you falsely report success and then have the audacity to return here and pretend you fulfilled your mission?" the emperor asked in a heated voice.

The guards shifted into a more balanced combat stance rather than standing at attention as they had done thus far. Lucius mirrored their movement. *If they were to die here, then he intended to squash a cockroach or two before he fell.* Martinel's jaw tightened, and his lip curled into a sneer as the situation played out as they had feared it would.

The general kept his eyes locked on Valentinian. "Your Majesty commanded me to deal with the situation in Mantua, not to kill. The people there were no allies of the Huns, my lord; they offered tribute to Attila to save their families. They

179

had no legions to protect them. Their lands were blighted, and what little remained was ravaged by war. They could not meet the barbarians' demands and did what they had to in order to save their wives and children. They had no money to pay, but the villagers provided services to the horde equal to what was demanded in tribute. The fletchers, armorers, blacksmiths, cartwrights, and even the seamstresses provided necessary services. They fled the Huns' encampment when my forces approached. Nothing was lost, my lord, and the people were grateful for your leniency. I did what I thought best."

Valentinian's face creased in an angry frown. "You were supposed to butcher those traitors, you placid fool. No one can contest my word! Leniency? My word is law, and my desires must be obeyed without question." The emperor smiled slowly. "Which is why all of those fools you teased with the thought of life now lie dead at the hands of my imperial guard. Every man, woman, and child has been slaughtered. A few escaped my will. Oh, that precious company of legionaries you stationed there tried to intervene. They held the bridge while a pack of panicked peasants fled. But, alas, they're all dead, too."

The general closed his eyes, and when he answered, his voice sounded more like an animal's growl than a human. "Centurion Peyago was more of a Roman than you could ever dream of being. You are mad. I should have stood against you years ago, but out of loyalty to Rome and the need to remain united against the barbarians, I sublimated my own good judgment." Aetius stared with eyes harder than the most compressed granite. "One final question: Do you have the faintest idea for what Rome stands?"

The emperor rolled his eyes. "What kind of question is that? I *am* Rome." When he glanced over to where Heraclius stood, watching like a hawk, the chamberlain responded with a single brisk nod, and Valentinian rose on shaky legs. "General, please come closer. We need to come to a common understanding. Perhaps this conversation started on the wrong foot."

With his temper barely constrained, Aetius closed the last few steps and stood nose to nose with the emperor. However, at the sound of a scream from a familiar voice, all eyes turned to a woman who burst through the semi-open doors.

The woman cried, "General, it's a trap! Your wife and son have been murdered!"

No other words escaped her lips as the two imperial guards who had ignored her just moments before cut her down. The realization that she was not a slave on a routine errand came too late.

Satewa gasped as he spun around. "My Brenda!"

Their eyes met for but a moment before blood sputtered from her mouth, and she collapsed on the mosaic tile floor.

Aetius turned at the shout, inadvertently dodging the emperor's strike. Instead of plunging into his heart, it went through his arm and scratched his chest. As the general spun, he also pulled the knife out of Valentinian's shaky grasp.

The startled emperor leapt away screaming, "Kill them! Kill them all!" At the same time, he fled to where Maximus stood among the confused and frightened senators.

A frenzied Heraclius ran to the emperor's side. "Sire, we must move you away from this fighting. Let the Praetorians do their job." As he lifted the bar of the bronze door behind the throne, he called out, "Defend the emperor!"

Maximus nodded and raised his sword. "Praetorians, to me!"

The soldiers glanced back in confusion. They circled Satewa like wolves around a wounded bear. The two guards at the door lay dead already, and a third lay on the now slick floor with blood gushing from his neck, but they had Satewa cornered. They halted their attack, and with slow, deliberate moves, backed toward the door the emperor and his chamberlain had scurried through.

Satewa roared and pressed after them. Martinel gutted the man facing him and moved to Satewa's side. Lucius skewered the Praetorian in front of him and then stood before the wall of swords. A high-pitched scream startled Lucius, and he looked up to see Satewa tossing a bony senator through the air at the Praetorians. His screech came to an abrupt halt as he landed on a long Praetorian blade. With the opening made, Satewa charged in, crazed with grief.

Maximus took three large strides backwards. "I need to see to the emperor," he shouted as he slipped through the open door.

For the first time, fear crept into the Praetorians' eyes when they heard the bar slam down on the other side of the exit behind them.

Aetius hamstrung a dagger-wielding senator who tried to sneak up on him. The man shrank back, and the general started to pursue, but his sword clattered to the floor and he stumbled to his knees. Lucius moved to the general's side in a flash and drew out the blade still jammed in his flesh.

"My arm's numb," the general gasped, watching his blood-soaked fingers spasm.

The wound itself didn't appear to be fatal, but Lucius noticed that the knife carried a peculiar scent. "This smells of belladonna. You've been poisoned." Lucius whipped his head around at the combat swirling around him and spotted a clear path to the main entrance. "Martinel, the general's gravely hurt. I have to get him out of here. Hold them as long as you can!" He hoisted Aetius up and helped him stagger past Brenda's still body and into the deserted hallway.

Lucius didn't like how pale Aetius grew with each step, but he forced himself to stay calm. "Please, General, don't give up. Rome needs you."

Aetius stared at nothing, his eyes glistening with tears. "Rome has taken everything from me that I love. I don't care what it needs."

The words sounded all too familiar; Lucius had made a similar assertion to Dervla a short time earlier. "Sir, Valentinian isn't Rome. He and his lackeys have transformed it into this grotesque monster. Without you, we're all doomed to their world. Don't leave us."

The general's eyes hardened as a faint light returned to them. "The emperor wants a war? Then I'll give him one. The main entrance will be closely guarded. Help me to the slave quarters. Phokas should still be there, or it'll be a very short war."

CHAPTER XXVII

ESCAPE FROM RAVENNA

Dervla perked up when the filthy sheet that hung over her apartment's entrance parted. However, any joy she felt died out as a blood-splattered Lucius staggered in, half carrying Flavius Aetius. "Lucius…"

"My dear God, man, what happened?" Doctor Phokas sprang to the general and helped the tribune ease Aetius down on the rancid straw mat that served as a bed.

"The general's been stabbed and, I think, poisoned," Lucius groaned as he handed the dagger to Phokas.

Phokas scowled as he sniffed the blade. "This is serious. There're a few different poisons here." The doctor handed the knife to a worried Father Patricius, who studied the glyph marks on the handle.

"This is a druid blade," said the priest. "These markings are a curse, and it appears whoever crafted this was not very fond of us. It says, 'Deliver death to the great Roman.'" He gave the weapon to Seamus. "Hang onto the knife, lad. We may need to examine it later."

"I guess the emperor was pretty safe toying with it," muttered Lucius.

"What? Oh, that's for sure." Phokas arched his eyebrows but continued probing the wound in Aetius' arm. "You better tell us the story, son."

Lucius turned his head toward the entrance. "Can you save him? We're going to have to leave soon. I bribed the slave quarter guards, but I'm not sure how long they'll hold their tongues. The assassin was the emperor himself."

The former imperial physician grunted. "I'm surprised the worm had the courage to do his own dirty work. In a sense, we're lucky. If he'd used a professional killer, Aetius would be dead."

Lucius relayed the events of what occurred in the throne room, and solemn stares followed his tale. Dervla's voice came out choked when she broke the silence. "Oh, poor Brenda. She was such an open-hearted soul."

Phokas pulled a small vial from the satchel he wore on his side, broke the wax seal, and poured the amber contents in the general's mouth. A satisfied breath escaped him as the near unconscious man choked down the liquid.

"What's that stuff? It smells terrible," the curious priest asked.

"It's *mithridatum*, more precious than gold. According to the writings of Pliny the Elder, it's an antidote for almost every poison. We'll see how true it is. Your druids can have their curses. I believe in modern science."

Patricius stole a nervous glance at the entrance. "Can the general be moved? I agree with Lucius. This place won't be safe much longer."

"He *shouldn't* be moved, but you're right. All our lives are forfeit if we're caught. We'll have to take the risk and carry him out of here. But where can we go?"

Lucius met Dervla's eyes. "Padre, one thing first. Marry Dervla and me. If we're to die tonight, I want to be with my wife."

Father Patricius looked over at Dervla, who nodded, her eyes gleaming with emotion. "And who will stand for the bride?"

"I will." Seamus stood and hugged his sister.

"Then will the couple please join hands?"

* * *

The slave guards hoisted their cudgels and stared at the stretcher bearers carrying a shrouded man.

"We have to get this corpse out of here," Doctor Phokas intoned with authority. "It's the pox. It wouldn't do to have that spread around."

The guards rested their hands on their swords and eyed Lucius and Father Patricius, then each other. "Go ahead. Get outta here, but we're going to report this."

Lucius knitted his eyebrows. "Just don't tell anyone until morning. If caught, I'm sure I'll give up the names of those to whom I gave a pocket full of coins."

The guards stiffened as the small group vanished up the stairs.

Phokas took the lead but said nothing more until they were well away from the guards. "I know a way out of here that won't be guarded yet." Phokas led the small troop down a dark flight of stairs. Lucius gagged on the stench when he reached the bottom. A glance around revealed to him many carts, all of which carried some kind of cargo with a fetid scent. One look at the vague mound in one cart, and Lucius put two and two together.

"Are these refuse carts?" he blurted out.

"It's the only way," the doctor replied. "Everything going through the palace gates will be checked. Now hurry. We don't have much time before someone comes."

Lucius exchanged a look with Dervla, sighed, and shuffled to the nearest cart with everyone else. Seamus took the reins of the horse, and the group went on their way. Lucius held his breath as much from the smell as to ensure he wouldn't draw any undue attention to the group, and he didn't release it until they were past the gate.

After spending an hour lying at the bottom of a refuse cart, the whole group bore an interesting aroma. Doctor Phokas even sniffed himself. Lucius sighed, at once relieved and tense. They hadn't had time to concoct a more sophisticated ploy, but the foolish plan had worked well enough to get them away from the palace. Now they had to figure out how to leave the city.

Lucius surveyed the wharf that they had arrived at, watching for any signs of trouble. Although still dark, the harbor was busy with fishermen preparing to sail out with the tide. Plenty of boats bobbed in the water, and a part of Lucius groaned as he realized what they would have to do next. *I hate boats. This is another stupid idea.*

Phokas joined him soon after. "The general is breathing a little easier, but it won't be long before even that idiot, Maximus, thinks of the sea. I doubt it took long for those guards to work up the courage to tell their overseer about our departure. They'll both be dead as soon as they report to the Praetorians."

Lucius walked down the long pier, glancing about as curious seamen watched him pass. He paused near a gnarled old man with dark, weathered skin, and his snow-white hair cut short in the military fashion. "Did you serve in the legions?"

"Aye, I spent eight years under General Stilicho," came the wary reply as the old sailor stood straight. "Those charges of treason against him were lies. He was a good man who loved Rome. They knew they could prove nothing. That's why they murdered him."

With their time running short, Lucius decided to take a gamble. "Would you have tried to save him, if you could?"

The sailor looked Lucius in the eye with a defiant glint. "The name's Polo, and I'd do it in a second. Rome needed him. There's no one left in this sick country that stands for those ideals anymore."

"There is one other, and he needs you."

Polo responded with a cock of his head and a quizzical stare.

* * *

A small, single-mast skiff was the first boat to sail out of the harbor. Predawn had only just touched the horizon, but they had no more time to delay. A column of imperial guards trotted down to the docks.

Just as planned, Father Patricius stood aside and greeted them. The Praetorians didn't notice him sweating profusely as he bestowed a blessing on the detachment as they passed by. They also didn't notice his brisk walk that was almost a run once they passed.

The fisherman watched Seamus tie down the knot for the hoisted sail. Grunting in satisfaction, Polo jerked his head to Lucius. "I'll do you one better, soldier. I'll take you to a small town hidden on some islands in a lagoon north of here. It's very hard to find. They named the place Venice. The folks there were tired of the constant raids and moved to where no one could find then unless they want them to." While he adjusted the jib on the sail, he added, "I was planning on moving there myself someday. You just helped me speed up my decision."

"I don't know how we can thank you. I have very little money left, but it's yours."

"Keep your money. I won't have those bastards murder Aetius the way they killed Stilicho. Rome's going to run out of heroes one of these days, and then where will we be?" Polo turned toward the sun cresting the ocean. "I love my country. I just pray someday we'll have an emperor who'll care as much for it." Polo put his hand on Lucius' shoulder, tears in his eyes. "Protect that man. He may be Rome's last hope. How many chances do you think the Good Lord will grant us before He lets us be overcome by darkness?"

Lucius looked back at Flavius Aetius, whose skin was drawn and breathing shallow. Doctor Phokas and Dervla knelt beside him, trying to get more of their scant supply of drugs into his body. Lucius smiled as his wife looked at him. She returned it and went back to a thoughtful discussion with the physician.

Lucius sighed and looked out to sea. The rolling water was already making him sick. "Merciful God, please help us."

* * *

Father Patricius stood ashen in a dark alley across from the inn. The city militia dragged out the bodies of Red Fist legionaries one by one and stacked them in a cart. "They're all dead. What should I do now? Maybe I—"

A large, calloused hand covered his mouth and dragged him deeper into the filth-strewn lane. "Padre, quiet please."

Father Patricius swung around and found himself face to face with two blood-smeared men he recognized. "Martinel, Satewa! Thank God you're still alive."

Although covered in gore, they didn't appear harmed; Martinel in particular looked as ready as ever. However,

Satewa's eyes revealed where his real wounds lay. *Those are the eyes of a dead man.*

"What news?" Martinel whispered.

Father Patricius sighed and described their desperate escape, his role as a distraction, and the general's condition.

Satewa finally stirred to life. "Venice? I must follow him. His life is my responsibility. I must not fail him the way I failed my wife."

Martinel gripped Satewa's arms. "To Venice, then." He turned to Patricius. "Do you think you could get us a couple more of those monk robes? Soldiers never look priests in the face. I think it's our guilty conscience. Also, where the hell is Venice?"

CHAPTER XXVIII

WHEELS IN MOTION

"Sire, he must be dead. You struck him with a poisoned blade," Publius shouted. "We killed his wife and son and confiscated his property. Do you think that man would sit idle without raising a stir if he still lived?"

Sweat beaded on the emperor's forehead. "Yes... Yes, the blade was poisoned. Of course. What kind did you use?"

"The deadliest I could find without rousing suspicion. If you cut him at all, he'd be dead within the hour. Whether your blow was mortal or not, he would've had to reach a healer with an antidote within minutes of you striking him."

Valentinian recalled the blazing hate in the general's eyes, and his voice quivered. "We never found his body."

Publius huffed. "There was a body carried from the slave quarters. His lackeys must've spirited the corpse away in the confusion. The slave guards we caught trying to hide told everything to the torturers before they died. It was a corpse."

None of that allayed Valentinian's nervousness, and he rubbed his sweaty hands along his scarlet robe. "What about those men who slaughtered our Praetorians? Those were Maximus' elite warriors, and they're all dead. Have they been found yet?"

Fear briefly flicked in Publius' eyes. "They've been branded as traitors, and we posted a hefty reward."

Valentinian shuddered at the memory of seeing the throne room in the aftermath of the fight. Everyone lay dead, be they soldier or senator, and some didn't die on the spot. He took a breath or two to push the nightmarish image out of his mind.

"The description of the men who fled the slave quarters with two of my slaves doesn't quite match, but the numbers are right," said Publius. "It must've been them. Don't worry. They'll be found and silenced."

"Very well, then. I'm putting Maximus in command of the Red Fist. With those troops behind me, I don't think we need to fear any incipient civil war breaking out." The emperor lifted his chalice of wine to his lips with a shaky hand. "Put out a proclamation that anyone found speaking well of the traitor Aetius will be executed. Also, find someone who looks like our deceased general and stake his head next to the wife and son. That should send the right message."

Publius bowed and departed. A cruel smile crossed his lips.

* * *

King Genseric lowered the parchment and gazed out his window. The warm Mediterranean breeze wafted into the room, and he watched the large fleet of ships rock in the Carthage harbor. *Ten years ago, that navy belonged to Rome, and now it's mine.*

His grin broadened and he turned to his aide and nephew. "This is sweet news, Axise, and it's long overdue. Flavius Aetius has been a major nuisance and thwarted my plans for as long as I can remember. I sent assassins, and they became his devoted bodyguards. Now that imbecile Valentinian gets rid of him for me. Tell me, who is the new imperator of the Roman armies?"

"The proclamation said the Praetorian Commander, Petronius Maximus, has been put in charge of the army."

Snickers of derision bubbled from the other men in the room. The Vandal King couldn't help but join them.

"This gets better and better. I've met the man. He's no more than the emperor's lap dog. How did Rome ever conquer the world with simpletons like him in charge?" Genseric tapped his knuckles on the carved arm of his dark wood chair.

He spent a long time contemplating his fleet, bobbing at anchor. His war council whispered among each other until he spoke in deliberate terms. "The Goths and Huns are at each other's throats, and the Franks are still licking their wounds. This will be the age of the Vandal." Genseric's eyes knitted as he looked around the table at his generals. "I will do what the great Attila could not. I will take Rome itself. Gentlemen, by this time next year, I'll sit on the imperial throne, and the Vandals will rule the world!"

His warriors responded with deafening roars.

Axise murmured in his king's ear, "Uncle, we can hardly go back the way we came. Iberia is hostile, and the Romans will be forewarned."

"We'll strike where they least expect it. We're going to sail straight into Rome's port at Ostia."

Axise's mouth hung open in surprise for fleeting a moment. "We'll have no line of supply. If we don't take the city by surprise, we can't sustain a siege."

Genseric leaned back on his silken cushions and bit into a ripe fig. "Then we'll have to ensure the first blow counts. Rome's an empty shell. Now is the time to strike."

As the shouts of his military captains subsided, Genseric leaned on his elbows. "It took Rome over a hundred years to conquer Africa. We took it from them in one. When this campaign is complete, history will record us as the greatest empire the world has ever known."

Axise nodded. "Commanders, you have your orders. Gather the army. Wealth beyond your wildest dreams awaits you!"

* * *

"Prefect is quite an impressive rank for one so young, but you earned it." A smug Petronius Maximus smiled at Marcus Carloman as they rode past the sullen guards into the camp of the First Legion. "You were wise to recognize Aetius as a traitor and resign your Red Fist commission."

Marcus patted his new commander on the shoulder. "I'm now one of the wealthiest men in Gaul and favored by the emperor himself. Albinus will stay in line. There'll be no opportunity for sedition."

Maximus, Marcus, and a string of new officers came to a halt before the stout, stone cabin that served as the legion's headquarters and dismounted. A downcast Legate Albinus and his senior centurions greeted them with curt salutes.

Marcus recognized one of those centurions as Cilla. The man looked at him with grave disappointment. Cilla and five tribunes who had been stripped of their cohorts stood in civilian togas across the road.

Marcus regarded the group of men and tentatively nodded. The old prefect spat on the ground and mouthed the word, "Cockroach." The others returned his recognition with pure malice in their eyes.

Marcus pursed his lips and turned to Maximus and Albinus, who were engaged in a stilted conversation. "Imperator, with your permission, I would like to keep the deposed officers on for a while. Our tribunes are green and will require a few weeks to adapt."

Albinus gave Marcus a flat stare. "Whatever my new prefect recommends is fine with me."

A wary Maximus responded, "Those men aren't trustworthy. They all spoke for sedition at the proclamation regarding the previous imperator's crimes."

"They now stand disgraced. I'll give them a small chance at redemption and make a full report to Rome of their actions. Perhaps with the proper devotion and contributions to your personal treasury, they could regain some stature."

Maximus gave a cruel smile. "I like that idea. Very well, see what you can do with them." To Albinus, he added, "I want your legion on the Rhine within a fortnight."

"Aye, sir, it shall be done. With the Goths and the Huns fighting for control of Germania, I'm sure we'll be very busy."

Marcus caught the hint of sarcasm in the legate's voice and gave Albinus a warning scowl. He understood the man's frustration well, however. *The Rhine is about as far away from Rome as they can put us.*

Maximus regarded the two officers glaring at each other. "Well, I'm sure everyone needs to get reacquainted, and it's a two-day ride to the Third Legion. I'm leaving now." He moved close to Marcus' ear and whispered, "I want frequent reports on the progress here. The new tribunes are of the finest families and can be trusted implicitly." He waved a haphazard salute and rode off with his escort.

Marcus watched the new imperator make his hurried exit. He drew in a deep breath and hailed the gathered officers. "Centurions, escort the new officers to their cohorts. Cilla, stay with me. I'll be taking personal command of your cohort. Albinus, we have to straighten out some priorities. Let's go inside." He strode into the headquarters without looking back, but he heard two pairs of feet follow.

Once inside, Marcus stood in silence, staring at a map of Gaul pegged to the coarse stone wall beside the warming hearth. After a minute, he turned and studied the two men and cringed inwardly. One glared with simmering rage, the other with manifest disappointment.

I've never gambled, but my life depends on guessing these men's hearts. Marcus braced himself and declared in an even voice, "He lives."

The confusion on their faces transformed into hope fighting with wariness. His shoulders sagged with relief upon seeing he made the right choice.

"Pull up a stool; I've much to tell you. Imperator Aetius was at death's door for several weeks and is still very weak, but Doctor Phokas sent me a detailed letter. He believes the danger has passed and our general is on the road to recovery."

"I knew you wouldn't betray us," Cilla exclaimed. Marcus gasped as he was crushed in a bear hug by the bull-necked centurion.

Albinus arched his eyebrows. "Marcus, you've missed your calling. You should be on stage. Half the men want to slit your throat. I was one of them, I might add."

Marcus plopped onto a rough-cut pine chair. "Fortunately, there wasn't much acting required. Literally the day before Maximus approached me, I received a message from Lucius saying there's a small band of loyalists in hiding with the general." The corners of his mouth tightened. "With my parents dead, I've become a very wealthy man. Maximus is the kind of person who's very impressed with money. I stroked his ego, praised the emperor, and threw him a banquet. We were soon the best of friends."

Albinus edged forth with intensity burning in his eyes. "Will you tell us where? There are many things I need to discuss with the general. He's the one man the legions will unite behind, and time is running short. We have to remove that imbecile from the throne before Rome is destroyed."

Shaking his head, Marcus frowned. "In all honesty, I don't know. Lucius was very circumspect in his letter. The message was delivered during the night by one of Martinel's Franks. The man said little and was gone as soon as I sealed my response. They're being very cautious. If those letters fell into the wrong hands..." Marcus shifted his eyes to Cilla. "I believe it's somewhere near the eastern border. Lucius made a specific request for his original gang to be transferred to the Second Legion, and that's where they're posted now."

Satisfied, Cilla leaned back and grunted. "Aye. The boys and I will look after them, and there won't be any loose tongues wagging, either."

"Be careful, and don't trust anyone you can't vouch for yourself. The emperor has infested the Red Fist with his own men, and they'll be listening for any plots."

"Like that collection of fops who rode in with you?" said Albinus. "When they're not preening around in their new uniforms, they'll most likely send the men on useless missions and make their equipment look pretty."

"Actually, that wouldn't be a bad idea. Just make sure they're leading those patrols themselves." At last, Marcus let himself smile wide. "Tell them it'll develop their leadership experience. It'll also keep them out of camp for as long as possible, and getting new equipment will be useful. When the order comes to march, we'll need to move fast."

"How about the decommissioned tribunes? They're loyal to our cause."

"They showed that they're also hotheads. Keep them in the dark, but keep them around. Their cohorts will need commanders. I don't expect any of the new officers will be making the trip to Rome with us."

A vicious smile crossed the centurion's face. "That'll be a small payback for what they did to Vidin."

"A very small measure of the payback needed." The corners of Marcus' mouth turned down. "Gentlemen, tell no one where I stand. Men talk when wine flows freely, but I would also appreciate it if you would spread word through the legion that I'm a useful puppet who should be kept alive. I'd rather not receive a knife in the back from some firebrand. I don't believe we'll need to hold this secret too long. Rome will have a new emperor, and it'll be very, very soon."

CHAPTER XXIX

VENICE

Lucius studied the sleeping general, who shivered and burned with a high fever. "I thought he was recovering?"

The usually abrasive Doctor Phokas was silent and focused on his patient. "His body is weak and susceptible to every malady floating around here."

"It's been days now. How much longer can his body endure this?"

Dervla sat on the opposite side of the bed, sponging Aetius' forehead with a damp cloth, and responded with a clinical tone. "His spirit is strong. I think the fever's breaking now." She looked over at Phokas. "Should I grind up more willow bark?"

"Yes, my dear, that's an excellent idea. And how about some broth? I agree the fever has run its course."

Lucius released a breath he'd been holding without realizing it. "I'll get it." He sprang to his feet, wanting to do whatever he could to help but felt helpless. He worried about Dervla, too. She'd learned about the death of her parents from young Titus when Father Patricius brought him on his last trip to Venice. She took the news hard. Since then, she'd cried every night while in bed, and by day, she worked alongside Phokas with a rigid focus. Lucius caressed her cheek, and she held his hand there for a moment.

Lucius left the curtained alcove and met a score of concerned eyes. "Phokas thinks General Aetius has turned the corner."

The gathered men sighed in a chorus of relief. Lucius looked over at the gray-haired priest beside Father Patricius, who was the abbot of the monastery they had taken sanctuary in. "Abbot, could we have some soup and ground willow bark for General Aetius?"

"Certainly. I'll see to it now." The abbot disappeared down the simple, wooden staircase. A new building, the interior of the monastery was only about half finished, but it served their needs well enough.

Lucius saw concern in Father Patricius' drawn face and guessed the reason. "Padre, how's the boy doing?"

The priest responded in a troubled voice. "Seamus consumes himself with hate. Right now, I think he would tear Rome down brick by brick if he could."

"Would it help if I spoke with him?"

"Yes, but not now. He hates you along with every other Roman. He'll just strike out and say words he won't be able to take back. Let him grieve for a while more."

Lucius nodded in resignation. *So many problems, and all I can do is sit and wait.*

His thoughts brightened as he approached the small group of familiar legionaries who had arrived that morning. They stood in respectful silence. Lucius nodded to them, and his jumbled thoughts untangled themselves. "I'm glad my message to Tribune Carloman got through."

Cilla laughed somewhat sheepish. "Well, it's *Prefect* Carloman now, and even with your directions, we had a hell of a time finding this abbey. There must be a hundred islands in this lagoon, and no one seems to have ever heard of a Saint Mark's Church or any monastery associated with it."

Lucius arched his eyebrows. "Prefect, is it? He's moving up the ranks pretty fast for someone who didn't even want to be a soldier. Is he over in the Second Legion with you?"

"No, sir," said Decurion Gentilius. "Legate Albinus was able to transfer your old gang easily enough, but moving the new prefect would have needed imperial approvals."

Gentilius looked at Martinel, who sat in a corner with Satewa, whittling a piece of wood into a toothpick. "Captain Martinel, all your boys came with us. We've settled in pretty well together."

Martinel looked up with real gratitude. "Thanks. My honor is hurt, though. I want to know why Lucius and Satewa each have a reward twice as large as mine. Do I have to kill more cockroaches to raise my value?"

"I suspect you'll get that chance soon enough," Lucius said. "What's the mood of the troops? Are they with us?"

Centurion Cilla replied as if he were making a quartermaster's report instead of plotting an insurrection. "Sir, you know the First. They were ready to revolt as soon as they heard General Aetius was branded a traitor. Legate Albinus has his hands full stopping them from marching on Rome now. I have friends in the Third, and they're in much the same mood. The Second is a little harder to read. Mind you, we've been there for just two weeks, and it's a topic folks don't discuss with strangers. At any rate, the old legate is dead. He apparently had an accident and stabbed himself in the back. He's been replaced by an imperial loyalist, but I can say that none of the junior officers seem fond of him. Any mention of Maximus just brings sneers."

Lucius digested the information and nodded. "It's as good as I can hope for. Okay, men. I don't want any heroes here, but do what you can to prepare. When General Aetius regains his strength, we will strike, and we must do it before Valentinian has the chance to wrap himself in a cocoon of Praetorians."

Gentilius gritted his teeth, an angry passion in his eyes. "Begging your pardon, sir, but after what those cockroaches did to Vidin, I hope he does. I want to squish as many of those vermin as I can."

Lucius drew breath to respond when he noticed all eyes shifted at once to something behind him. In the doorway stood none other than General Aetius himself, haggard and emaciated but supported by the physician and Dervla. Through his weariness, his eyes shone clear and true.

Aetius spoke in a soft voice. "The time for Romans killing Romans is coming very soon, and the ones who'll benefit from this are our enemies." He lifted his chin and added with determination, "Head back to your base before you raise suspicions about your patrol being gone too long. Just be ready, my loyal friends. Be ready."

CHAPTER XXX

CONSPIRACY

Aetius leaned against the warm brick wall, enjoying the midspring sun in Venice. A year ago, the place had nothing more than a few fishing huts, and now it had grown into a full-sized town. Across the piazza, villagers broke ground on the new church. *Someday, that'll be a beautiful cathedral.*

He sipped the brew Phokas had been forcing down his throat for the past three weeks. A smile crossed his face after the first tentative taste as it didn't have its normal bitter tang; in fact, it held a hint of honey that sweetened the taste. The general concluded Dervla must've prepared the brew, and she confirmed it herself when she came to collect his food tray and winked at him. Grateful, he whispered, "Thank you."

She responded in a voice that carried across the room. "You're very welcome. Sometimes, I think the good doctor goes out of his way to make his potions unpalatable."

Phokas arched his eyebrows and offered her a crinkled smile. Nearby, Aetius laughed at the exchange. *I hope Lucius knows how lucky he is to have a lady like her for a wife.*

Phokas came out of his ruminations to see the general grinning at him and scowled. "Patients should have more respect for their physicians. Wait until you taste tonight's medicine."

Aetius hid his mirth and turned to Father Patricius. Covered in dust, the exhausted man slumped from several days on the road. "Padre, sorry for the interruption. Please continue. What news from Rome?"

Father Patricius took a long, thirsty gulp from the mug of wine set before him, and then handed the general a pouch of sealed letters. "Pope Leo sends his greetings and prays daily for your full recovery. His sources tell him the emperor and his advisors believe you're dead. As far as he can tell, there's no search for you." He glanced at Satewa, Martinel, and Lucius sitting across from him. "There's still a price on your heads, but the hunt has stopped. They believe you've fled the empire."

"If we had any brains, we *would* be long gone," grumbled Martinel. "My eldest brother has a fine estate. We could be eating fat roasted meat and drinking fine wines every day."

Aetius locked eyes with him. "That is very true, my friend. You've done more to help me than many who call themselves Roman citizens. I'll be fit for travel soon. Go. You have my heartfelt gratitude for all you've done."

Martinel flushed and twisted his hands in a nervous fashion. "My brother is a bit of an authoritarian, and I bet we'd start tearing at each other's throats within a week. I also promised Lucius here that I wouldn't leave until I bested him in a duel, and I'm guessing that'll take me a very long time." Smirking, he rubbed his chin and looked sidelong at the tribune. "Besides, who else can keep that hide of yours from getting poked full of holes? You know you're always showing up in places where people are trying to hurt you, and no one wants to see that new bride of yours crying."

"I'll always have your back, too, my friend," Lucius replied.

Martinel huffed, sliced a wedge of cheese with his knife, and shoved it in his mouth, halting all further conversation.

Aetius closed his eyes. It was early in the afternoon, but weariness lay on him like a cloak. A wistful smile crossed his face, and Aetius wondered, *With men like this during Rome's waning days, what were they like during its full glory?*

Father Patricius raised his hand. "There is one newsworthy item His Holiness wanted me to bring to your attention." The priest pointed to the mail pouch. "The details are somewhere in those dispatches, but in essence, there's a concern the Vandals are plotting an invasion."

The general snapped to full awareness and exchanged worried looks with Satewa. "What's Genseric up to?"

"There's little we know for sure. King Genseric is marshalling his army and has assembled an enormous fleet in Carthage. To counter this move, Imperator Maximus withdrew every legion from the Italian provinces and is rushing them to Iberia."

"The damn fool." Aetius leaned his forehead onto his steepled fingers. "The Vandals won't go to Iberia; they abandoned it years ago. Genseric is ambitious and wants to be remembered in history." He raised his head to face everyone around the table. A chill ran down his spine despite the warming sun. "There's only one place he'll bring his forces: Rome."

Aetius grabbed a sheet of vellum, dipped his quill in a pot of ink, and scrawled a long message. "Father Patricius, I know you just got here, but tomorrow morning, I need you to take my letters straight to the Pope. I need to know who in the army and the senate will stand with us and who will remain beholden to Valentinian."

Moaning, the clergyman rubbed his sore backside. "I'm a priest. I didn't know it entailed being a messenger and a spy." He sighed as he straightened. "Of course I will, but when this is over, I will need a long vacation. Perhaps the Pope could give me a nice missionary assignment to some distant land." He glanced over at Seamus, who approached the inn along the newly cobbled street. "Perhaps His Holiness could send me to Hibernia. An island full of terrifying pagans would have to be easier to deal with than the civilized people around here."

When Patricius rose, Seamus ran to him and greeted the priest with a tight hug. "Lad, would you be so kind as to help me with my bags?" Twisting the kinks in his back, Father Patricius walked into the inn and shouted behind him. "And don't bother me until morning."

Aetius turned to Phokas next. "Doctor Phokas, I have a tougher assignment for you." The physician sighed and cocked his head before the general went on. "The Byzantine Emperor, Marcian, must be appraised of the situation. I'm sure his spies are providing ample information about King Genseric's moves, but he's a good friend. He needs to know what I think the Vandals' move will be, and he needs to know what I plan to do."

"I'll do it. It's about time we have an emperor whose worthy of that title. I'm getting very tired of these small-minded buffoons running the country." Phokas leaned back and raised his head as though in thought. "There's a trade ship leaving for Corinth with the tide at dawn. I have family there, so I'm sure I can acquire transportation to Constantinople." The doctor frowned at Aetius. "Don't think this will get you out of your medications. I'll leave detailed instructions with Dervla, even though she puts far too much honey in them." He stood, grumbling. "I'm going to find that ship's captain and let him know he has a passenger."

Aetius turned to Lucius. "Tribune, I'll give you letters to send to Marcus Carloman and Legate Albinus. Tell them the time is now for the Red Fist to march on Rome. They must bring the First and Third Legions with all haste."

"Don't worry, sir. I'll take the dispatches myself." Lucius hopped to go.

However, Aetius stopped him. "No, you won't, son. You've a price on your head. You won't get twenty miles, and then the emperor will have all my nice, clear directions."

Martinel raised his hand. "I have a man who can do it. He's the same fellow who delivered the first dispatches. Marcus will recognize him. He rides like he was born in the saddle, unlike *some* people I know." Martinel tossed Lucius a sly smile, then turned back to Aetius. "My men have been serving you for close to four years now. God help me, I believe they think of themselves more as Roman legionaries than Frankish warriors nowadays. Your message will get through."

"Then may the Good Lord see justice in our cause as we go to war with our own people." Aetius observed his men, his expression grave. Each responded with a silent nod, and he sighed. "So be it. You have your orders." He rose on shaky legs. "I'm going to rest. Hard trials await us."

Dervla met Aetius at the abbey's entrance and supported his walk to the rickety staircase. Aetius glanced back as the other men rose to see to their tasks.

Martinel draped his arm around Lucius' shoulder. "Don't be so glum, my friend. Think about our little adventure in that fort near the Catalaunian Plains. It was you and me with our boys against the entire Hunnic horde. I think that bunch was a touch more dangerous than Maximus and his band of toadies. Besides, you're already branded a traitor, so what do you have to lose?"

Lucius threw his arms up. "Can't you be serious about anything?" Despite his words, he smiled.

"Don't worry. If things go bad, I'm sure my brother will give us a job cleaning out the pig sties on his estate."

Lucius stormed off and Martinel ambled to the table to finish his wine. Aetius kept a chuckle to himself as Dervla helped him climb the stairs.

CHAPTER XXXI

MOVE IN THE SHADOWS

Doctor Phokas stood on the dirt lane and admired the newly completed manor house before him. *My brother has done pretty well as a merchant.* He wobbled to the freshly whitewashed gate and cursed. *I grew up by the sea, and here I can barely walk after a few days on the Mediterranean.*

He hesitated before passing through the villa's low walls. Long ago, he and his brother, Ionnes, hadn't parted on the best of terms; in fact, he could still recall the yelling, insults, and door slams from their last talk, as well as the regret that had followed. However, he couldn't let the past burden him now—not when he had but a day before he traveled to Constantinople.

Phokas looked at his aged hands. *When did I get so old? What are the odds of me ever coming to Corinth again?* He walked toward the white stucco building and noticed new mulberry bushes planted along a crushed stone walkway.

Ahead of him, the door of the house flew open, and an old man ran to him with open arms. Phokas got out, "Brother, I—" before the older man buried him in a bear hug.

The two brothers clung to each other, refusing to let go. Both wept, all past troubles forgotten. The household gathered at the door, watching their stern patriarch and the mysterious stranger whose face greatly resembled his.

Ionnes stepped back but kept his hands on Phokas' shoulders. "Brother, have you come home? Are you here to stay?"

Phokas felt like a knife pierced his heart. For the first time in many decades, he felt the need to belong, but he couldn't right then. "Alas, Ionnes, I can't stay more than a night. I sail for Constantinople on an important mission and it can't wait. I need to speak with Emperor Marcian."

Sorrow crossed Ionnes' face, and it didn't quite leave when he smiled. "Then you shall be regaled as you never have before. Still neck deep in Valentinian's intrigues?"

Phokas chuckled without mirth. "More of the opposite, I would say."

Ionnes gave his brother a sly appraisal. "I have another visitor here I think you should talk to." He turned back to those who watched from the doorway, and from that group emerged a tall, rawboned Byzantine officer. "Zeno, come here please. There's someone I want you to meet."

* * *

It had been far too easy to slip into the camp, but Lucius willed himself to stay quiet. Decurion Gentilius led a patrol out and in. The fact that Aetius, Satewa, and Lucius were three of those cloaked legionaries went unnoticed. Martinel had ridden in a week earlier with a troop of his own cavalry to test the wariness of the senior commanders, and not much had changed since their assessment earlier.

They settled into the barracks assigned to Centurion Cilla's command. The eight-man cabin sat against the inner rampart close to the main entrance, the *porta principali*.

It had been a busy morning. One at a time, centurions from the Red Fist's Second Legion entered with looks of confusion. They all left with grim determination and gave curt nods to Gentilius, who lounged outside the building with a group of his men. Those legionaries appeared to be engaged in the normal activities of repairing equipment, but by their hardened faces, the centurions had no doubt what they would do with those sharpened swords if the meeting inside went wrong.

At noon, the procession of visitors to the nondescript barracks stopped. Inside, a small group of men sat around the makeshift plank table for lunch. The fresh bread and olive oil, along with a not-so-sour wine, was better fare than normal.

Upon hearing the latest update, General Aetius arched his eyebrow at Cilla.

The centurion bit his lip. "Sir, that's all the officers I was confident would be with us. I could bring more, but if word reaches the new legate that you're here before we make our move, we'll have real trouble on our hands."

Lucius shuffled in his seat. "General, you have the sworn allegiance of a mere fourteen centurions. There're sixty centurions stationed here, plus a half dozen tribunes. How can we move with that little support?"

General Aetius returned a calm look to the young tribune. "Lucius, fourteen will be enough. I knew these men would be with us before they walked in, but I needed to get a feel for the camp. The others will join us. Did you see how readily they accepted me? These men are all old veterans. They were each here alone, and none of them paused to consider who they might have to draw swords against. They all seemed confident their fellow officers will enlist in our cause."

Still unconvinced, Lucius frowned. "But there'll be confusion. The legate will give orders, and those officers will follow them. They'll realize who they're fighting far too late to do us any good."

Satewa pounded the table. "That's why we need to be sure such orders are never issued. You Romans have loose tongues. If we speak to more, word of some unrest will sweep the fort, and that fool of a legate will have a full cohort surrounding his Praetorium headquarters."

"Then we should move now, before anyone starts whispering. I can't stand this waiting. My nerves can't take it." Lucius hopped up and paced around the tent.

Aetius spoke in an even voice. "Lucius, sit down. The plans are in motion. We'll close on the command center at midnight. I want as many of the Second Legion soldiers out of harm's way." His voice rose. "It'll be men who have sworn to me on the ramparts, and it'll be *our* men sealing off the Praetorium. Until the deed is done, I'll have no innocent slain for doing his duty. I'll not spill Roman blood unless I must."

Lucius plopped down on his camp stool and swirled the wine in his earthen mug. "This is going to be a long afternoon."

Martinel walked over and slapped Lucius on the shoulder. "Come on and dice with me. You're a terrible gambler, so you can worry about losing all of your money instead of starting a revolution."

The corners of Lucius' mouth curled up. "I don't part with my coin easily."

Martinel proved prophetic that afternoon. Lucius' purse was empty by the time the sun set, and he spent the evening glaring at the Martinel's broad smile.

* * *

An hour before midnight, the torpid pace around the nondescript barracks shifted into a beehive of activity. Centurions entered and reviewed the planned disposition of their men. The general gave them their assignments with brisk instructions and sent them on their way. Shortly before the appointed hour, Aetius donned his cleanest scarlet cape and polished armor, sighed, and stood.

Now's the moment of truth. Lucius exchanged a glance with General Aetius, and for a fleeting moment, he was taken aback by the leader he idolized. *He looks so serene and majestic. There's no doubt in his eyes.*

They walked out the cabin door together. Cilla was there waiting with his century in parade formation.

Martinel shared a quick conversation with his cavalry captain, who jogged off, and then approached Lucius. "Don't worry, Roman. My boys will have control of the stable yard just in case we have to make a quick escape. Remember, if things go wrong, my brother can always use new swineherds."

Lucius laughed, though the sound was high and tinny, and they fell in behind Aetius.

Satewa joined them. "Let's hope this doesn't turn out like Ravenna."

All three tightened their grip on the pommels of their weapons, and Aetius strode ahead without a glance back. Eighty men followed without hesitation. Despite the late hour, legionaries lined the via principalis at stiff attention. Keeping quiet, they saluted with their spears as the general led his small procession past.

As they entered the torchlight of the Praetorium, Aetius raised his hand to call a halt. The guards before the headquarters sprang to their feet, and one runner sprinted off. Lucius saw the direction the soldier took and knew he would not travel far.

Aetius nudged Lucius. "It appears our legate isn't a complete fool. His guards are Praetorians. Will you be so kind as to announce us and demand their surrender?" His eyes shone with a hard, serious glint. "Lucius, I make this offer in all seriousness, but just once. Be careful."

Lucius walked on, his shoulders a little too stiff, and his mouth dry. The guards raised their weapons and tracked his approach with wary eyes. One went inside to rouse the legate.

Ten paces from the guards, Lucius halted and announced, "Imperator Flavius Aetius declares Emperor Valentinian is a corrupt tyrant who has brought about the ruin of our empire. By his actions, the emperor has squandered his right to rule. Imperator Flavius Aetius commands all who love Rome to stand by his banner in the struggle to overthrow the despot." He stared at the black-clad soldiers and added in a quiet voice, "He makes this offer once. I would not make it at all."

One Praetorian elbowed his way past his officer and walked straight to Lucius. "I will take that vow."

I don't trust any of them. They're all snakes. Lucius tightened his grip on the hilt of his sword. "On what would you swear that would cause me to believe you?"

The man fell to his knees before Lucius, pulled off his helmet, and exposed his neck. "I am from Mantua. I swear by the lives of my family, both those who died and those who escaped, that the only honor I saw on that black day was by Red Fist legionaries. They perished to the last man aiding my people." He raised his head and locked eyes with Lucius. "I asked for this assignment so I could be close to real soldiers. If my vow is not good enough, then take my life. I'll give none better."

Lucius put his hand on the man's shoulder and sighed. "General Aetius was right. Every man should be given a chance. What's your name, Legionary?"

"Oxyntas, sir. Decurion Oxyntas."

At that moment, the door burst open, and the legate stomped out, planting his hands on his hips. He was a stocky man with a fringe of steel gray hair around a balding head. He strode out and spied Flavius Aetius in the flickering torchlight, then turned to the gathered soldiers. "Seize the traitor. Fifty gold pieces to the man who kills him."

A few men shifted their feet and shared looks with the other soldiers. None moved.

The legate flushed and roared, drew his gladius, and charged. "For Rome! For Emperor Valentinian!"

Satewa stepped up to meet him. The legate lunged but gasped in pain as Satewa slid to the side and grabbed the wrist of the man's sword hand. Lucius heard the bone snap in the legate's arm.

"For a better world. For my Brenda," Satewa intoned as he brought his one-handed axe down on the legate's neck. The camp turned deadly silent as the legate fell like a discarded sack of grain.

General Aetius regarded the band of imperial guards forming up in a defensive semicircle around the entrance to the Praetorium. He stepped forward with a measured pace.

Lucius made a grab to hold him back, but Satewa stilled his arm. "He needs to do this if he is going to rule all of Rome."

Lucius clenched his teeth but nodded his agreement and followed two paces behind his general.

Aetius surveyed the black-clad guards for the officers. One was a young tribune who appeared to have soiled himself already. The other was a swarthy centurion who sneered with disdain at him. In a soft voice, he asked, "Do you honor Rome?"

The young tribune's eyes lit with a desperate hope. "Yes, we live to serve Rome." He fell quaking to his knees. "When you rule the empire, I vow to follow you."

The Praetorian centurion returned a belligerent stare. "We made another vow, and some of us will not go back on it."

Aetius sighed. "Rome cannot afford the loss of any of its sons."

The centurion shrugged. "That's so noble of you. What would be your high and mighty words if I told you I led the raid on the inn where we killed your wife and son?" He made an abrupt move to draw his sword. The centurion's eyes went wide in surprise. Blood gurgled from his mouth, and the weapon fell from his lifeless hand.

Lucius had seen the move in the man's eyes even before the centurion made his first twitch. In a blur of motion, Lucius had stepped around the general and drove his blade through the man's chest. He kicked the lifeless body where it fell and turned on the remaining Praetorians. "The oath we took when we joined the legions was to defend Rome from its enemies. It was not to butcher its women and children."

The remaining Praetorians exchanged cautionary glances. Then, one at a time, they dropped their swords and knelt beside the tribune. One spoke. "Do as you will. We die as Romans."

Aetius' lips trembled. "You have half an hour. Choose. Lucius, please stay and handle the decision." He walked off on shaking legs.

The guards filed into the Praetorium half, carrying the limp tribune. A half an hour later, two Praetorians walked out and bowed before Lucius. "We swear by our lives and our honor to serve Imperator Aetius as the rightful ruler of Rome."

Lucius gazed over their heads at the door standing ajar. "And the others?"

"They chose death."

"The tribune?"

One Praetorian laughed with derision. "Oh, Troilus still lives. You'll find him curled up in a fetal position by the back wall."

Lucius nodded. "Your first job is to bury the dead—all but the centurion and the legate. Leave them for the carrion birds. We march on Rome at first light."

CHAPTER XXXII

HADRIAN'S PALACE

Tivoli was a small town eighteen miles from Rome. In its glory days, centuries earlier, Emperor Hadrian ruled the nation from his villa there, but those days passed long ago. The palace was still magnificent, and word that the emperor was to hold a masquerade ball here was an opportunity they could not pass up. Dervla knew as well and devised a plan, but convincing the Red Fist soldiers to go along with it proved difficult.

"I'll not allow it. This is far too dangerous!" Lucius roared.

Dervla glared at him. "Husband, you don't have a choice in this matter."

Seamus glared at Lucius. "Dervla, let the Romans fight their own battles. None of them are worth it."

She took Seamus' hand in hers, uncurling his fingers from the fist he'd made. "Scamus, this is my fight. These are the men who murdered our parents. They had me perform indignities that still make me vomit. No, brother, I have a greater claim on the death of these vermin than any other. I want Publius to see my face when he dies."

Sullen tears welled in Seamus' eyes. "And what if you're recognized? What if you're killed? These 'brave' warriors will still be safe and just start working on a new plan."

Lucius threw his hands up and scowled. "I agree with the lad. I say we rush the imperial palace and destroy the snake in his nest."

"Don't be a fool," Satewa said in a soft voice. "I don't like this plan any more than you do, but how are we to sneak an entire legion into the city? We'd flounder at the gates while the emperor stands on the wall and laughs. The best chance we have is to catch him away from the imperial palace. Hadrian's Palace is the ideal site. It has a network of long-forgotten underground tunnels we can move our troops through without being seen."

Aetius sat and listened, his gaze darting to each speaker with a dark expression on his face. "The boy is right. We cannot ask Dervla to take this risk for me. We need another plan."

Dervla turned on the general, her face flushed. "No one is making me do this. It is the one thing I must do if I'm ever to be free. Or am I still a slave who must follow the orders of her masters?"

Aetius threw open his hands. "It's your decision, Dervla. You know the risk."

Frustrated, Lucius curled his fists. "If anything happens to you, I swear I'll storm Palatine Hill myself." He stomped from the inn and fled to the streets of Tivoli.

Dervla lifted a gossamer silk gown with revulsion. "This is just the bait to lure him away from his guards. When I get him to the bed chambers, we'll have him."

* * *

Dervla stepped out of her coach and sauntered to the villa's gate on soft slippers. As she approached the two leering guards, she trembled and clutched the cloak at her neck. When asked, she mumbled an unrecognizable name. The guards' smiles broadened as she lowered her cape, revealing her thin gown, and approached the two guards.

She watched over the sentinel's shoulder as three silent shadows slipped from the side of her coach and disappeared along the wall where no torch light shone. The guards' leering eyes remained fixed on her as she stepped close to the nearest man.

Dervla put on a seductive smile as the shadows coalesced into men right behind the guards. One man grabbed at her, but his smile froze on his face as she drove a slim stiletto up through his exposed jaw into his brain. The other guard hit the ground at the same time with blood gushing from his slit throat. It was over in a second and without a sound. Three more Red Fist legionaries scrambled up from the floor of the coach. The six men dumped the bodies into the carriage.

Dervla looked up at the driver. "Cilla, tell Lucius the path is clear. He can get his men down in the tunnels now. Tell him the next time he sees me, I'll be a free woman."

Cilla nodded and watched his legionaries take up the posts of the dead guards. "That I'll do, ma'am. My boys will hold this position, and the tribune will have a full cohort down in the tunnels in no time."

Dervla took a few controlled breaths to steady herself. "Yes, I know the plan."

Cilla shot a sharp look at the six legionaries. "If anything goes wrong, holler like hell and run. We'll come for you."

She smiled and clasped his hand. "I know you will."

"Uh, ma'am, you might want to leave your cloak here."

Dervla looked down at her now bloodstained wrap, undid the clasp, and handed it to him. "Watch this for me."

"The knife, too, ma'am. The guards near the emperor will be checking any guest that approaches."

Dervla flipped the blade handle toward Cilla, who took it in short order. She composed herself, squared her shoulders, and stepped through the causeway.

Dervla walked down the inlaid brick path and took a goblet of wine from the tray of a passing servant. She took a sip to calm her nerves, but almost slopped the ruby-colored liquid on herself when the servant leaned in and whispered, "Don't worry, Miss. If there's any trouble, I got your back."

She hissed back, "Gentilius, I didn't even recognize you. Sweet Jesus, please try to act more like a slave."

The Red Fist legionary gave her a sheepish look and lowered his voice. "Just so you know, there are about a dozen of us scattered in with the servants."

Dervla nodded and swept her long hair, now dyed black, over her shoulders. She adjusted the masquerade mask covering her eyes and glided across the torch-lit bridge to where the festivities raged. In the darker corners of the room, fat old men pawed at girls no older than children. The sight reminded her of sordid incidents from her own past, sending shivers through her body. Dervla made a silent prayer for comfort to find those young girls before turning back to her task.

She pasted a vivacious smile on her face and strolled over to the couch where Valentinian lounged. He chatted with Publius, but his eyes locked on her with lust when he noticed her approach.

Dervla curtseyed before him. "Your Majesty, I bring you greetings from my uncle, Marcian, the Byzantine Emperor. I'm Olivia."

Valentinian snickered and leered at her. "Yes, my dear, I do know what lands Marcian rules. I must say, I definitely need to introduce the new Byzantine fashions here. Romans can be so staid in their attire. Come, sit with me. I want us to be very close friends before the evening is done."

She shuddered as she moved to lounge beside him. *This is it.*

As Dervla leaned toward the emperor, he ripped off her mask and playfully studied her face. She gasped as he pulled her tight against him.

He sat back smirking. "I've seen his family. Ugly, every one of them. With those blue eyes and fair skin, you're nothing more than a bastard child of some favored concubine."

A wary smile creased her face. "I hope I'm not too ugly for your taste."

The emperor brushed his hand across her flimsy gown. "He'll thank me for planting some royal seed in one of his harlots." He hoisted her onto his lap.

Dervla bit back her scream of fear, thinking of how to play along. She forced herself to coo into his ear. "Your Majesty, take me to your room, and I'll give you a night you'll never forget."

"That you will, my sweet cake," he grunted. "But first, my guests need a demonstration of their emperor's virility."

Her mind churned as she sought an excuse. The Red Fist had set up the ambush in the bedroom suite, and Dervla had to lure the emperor there. Putting a finger on his lower lip, she looked him in the eye and kept her voice steady. "That would be beyond my fondest dreams, Your Majesty, but I'm a little shy. How about some wine before we indulge?" She licked her tongue along his ear and pouted.

Valentinian grunted and then laughed. "Who says I'm not a gentleman?" Nonchalant, he looked down the table at a servant there. "You, slave, bring more wine for the lady and me."

The emperor leaned back and had his goblet refilled. He didn't notice the servant slip a thin dagger under the cushion behind Dervla, but she did. The slave left before she had a chance to look at his face.

"So tell me, my Greek jewel, how goes construction of the Theodosian Wall? Is it complete yet?" Valentinian asked as he stared at her scantily clad chest.

Theodosian Wall? What in the name of the Blessed Virgin is that? "It looked done to me," Dervla mumbled.

"You're no niece of Marcian." The emperor shoved her off his lap and glowered at her. He was about to say more when a military courier ran up to him. Valentinian glowered at the breathless messenger. "This better be important."

"Yes, sire, I came straight from Ostia. The harbor master said it was urgent," panted the dust-covered rider.

"Out with it, then."

The messenger handed the emperor a scroll. Valentinian ripped open the wax seal and scanned the document, then read it again more closely. He crushed the vellum and threw it on the floor, his face blanching as he hailed the chamberlain. "Publius, please keep this young lady warmed up for me. It's probably nothing, so I should be back soon." The emperor abruptly rose and barked to the courier, "Come with me. I'll have a response soon." He stormed off with his guards trailing behind him.

Dervla cursed under her breath with her hand under the cushion, feeling for the dagger. *I hesitated too long. What now*? She saw the contents of the note and could read some. Something about a lot of ships. Unsure of its importance, she resolved to tell Lucius about it at the first opportunity to get his assessment. How she would find that opportunity, she didn't know. *Should I wait for the emperor to come back? Should I leave? This whole plan's turned into a mess.*

A vise-like grip on her arm startled her out of her thoughts, and the fetid breath and mouth of her former master pressed against hers. Memories of abuse and unwanted advances flashed before her, and her mind screamed, *No, never again*. Her free hand groped for the hidden dagger.

Publius leaned back in confusion. "Say, I think I know you." His eyes bulged with sudden recognition at the same moment Dervla found the handle of the weapon.

She lunged and drove the dagger through the man's heart. As she leaned closer to him, she twisted the blade. "Publius, Satan is waiting for you with open arms. Burn in Hell!"

All chaos broke loose. Two guards ran toward what appeared to be a deranged, partially undressed woman, but were tackled by servants who started screaming, "Red Fist, to arms!" Armored men sprang from the ground, and guests fled in every direction.

Dervla was still stabbing a very dead chamberlain in her frenzy when Lucius approached her. He took off his cape and draped it over her shoulders. "Darling, it's all right now. There's no one left to hurt you."

Upon hearing Lucius' calm voice, Dervla dropped the blade and pulled the cloak tight around herself. She drew in a few deep breaths to calm her rattled nerves. "I-I thought I could do it. But so much came back at once. I couldn't let him touch me again. I just couldn't."

Lucius hugged her, and she buried her face against his chest. "Don't ever let go." Dervla lifted her face to his with a small smile. "How is it I keep ending up with your capes? Soon, you'll have no wardrobe left."

He answered with a passionate kiss. "Promise me you'll never do anything this reckless again."

Dervla nodded, but her thoughts cleared, and she pulled away. "The emperor left." She searched the ground and found the crumpled dispatch. "He read this and rushed out of here."

Lucius glanced over his shoulder. Fierce fighting sounded in the stable yard, but none of it drifted back toward them. Lucius took the letter and read it, then shook as his gaze darted over the paper. "Dervla, do you know who sent this note?"

"Yes. I heard the courier say that it was from the harbor master at Ostia. Why? What's the matter?"

"Possibly the end of our world. Stay here." Lucius ran off as if the hounds of Hell were after him.

As members of the Red Fist secured the villa, and her rattled nerves relaxed, Dervla picked up the note but couldn't make out more than a few words: *Enormous fleet. Vandals. Can't hold long.*

* * *

Valentinian pulled the reins from the dispatch rider and leapt into the saddle, kicking the man in the face. "Defend your emperor!" he shouted as he galloped out the gate.

The fight was lost. His guards were overwhelmed; some of the cowards even surrendered. He clung close to the horse's neck as he raced through the darkened streets of Tivoli. Those men wore the uniforms of the Second Legion, but he knew that group was stationed way to the north. That meant the warriors who had defeated his guards must've been the Vandals.

He kicked the horse for more speed.

x x x

Lucius arrived at the gate breathless. The fighting had ended, and prisoners were herded together against the wall by the pool. He looked around, spotted Martinel, and spoke fast. "The emperor's escaped. Go after him with your cavalry. If he gets there, the gates of Rome will be closed to us, and that'll cost us time we don't have."

The easy smile disappeared from the Frank's face and he sprinted, shouting for his men at the back side of the villa.

Lucius spotted Aetius next speaking with the sullen prisoners. He ran to him and blurted out, "General, we have a real problem." The tribune went on to describe the contents of the message he'd just read.

General Aetius' face turned grave. "Gentlemen, we're in for the race of our lives. We march to Rome now, and we must be there before the sun rises."

Aetius walked out the gate on unsteady legs. Sweat beaded on his forehead as he forced himself into a determined, open stride. Aetius leaned on Lucius' shoulder when the tribune raced to his side. "I'll be damned if I let this broken body of mine stop me now. My country's not going to perish while I can still draw breath."

The thundering hooves of the cavalry charged through town. He cocked his head and listened to the voices of frantic centurions and decurions rise in a crescendo from the villa and the town. Many footsteps rushed up behind Lucius and the general.

"I hope someone fetches me a horse soon," Aetius gasped through gritted teeth.

CHAPTER XXXIII

THE FINAL RACE

Martinel and his men closed some of the distance between the lone rider and themselves. The emperor rode a fresh dispatch rider's mount and moved like the wind. The predawn light showed their target would reach the looming walls of Rome before they could catch him.

Martinel patted the neck of his lathered roan stallion. "Come on, great heart, you can still do it." The horse appeared to respond by redoubling his efforts.

Martinel smiled wanly, realizing what the inevitable result would be of the task Lucius had given him. Kill the Roman emperor. Easier said than done because it sure doesn't look like that's going to happen. Maybe life as a swine herder won't be too bad.

* * *

With a roar of triumph, Valentinian drove his flagging animal through the Porta Salaria. He turned and saw his pursuers lagged behind by a long distance off. Meanwhile, the city militia stared at him with bored curiosity. None recognized him.

Upon spotting a Praetorian standing nearby, Valentinian breathed a sigh of relief and summoned the man. "Praetorian, do you recognize me?"

The legionary glanced at the emperor's rings and studied his face, then gave a stiff salute. "Yes, Your Majesty. I am yours to command."

Valentinian leaned over. "Close those gates and fill anyone who tries to enter full of arrows."

"Yes, sire."

"What's your name, Praetorian? I will see that you're handsomely rewarded."

"Oxyntas, sire. Decurion Oxyntas."

The emperor trotted off. Now I must go to the Senate. I'll need them to put together terms of surrender to Genseric. I'm sure we can come to some accommodation that won't be too odorous for the Patricians.

* * *

As Oxyntas walked over, the curious gate captain asked him, "So what did that dust-covered nobleman want?"

"Oh, he just wanted to let us know that a column of troops will be coming in today and to keep the gate free of civilian traffic."

The captain breathed a sigh of relief. "That's welcome news. I've been hearing rumors about some pirates raiding Ostia or something like that. Anyway, it'll be good to have real soldiers around."

Oxyntas smiled as he watched Martinel's cavalry approaching the portal. When he glanced over his shoulder, the emperor had already ridden out of sight. "It looks like the Second Legion's riders have arrived." He waved to the riders. "Hurry, the emperor is looking forward to seeing you."

Martinel shook his head with a tired laugh, then signaled his men. They paraded into the city, returning the smart salutes of the city militia.

* * *

Four hours later, Aetius rode through draped in a hooded cloak and led the exhausted Second Legion through the Porta Salaria to the cheers of a gathering crowd. The rumor had spread that Ostia was struggling with more than a simple pirate raid, and seeing the great general proved a welcome sight.

"Close and bar the gate, and have the city sealed. There's trouble coming," Aetius said to the portal's captain.

The captain hesitated at first, staring with surprise and confusion on his face. Once his gaze drifted toward Aetius' Red Fist commander insignia, however, the confusion fell away.

"Call in all your off-duty men. I want every catapult and ballista ready to fire by noon," Aetius roared.

Shaken from his stupor, the guard captain jumped and left.

Soon after, a cavalry officer approached at a slow trot. General Aetius eyed Martinel as he rode up. "Well?"

Martinel scratched his chin. "Well, General, Valentinian is holed up in the senate building, and it's pretty well guarded. I didn't think it would be wise for me and my boys to go charging in, especially since most of us are Franks." His mouth curled into a sly smile. "The local citizenry might get the impression that some barbarians were trying to do something evil, like kill the emperor."

Aetius returned a bitter grimace. "That's a pleasure I reserve for myself." Standing tall, he faced his gathered officers. "Lucius, you and your cohort are with me. We're going to the Forum. I want three cohorts occupying the imperial palace on Palatine Hill. Move the rest of the legion to the western gates along the Tiber. That's where the Vandals will strike first."

The legion split into three columns and headed in different directions. "Satewa, go with Martinel. Make sure no one leaves that building."

Satewa nodded and grunted at Lucius. "I'm putting the general's life in your hands. Guard him well." He trotted off without waiting for a response.

Aetius chuckled despite the incredible tension. His eyebrows lifted as he noticed the unusual legionary who appeared beside Lucius on a lathered mare. "They're letting some pretty undersized soldiers into the legions these days."

Curious, Lucius glanced over and almost jumped at the sight of the short legionary walking up beside him.

"Hello, husband," said the petite legionary in a soft soprano voice.

"Dervla? What in the name of God are you doing here? I left you back in Tivoli. I thought you agreed not to do anything reckless."

"You told me to come, my darling. Didn't you say we'll always be together?"

"Yes, but I didn't mean in the midst of a battle! There's going to be serious trouble soon."

"And who's going to look after you while you're looking after General Aetius?"

"Well, just stay back," Lucius said in an exasperated voice. "God, I love you, stubbornness and all."

He reached over and squeezed her hand. She looked menacing despite wearing a leather breastplate far too large for her. The slim sword on her hip and the strung bow she carried in her hand looked functional. Without time to argue, they followed the general out.

* * *

The cohort hurried through the city. Many citizens cast worried looks in their direction. General Aetius didn't pause when he reached the foot of the Forum's wide steps. A growing mob of onlookers gathered to follow the cohort. Some were curious, some were apprehensive, and some just sought interesting entertainment.

Aetius dismounted, and Satewa and Martinel jogged over and fell in beside him.

Satewa pointed up the marble steps. "There's perhaps a century of Praetorians and a scattering of bodyguards inside. They know we're here."

Aetius nodded and signaled some of his men into the wings. Two centuries led by Cilla formed a shield wall before him. They encountered their first resistance as they reached the limestone platform at the top of the paved stone steps. They conquered the uncoordinated assault and drove the defenders down the arched hallways. Inside the cramped space, the Praetorians fought with desperation, but their attacks lacked organization and effectiveness.

Aetius called for a halt as his force reached the barricades thrown up in haste around the assembly area. Many of the Praetorians facing him were already wounded, some more severely than others. He met the eyes of the Praetorian centurion opposing him. The man's face told him that he knew the situation was hopeless.

In a commanding voice, the general asked, "Will you yield? There is only one death I seek here."

From behind a marble statue, the shrill voice of Emperor Valentinian gibbered, "Kill the traitors! Kill them all! You must defend me!"

The Praetorian centurion glanced back and sighed, then looked at his wounded men and the opposing force crowding in. "General Aetius, the empire will soon be a better place when you assume the throne. Will you have pity on my wounded? They've done their duty and served with honor."

"Centurion, they will be accorded the same care as my own. If they swear to me, their rank and position will remain unchanged."

"General, you're a decent man. It would've been a pleasure to serve under you. Perhaps in the next life, we can be friends."

"You can still yield."

The centurion saluted. "You know I can't."

Tears glistened in the general's eyes and he glanced at Lucius, recalling the horrible death by stoning that had almost befallen another honorable man. "Rome can't keep butchering the best of us. Centurion, I need you."

The centurion breathed deep and bellowed, "Shield wall." Barely a dozen men could respond.

Aetius eyed his own soldiers. He had over a hundred archers in place but could not give the command.

"General, should I give the order?" Lucius asked in a quiet voice. Aetius answered with a silent nod, so the tribune roared, "Archers to the rear, fire!"

Bodyguards ran at the wall of Red Fists, attempting to breakthrough and escape, but they were cut down. Arrows struck down the senators and imperial courtiers as they sought refuge behind the statuary. In that open auditorium, no one could conceal themselves. After a few minutes, nobody moved in the bloodstained pit except a small circle of Praetorians and their wounded comrades.

The Praetorian centurion dropped his sword and shield and knelt, exposing his neck to the victors. His remaining men followed suit. General Aetius stepped around them with his sword drawn until he stood over the wounded emperor.

Valentinian quivered and shrank away as sweat beaded his face. "Aetius, spare me. The throne is yours. I'll make any oath you wish, just spare me!"

A snarl crossed the general's face. "You can plea for mercy before my wife, my son, and Almighty God."

Valentinian whimpered as the general drove his sword through the man's heart. The deed was done. After a moment's pause, Aetius turned to face the still kneeling Praetorians. "What oath will you give?"

The centurion stood and looked him in the eyes. "I need not give a new oath. I swore to protect the emperor with my life, and I shall." He thrust his arm out in a Roman salute. "Hail Flavius Aetius, Emperor of Rome!" A second later, the Forum shook with the thunderous noise of every throat there hailing him with the same salute.

Weary, Aetius sat down on a stone bench next to Satewa and Martinel and scanned the chamber. "I would've expected to see Petronius Maximus here. He's never far from the emperor's side."

"Ah... Your Majesty, may I answer your question?"

The general's mouth crinkled at the corners. "I guess I'll need to get used to being addressed like this." He looked up, quizzical, and met the eyes of the Praetorian centurion. "You're a brave man, Centurion. What's your name?"

He gave a stiff salute. "My name is Tacturnus, Your Majesty."

Lucius walked over with his wife by his side. "Where is Maximus?"

Tacturnus glanced at the gathering crowd, then gulped. "He went down to Ostia to direct the defenses there. We haven't heard anything from him since yesterday."

Aetius tried to stand, but his legs gave out on him. Lucius caught him before he fell. "Thank you, Lucius. I'm guessing the good Doctor Phokas wouldn't recommend an eighteen-mile forced march and a pitched battle as proper rest and recuperation."

Martinel wiped the blood from his blade and sheathed his sword, chuckling. "By the way, Your Majesty, as one of your first orders of business, could you cancel the bounties on

Lucius, Satewa, and myself? For that kind of money, I would slit my own throat, so it kind of wrecks my sleep at night."

Aetius didn't laugh, but a distant look crossed his eyes. "Help me outside. If we don't do something soon, I may earn the record for the shortest reign of any emperor."

With a sigh, the corners his eyes crinkled as he gazed at the people around him—Lucius, Martinel, Satewa, Dervla, everyone. "They say a man can be judged by the friends he keeps. Well, I must have great honor because you are the finest men and women I have ever had the pleasure to meet. Now come. We must prepare our city for war."

Lucius ordered his cohort ahead, and they worked their way through the carnage in the long hallway. Every inch of it had been contested. As they stepped into the bright midday sun, Lucius gasped. A crowd had followed them here, but that couple hundred had swollen to thousands with more rushing in from every side street.

As they emerged from the building's shadows into the blistering heat of Rome's summer sun, the piazza erupted with thousands of cheering voices. Aetius' head perked up at the heartfelt shouts of support, and surprise registered on his face. He gazed at the gathered throng. "Perhaps I have an army here already. But, will they fight?"

The mob of patricians and plebes stood shoulder to shoulder, all class distinction erased. Priests and thieves craned their necks in order to catch sight of the general. A mere day earlier, these people had despaired and awaited the doom that floated outside the city's harbor. This day, their eyes glimmered with hope. Their shouts subsided to a reverent murmur as they strained to hear their liberator's words.

The general released his grip on Lucius who served as his human crutch and grimaced as he squared his shoulders. "I'm no orator, but I must find the words to inspire these people to believe in themselves again." He sighed and faced Lucius. "My young friend, how do I remind them what it's like to be Roman? That meaning has been lost to most for so many generations."

Lucius thought on it for a moment, his eyes glinting as though looking into the past. "Show them your vision of Rome, what it's been and what it can still be. Then they'll remember those virtues and realize they're worth fighting for."

Aetius smiled and squeezed Lucius' shoulder. "Step back and stand alongside our co-conspirators. We'll see if the Good Lord will grant me the wisdom and words I need." He paused to collect his thoughts as he contemplated the gathering crowd.

The new emperor ventured with but a few words. "Fellow Romans..."

His voice could not carry over the din made by the throng below, so he held up his hands for quiet. A resounding cheer followed. "Hail, Emperor Aetius!" The cry shook the stone beneath the new emperor's feet.

When the noise subsided, Aetius raised his arms to speak again. "Romans, you all know the ancient story of Horatius. The Etruscans were at the city with an enormous army in a sudden attack. Horatius stood before the people and said, 'To every man upon the earth, death cometh soon or late. Though their army is forty thousand strong, I will hold the bridge entrance with two others while you destroy the span behind me and save the city.'" Aetius curled his raised hands into fists. "I will be your Horatius, but who will be the two to stand beside me?"

A legion officer with a bloodied head elbowed his way to the base of the Forum. "Your Majesty, I am Lartius, the commander of the marine legionaries. The port at Ostia has been lost to the Vandals, and they're unloading their army as we speak. I will stand at your right."

Aetius closed his eyes. "Merciful God, why couldn't you have granted me a little more time?"

Lartius straightened his back and saluted. "My marines have lost that battle, but we aren't yet beaten. Command me!"

Another soldier stepped forth, a grizzled old man with one arm. "I am Herminius, the commander of the city militia. I will stand on your left. Tell me where you want my men."

The black-clad Praetorian, Tacturnus, walked up to Aetius and bowed. "The Praetorians have always been the shield of Rome. Command us, my emperor."

A low murmur arose from the crowd as it parted for a small group of men surrounding the ornately clad Vicar of Christ. Pope Leo tilted his head to the new emperor standing between the mammoth pillars at the head of the stairs. "The church recognizes the rightful ascension of its new temporal ruler. With the crisis before us, we will render whatever aid we can."

Father Patricius stood at the Pope's side and roared, "Amen!" and swung his sword high. Thunderous cheers followed suit.

Tears trickled down Aetius' face as he turned to face Satewa. "Infirm, old, and battered, but they're true Romans. I must find some way to save them."

He signaled for the commanders to come join him and then waved to the crowd. Aetius shuffled back inside, sat down, and leaned his head against a stone pillar. "Jesus, thank you. I needed them, and they were there. I never said a word, and they came to me."

Once he collected himself, he faced the men standing before him. "This is what we're going to do now."

※ ※ ※

Lucius' vision misted as he listened to Aetius' speech, and tears flowed as the crowd's cheers swelled to a triumphant roar. The sound lifted something in his chest as well, causing him to stand straighter and taller than he had in a long time. What that feeling was, he could not say, but it filled him with a sense of pride he hadn't felt since his first engagement. Had it really been just four years since then?

Lucius turned to Dervla when he felt her hand brush a tear from his face, and he answered the question in her eyes. "I wish my father and mother had lived to see this. This is the Rome they spoke of so often. This is the Rome I would fight and die for. Ever since I joined the army, I've been fearing and preparing for this moment. Now it's here. The fate of the world balances on the edge of a knife, and God in Heaven alone knows whether civilization will stand or fall into the abyss today."

Dervla hugged her husband. "Lucius, Emperor Aetius is a good man. He'll make this dismal world a better place. Why don't you say, 'This is the Rome I want to live to see?'"

He hugged her back. "It is, my darling. With my whole heart, it is."

* * *

King Genseric fumed as he paced before his striped pavilion. Everything had gone according to plan until now.

Genseric whipped around to face his gathered commanders and bellowed, "What do I do now? Instead of that fop, Valentinian, I find that not only were the rumors of Aetius' death wrong, but now he's their emperor. The one Roman in the world with backbone, and he's their ruler." He threw his hands down. "Must that man always vex me?"

Axise cleared his throat. "We could hit them again. They'll break."

Genseric made a curt shake of his head. "The best general in the world is sitting behind a fat stone wall, and you want to hit them again. He drove off our last assault with little trouble, and their catapults have a much greater range than ours."

"We must outnumber them at least ten to one. If we can get close to them, victory will be ours."

"And how are we going to do that? We could lay siege to the place, but I know that old fox is marshalling his legions in Gaul. When they show up, we'll be cut off. We'll be alone in a countryside swarming with enemies. No, we must take Rome soon or depart. Once inside, we could hold forever, but out here in the open, we're dead."

Axise scratched his cheek in thought before snapping his fingers. "Do you remember the old Greek story about the Trojan Horse?"

The king rolled his eyes to the heavens. "I don't think leaving a large wooden horse at one of their gates will be very effective. I'm sure someone in that damned city knows the story."

Undeterred, Axise went on. "Oh, this would be much better. We could use a live man."

"Will you just speak plainly instead of in riddles? I'm not having a very good day, and you're giving me a headache."

"Yes, sire. Do we still have that inept Roman general as a prisoner?"

Genseric scowled. "Yes. The little weasel was somewhat useful. He gave my interrogators every piece of information about the city's defenses the moment they started honing their blades." The Vandal King grew thoughtful. "He seemed rather disconcerted when he was informed about Rome's recent change in leadership." He slapped his hands together in excitement. "How many Roman uniforms do you think we acquired in the harbor?"

Axise gave a triumphant smile. "Oh, at least five hundred, sire."

"Let's see... there will be a half moon tonight, so we'll have a little light. Do whatever you need to convince our 'guest' to help. Promise him riches, threaten him with torture, or do both; I don't care. But after dark, work your way around to the northern gates. Use the Porta Salaria, and have him gain your force entry. Once inside, overpower the guards and open the gates. I want you to light a beacon once you're successful."

Genseric pumped his fists and spun in a circle, his smile growing broad. "When old Aetius awakens in the morning, we'll have our entire army sitting inside that sweet little treasure trove of a city. Axise, go choose your men from the greatest warriors we have. The rest of you, listen up. I want sorties harassing the southern walls to keep Aetius focused somewhere else."

CHAPTER XXXIV

TROJAN HORSE

Seamus sat on a crate nestled deep in a dark alley. It stank, and he couldn't sleep. His mind roiled with conflicting emotions from the news his sister had told him in secret after dinner. Seamus stared up at the starlit sky as though it held answers.

She's six weeks pregnant. I hate this rat-infested city and everyone in it, and now even Dervla's one of them. I'm going to be an uncle to a Roman. Frustrated, he threw a pebble against a stone wall, then pulled out the knife Lucius had given him and twisted it in his hand. Though Lucius was decent enough, and Dervla was madly in love with him, Seamus still thought the situation felt wrong. He tugged at his flaming red hair.

We should be in Hibernia with our own people. Here, everyone points at you and stares. She'll never want to leave now. Since he could do little about the situation, however, he hopped off the crate. Might as well try to get some sleep.

The inn was a short walk away. Seamus knew Lucius had chosen it so that they would be close to where his cohort was camped out in the Sallust Gardens. It also wasn't far from the Porta Salaria where Seamus had taken his moment to think.

He stopped in midstep when pair of silhouetted men gathered at the mouth of the alley. Seamus slipped back into the shadows and ducked behind the crate.

Two heads glanced into the darkened area and then continued their conversation. "All right, Captain, here's your money. Your task is easy. In about an hour, a unit of legionaries will beg to be let in. All you have to do is allow it."

"But we have strict orders to keep the gates sealed. My men will never obey such an order. The Vandals are roaming all over the place out there."

The first man chuckled with a cold, soulless voice. "Oh, yes, they will. This Roman unit will be led by General Maximus himself."

The second person said with relief, "General Maximus? He was fighting in Ostia. Has he escaped?" Suspicion entered his voice. "How do you know this?"

"I have my contacts. Look, since the beginning of time, this city has had bloody political spats. General Maximus was unfortunate enough to be on the losing side of the latest one, but that doesn't mean he isn't a loyal Roman. As you said, the Vandals are out there, and we need all of our soldiers. You can't leave him and his men to be butchered because of politics. The command structure is in chaos, so approval would take hours. If you wait, those brave men will die, and their blood will be on your hands."

"That makes sense. I often have trouble remembering who's in charge. Nothing ever changes."

The first man grunted in sage agreement. "Look, when this is over, not only will you be a wealthy man, but many well-connected people will consider you a hero."

Seamus heard the clink of a coin bag sliding into a satchel.

"All right, my shift is about to start. I'll meet you here tomorrow for the other part of the bounty." Both men walked away in separate directions.

Seamus slipped from his hiding place and cautiously approached the alley opening. He had no idea what to do, though. The conversation he'd overheard sounded like more Roman political games. *Maybe they'll all slit each other's throats. Then the world will be finally free of their stench.*

He pulled the knife from his belt and regarded it, remembering the desperate night it was given him. *I should tell someone. I'll see if Dervla's still up.* Seamus continued his slow walk to the inn, deep in thought.

When he entered the building, he glanced around the near-deserted common room. He guessed Dervla and Lucius were upstairs, so he didn't want to run the risk of interrupting them. The tired Seamus considered going to bed first and inform someone after waking up, so he headed toward the stairs.

On the way, he spotted two men talking over mugs of mulled wine by the crackling hearth and recognized them as

Martinel and Father Patricius. He liked them, and neither one was a Roman. *Maybe they'll be interested in what I heard.*

Seamus grinned when Father Patricius' face crinkled into a smile as he approached. He felt a kinship to the priest, who once said he'd been a slave to a Hibernian chieftain when he was about the boy's own age. Seamus always held an interest in hearing about his people, who he'd never seen. The priest had said they were a hardheaded pagan people but had good and loving hearts, and he dreamed more and more of returning there to bring them the word of God.

His reflection ended when Martinel put down his mug. "Well, lad, what's keeping you up at this late hour?"

With a side glance at the priest, Seamus dug his heels into the floor. "Father, is it a sin to repeat an overheard conversation?"

Patricius stroked his beard. "That's not an easy one to answer. I suppose if it will save someone from being hurt, it would be good to tell."

Seamus sighed. *Never a straight yes or no.* "Okay, I don't know for sure. I'll tell you, and you can tell me if I've sinned."

Martinel cleared some space on the bench, and Seamus sat down and revealed what he overheard. When he finished, he expected the two men to laugh at him, but they both looked deadly serious.

"The marine legionary commander said he saw Petronius Maximus being captured by the Vandals a few days ago," said Martinel, looking hard at the boy. "How long ago was this?"

"About an hour, I guess."

Martinel leapt from his seat. "Padre, rouse Lucius. I'm going to gather my men." The door slammed against the wall as he rushed out.

Father Patricius raced up the stairs, taking two at a time. Seconds later, Lucius flew down the same flight of stairs, belting on his sword over his night shirt. Dervla and Father Patricius followed close behind.

The tribune called over his shoulder, "Padre, alert the city. If we're not in time, we're going to need a lot of help very soon." He burst through the open door and started bellowing to his cohort's guards. "To arms, to arms! The enemy is upon us!"

Soon, clarions blared, and legionaries formed into ranks still tying down parts of their armor. Lucius moved barefoot, but he'd put on his breastplate and helmet that Dervla brought with them. His men readied themselves in seconds, but it felt like hours before they moved.

* * *

The nervous militia captain looked down from the barbican, or gate house, and patted the purse of gold tucked inside his tunic. "This city stinks of its constant politics." Upon observing the legionaries standing on the outer side of the barred entrance, he rubbed his chin. "That definitely looks like General Maximus leading them." He roared to his soldiers, "Lift the portcullis and open the gate. Be quick about it! That's General Maximus out there!"

With his dagger prodding Maximus in the back, Axise grinned wide as the portico lifted and the massive doors creaked open. He whispered to the Vandal captain beside him, "The gambit's working. This fat city is ours." He barked in his best Latin, "Legion, forward!"

Five hundred Vandals in rent and bloody Roman armor surged through the gates. They glanced nervously at the eyes watching them through the murder holes in the gate house walls. They passed beneath the walls and into the open square inside the city.

* * *

An old guard standing by the lift pulleys in the gate house ceiling studied the legionaries passing through. He'd served twenty years in the legions before he retired, but his senses hadn't dulled with time. He scratched his jaw and called over the other two guards in the small room. "Something doesn't smell right. Their armor looks like it's been through bloody hell, but I don't see a scratch on any of those men." The murmur from the soldiers filing in below sounded off. "That's not Latin they're speaking. It must be more mercenaries. At least we have more troops to fight the Vandals."

The guard moved to the release lever that would drop the portcullis, but he had to wait until the outer gates were closed. He wanted to be ready in case a Vandal raiding party showed up.

When he heard terrified screams in the bailey, he froze for an instant. The old guard looked out the murder hole and gasped. The militia captain breathed his last as gold coins from a torn purse glistened in the pool of blood that spread around him. The newly arrived legionaries went crazy and began slaughtering the city militia men. The truth of the situation hit him as a number of them pounded up the gate house steps.

"We are betrayed. Bar the door!" he called to the two men in the barbican with him. The iron bar dropped into place just as a heavy thud slammed into the door. It was stout oak, but it would not hold long against the axes hammering on it from the other side.

The old guard looked back down. All of his friends in the bailey lay dead. However, his heart lifted as the invaders formed a defensive line. Roman legionaries approached—real legionaries.

The axe work began to splinter the door. He walked to the portcullis wheel and released the lever. The grate winched down at a crawl. If the invaders made their way in, they could raise the portico again with ease.

The old guard made eye contact with the two terrified men holding their swords by the entranceway. "Good-bye, my friends. Die well." He threw himself onto the chains of the grate's rising counterweight stone. Just before he was crushed in the housing high above, he jammed his sword in the mechanism's gears.

* * *

Axise laughed and gathered up the coins and the torn purse from the dead militia captain. "I hope you enjoyed your wealth while you had it." With that done, he walked over to

Petronius Maximus and drove his blade though the Praetorian general's chest. "Thank you for your service."

As the Roman slid to the ground, one of his men rushed up. "Captain Axise, there's a troop of legionaries advancing on our position. They're coming fast."

"That's sooner than I expected, but they're too late." Axise studied the oncoming force for a moment and remained confident that they could hold the gate house long enough. "Raise the portcullis and light the beacon! Archers, up on the ramparts!"

* * *

Lucius didn't like the looks of the situation as he approached. A couple dozen militiamen lay dead in the courtyard, and obvious non-Roman legionaries formed up to meet them.

A man behind him screamed in surprise and fell when an arrow shot through his chest. Lucius cursed and looked up at the battlements before turning to the centurion beside him. "Cilla, in the name of God, clear those ramparts! We're easy prey for their archers!"

Lucius knew he had to move fast. The Porta Salaria portcullis was down, but the gate sat wide open. *If that grate lifts, the entire Vandal army will walk right in.* "Shields up! Forward!"

The two sides closed on each other in seconds. The Romans fought as a coordinated unit while the Vandals dueled as individuals, but they were the greatest warriors that army had. Lucius groaned and realized time was his enemy. He led a fresh assault, but his group had to pull back.

The tribune glanced up at the gate house, which swarmed with Vandals. *Why haven't they raised the portcullis yet?*

Shock hit Lucius when he caught sight of his counterpart. It was the Vandal who had led the raiding party on his first engagement four years ago.

As those thoughts crossed his mind, a few of the barbarians yanked a crushed human body and a broken sword from the mechanism. Both hit the ground by the gate house, and the grate started to rise at a slow pace. Meanwhile, the Vandal leader roared, "Light the beacon!"

His fear at seeing the fire blaze turned to confusion as the ground trembled beneath his feet. The confusion turned to a triumphant smile as a wild pack of Frankish lancers charged up a side street into the Vandal flank.

* * *

Father Patricius gasped for air as he tried to keep up. When he left the inn, the first Roman officer he found was Satewa. *Why doesn't that surprise me? The man's every-where.*

The nervous priest encountered Satewa near the Castra Praetoria where the Praetorians who served the former emperor had been sequestered. A full cohort of these men now raced along the battlements, following Satewa. The frantic priest searched his surroundings as he tried to catch his breath.

A day earlier, they fought for the old emperor. Now they fight for Rome, but I'd still feel a lot better if they were Red Fists.

As they came into sight of the wild melee, Satewa unleashed a war cry that chilled Patricius down to his blood and sprinted ahead. The Praetorians picked up the yell and swarmed past the priest. They closed in on the Vandals, heedless of the missile volleys scything through their ranks.

Father Patricius paused to wipe his brow and gazed out over the ramparts. At first, he stared hard into the moonlit darkness, confused at how the ground trembled under his feet. *Is the ground moving?* He recoiled in terror. *It's the entire Vandal Army coming this way.*

He screamed Satewa's name, and the Mohawk somehow heard him over the din of battle and followed where the priest's wild gestures pointed. The Mohawk warrior pulled himself up the outside wall of the gate house. Soon after, three bodies fell below and the beacons were extinguished. However, the black wave of Vandals didn't slow their advance toward the open portal.

* * *

In the courtyard, the fight had almost ended. Lucius nodded in grim determination. His Romans ground into the shrinking enemy force, and now arrows from the battlements rained down upon the Vandals. His heart sank as he looked through the gate at the shadowy vast horde approaching. *We can't close the gates in time now.*

He scanned the field and saw the Vandal leader charging at him. With a berserk roar, Axise ran across the bailey followed by his remaining men.

Lucius moved slowly, weighed down by fatigue. Seeing the gashes in his armor brought to mind an unhappy Dervla scolding him. The remaining Vandals advanced in his direction. Despite the crowd in the battlefield, Lucius felt horribly isolated.

Romans fell on the charging Vandals like a pack of wolves, but their leader brushed aside all who opposed him and focused on Lucius with a burning hatred in his eyes. Lucius raised his sword, and their blades crashed together many times. The force of the blows drove the weakened tribune back. His bare feet slipped on the blood-smeared ground, and he fell with a heavy impact. Lying almost supine, Lucius extended his weapon in a futile effort to defend himself.

The Vandal leader raised his sword and smiled in triumph.

Then Lucius caught Seamus out of the corner of his eye. The boy clutched his knife, leapt on the Vandal captain's back, and drove the blade in deep. He kept stabbing as Axise fell dead, much like what Dervla had done to Publius. A few moments later, Seamus stopped his vicious assault.

Lucius met the boy's eyes and groaned out, "Thank you."

"That was for my sister," came the stiff reply. "Treat her well."

Lucius opened his mouth to answer when Centurion Cilla ran up. "Tribune, we have a big problem. The entire Vandal army's going to be here soon, and we can't close the gate."

Lucius staggered to his feet. "What do you mean? Just shut the damn thing!"

"Sorry, sir. The winch on the portcullis is broken, and the gates are jammed open."

"In the name of the Lord Jesus, how long will it take to unjam them?"

"It'll take us ten minutes, sir, but we don't have ten minutes."

Lucius' exhaustion exploded into frustration and rage. It cooled, though, when Praetorian Tacturnus approached him.

"Tribune, I can buy you those ten minutes," he declared in a flat voice. "My men will hold the road until the gate is closed."

A vast chill locked Lucius in place. "But you'll be trapped on the wrong side when that happens."

The Praetorian stiffened to attention, showing a half smile. "We committed much evil in the name of what we thought was right. Let this be our penance. Perhaps we can earn a better name than cockroaches from the Red Fist."

Tacturnus pivoted and ordered his troops to move. The black-clad cohort marched out the gateway and formed into a square bristling with spears.

Tears welled in his eyes, but Lucius turned away to meet the officers around him. "I want every man who has a bow up on the ramparts. And close that godforsaken gate!"

He crouched down in silence as he heard the snap of a hundred bows and the screams of pain that followed. Bitter tears left him when the enormous gates closed and steel bars locked the two groups of soldiers in their places. When the portcullis grate at long last clanged down into its moorings, the cries from the far side of the wall had already ceased.

CHAPTER XXXV

MOVES AND COUNTER MOVES

"Your Majesty, we can still crush them," the burly captain pleaded. "They were lucky at the Porta Salaria. If we'd been just minutes sooner, we would've won our way in."

King Genseric chuckled without any mirth. Ahead of him and his soldiers loomed the walls of Rome, whose battlements teemed with angry men. "No, Captain. Two days ago, we could've strolled into the city and would've been offered whatever treasure we desired. Yesterday, five hundred of them fought against our numbers to buy those precious few minutes. Today, we would have to rip it from their dying hands."

The king examined the map of the area. "A long siege will never work. We must draw that damned Aetius out in the open. He's the one who's giving them a spine. When he falls, those fat Romans will be like sheep, ready to be sheared."

The captain crossed his arms and studied the map himself. "Your Majesty, if he's so smart, how are we going to get him out here in the open?"

Genseric met the captain's eyes, then those of all his commanders. "The greatest weakness Aetius has is his loyalty. I have good reports that two Red Fist legions will be here soon, and we stand between them and the city. When they get here, we'll annihilate them. Aetius will believe he has no choice but to attempt a rescue. He'll lead whatever troops he has inside the city to save them. That's when we'll strike."

* * *

Emperor Aetius smiled at the consternation on his friend's face. "Satewa, most men would consider this a great honor."

"I am not 'most men.' I vowed to protect your worthless hide. How can I do that if I'm the legate in command of the cockroaches— I mean, Praetorians?"

239

"Isn't it the responsibility of the Praetorians to look after my well-being? Now you'll have five thousand men to do so with."

"It was never my plan to sit behind thick stone walls and grow fat," Satewa retorted.

"Well, since I'll be going after Genseric when the other Red Fist legions arrive, I think you'll be plenty busy keeping my 'worthless hide' from getting poked full of holes."

"Bah! I had hoped you'd become more reasonable when you became Chief of the Romans, but you're as stubborn as you've ever been." Satewa jumped and headed for the throne room exit.

He almost ran over Lucius, who limped his way in.

Satewa paused and examined the bandaged tribune. "How are your wounds, Lucius?"

"Not too bad. I think the lecture I got from Dervla hurt more."

Satewa's face softened, and his eyes glistened. "She reminds me much of my Brenda. Be good to her. One never knows when your paths will part."

Lucius nodded in understanding. "I will, my friend. I will."

Recollecting himself, an idea came to Satewa. "I've just been put in command of the Praetorians. I could use you as my second-in-command. Join me."

The emperor walked up to them then. "Oh, no, you don't. I have another job for Tribune Bernius."

The one in question gawked at the emperor, confused. "Your Majesty?"

"Lucius, I want you to be the Legate of the Second Legion. I need a good, levelheaded commander who I can trust completely, and that's you."

"Sire, I've been in the army for just five years. Surely there are many others who are far more experienced."

Aetius and Satewa's eyes met and both men smiled, but it was the latter who spoke up. "I dare say there are very few men who have found themselves in as much trouble as you and gotten out of it. For once, the emperor has shown wisdom. Besides, now I'll have someone to take notes while I sleep during those tedious commander meetings." The Mohawk warrior slapped the newly promoted legionary's shoulder. "Congratulations, Legate. It looks like we're both being punished."

* * *

Two days later, Lucius sat next to Satewa at the emperor's war council meeting. His new prefect and second-in-command, Martinel, sat on the other side of him while the city militia captain sat across from them. At the head of the table, Emperor Aetius scowled at a detailed map before him. Small wooden markers showed the known locations of enemy troop placements along the Tiber River from Rome to Ostia.

"It looks like the Vandals are definitely digging in," said Aetius.

The city militia commander cocked his head. "They can't hope to starve us out with a siege. You said yourself that two legions will be here soon."

Without taking his eyes off the map, Aetius released a grim sigh. "That's our problem. Those troops will have no way to reach us. They'll march right into a deathtrap, and we'll be stuck watching it from the walls. We must warn Legate Albinus, but the scouts I sent out last night were returned headless this morning. They can't get in, and we can't get out."

Martinel stroked his beard and studied the markers on the map. In a quiet voice he said, "I'll do it."

Aetius shot him a look, his eyebrows knitting. "Martinel, we had skilled scouts who tried. They're all dead now."

"With all respect, sire, I can get through where your men could not because I can pass for a Vandal. I speak their language without an accent and know the names of some of their commanders."

"You would do this for Rome?"

"No, but I'll do it for a friend."

Aetius dipped his head to the Frank. "Then go see the quartermaster and get what you need. May God be with you."

With haste, Martinel bowed and excused himself.

* * *

The cloud-covered night sky helped. Martinel slipped from the well-oiled sally port door and dropped down outside the city's walls with nary a sound. He adjusted his Vandal nobleman's garb, pilfered from a previous skirmish with the Vandals some years ago. The quartermaster had wished him better luck with the breastplate than its previous owner, though the Frank didn't find much comfort in the remark. Sighing, he scanned the field for any sign of movement from the pickets he knew were out there. *I really stuck my foot in it now. Hide in plain sight. Should be simple enough.*

Martinel crept along until he detected a telltale shift in the shadows to his left. He straightened himself out and called, "Who goes there?"

Three wary men approached him. "And who are you?" asked a short, barrel-chested man with a broadsword.

"Not so loud. Those damn Roman ballistae can reach this far," Martinel replied in an authoritative voice. "Have you seen anything suspicious yet?"

"Nothing, sir."

"Well, I don't like it. Those Romans are sneaky bastards. Keep your heads down but a sharp eye open." Martinel began to walk off. "I need to check the other pickets. Carry on."

The short one shrugged at the others. "Damn nobles, popping up out of nowhere like that. It scares me half to death."

"Yeah, but he's right about those Romans trying something," said another of the three nervous men who looked around. "I just hope they don't try it here."

Martinel continued on stilted legs, waiting for the bite of an arrow to strike his back and feeling relieved when it didn't come. A short while later, he used the same ruse on another set of watchmen, and not only did it work, but he acquired one of their horses and rode at a canter down the Via Tiburtina.

It was a hot and muggy night, but he would've been sweating profusely even if it were the middle of winter. After traveling for some time, he noticed he hadn't seen any Vandals in quite a while, but he stayed his course. *Another hour this way, and then I'll cut north. How hard can it be to find an army?*

At dawn, he found a cart trail running through the rolling hills and scrub forest that appeared to go in the right direction. At midmorning, he found the Red Fist. More precisely, they found him.

"Hold, stranger. State your business," commanded a decurion. The voice spoke in guttural but clear Latin.

Martinel sighed in relief at the sight of the decurion standing on the path with crossed arms. However, the spears pressed against his side and the hard glares put him back on edge. Somehow, he kept his voice steady. "I need to speak with Legate Albinus."

"So how does a fancy savage like you know the legate?" The comment elicited a lot of appreciative chuckles.

Martinel's temper flared near its breaking point. "Will you take me to the legate, or do I have to ride over you?"

The decurion's eyebrows arched, and then his mouth tightened into a thin line. "Well, friend, I'll take you to headquarters. But if no one there knows you, I'll take personal pleasure in being the one to kill you. We can pile your corpse on top of the other Vandal spies who tried to sneak through here earlier. Now get off the horse."

Martinel grudgingly complied. The legionaries took his sword and bound his arms with rawhide thongs.

"I grant you this much, barbarian: your Latin is far better than the ones who came before."

"Decurion, I am Prefect Martinel of the Second Red Fist Legion. Trust me, you will regret this insult."

The decurion paused and stared at Martinel. "I met the prefect of the second. He was a skinny greybeard from Sorrento. That's not you, but for the sake of argument, let's say you are who you say you are. I would expect you would be thanking me for doing my job well."

Seeing no ways out of this, Martinel sighed in resignation. "Okay, let's just go, then."

When they entered the camp, Martinel glanced at the standard and grew more nervous. *It's the Third Legion. I don't think I know any of the officers here.*

The legionaries marched him to the Praetorium. The legate was sitting on a camp stool reviewing a crudely sketched map with his centurions. The legate lifted a questioning eyebrow toward the decurion.

The decurion saluted in return. "Sir, this man claims to be the Prefect of the Second Legion."

Martinel nudged his way to the front. "Aye, that's true, and I bring you important information from *Emperor* Aetius."

The legate's eyebrows shot up his bald forehead. All eyes locked in on Martinel, including one who jumped up with a broad grin.

"Hello, Martinel. It's very good to see you."

Martinel looked upon the familiar and friendly face with relief and recognition. "Hello, Marcus. I hear congratulations are in line. A son, as I heard it."

Marcus beamed. "And an incredible set of lungs he has, too. Julia is getting little sleep." His smile dropped somewhat. "We named him Takumi."

Martinel bowed his head. "That's a good choice. He was among the finest men I'd ever met."

The stern legate eyed Marcus, who had recently transferred over from the First Legion. "So, Prefect, I take it you vouch for this man."

"Aye, Legate Justinian. My dearest friend trusts his life to this man, and so do I." Marcus turned to Martinel. "Prefect, is it? Lucius must be twisted in a knot knowing you outrank him."

"Well, Marcus, that's not quite true. Lucius is now the Legate of the Second Legion."

The bald commander spluttered, "Lucius? Lucius Bernius is the Legate of the Second Legion? That boy is still wet behind the ears. Is Aetius crazy?"

"*Emperor* Aetius may believe he can do the impossible, but he is as sane as he ever was. Also, the Praetorians have a new legate—Satewa."

A stunned Justinian settled back on his stool. "That appointment is a major upgrade from Maximus. And Valentinian?"

"Dead, along with most of his lackeys."

"There'll be few tears shed for that one. At any rate, it appears you have much to tell us. You better sit down."

Justinian caught the eye of one of his orderlies. "Get this man some hot food and a proper uniform." He turned back to Martinel, frowning as he studied the Frank's face. "It's disconcerting to be talking to the image of a Vandal noble."

Martinel settled in and moved some of the markers on the map, then added several more to the positions held by the Vandals. He took a sip of wine from a goblet offered to him and relayed the events of the last few days. An hour later, Legate Albinus joined them.

Once he was caught up to speed, a frustrated Albinus growled. "I don't see what we can do. There's too few of us. We can't get in, and the emperor can't leave. Genseric can sit back and pick us off at his leisure. He knows Roman tactics far too well."

Prefect Carloman had been calm through the whole report, turning thoughtful, and he cocked his head. "Perhaps we can use that against him." All eyes swung over to him, and he leaned forward and returned their looks. "Here's my plan."

CHAPTER XXXVI

LEGIONS

Lucius stood at the battlement, watching the distant horizon fraught with worry. With the Tiber River behind them, Genseric's troops worked hard to construct breastworks facing both toward the city and north.

His concerns dulled a bit a as two slim arms wrapped around his waist and a head leaned on his back, prompting him to smile. "Dervla, you shouldn't be up here."

"And Lucius, nothing is going to change with you staring at it."

Lucius sighed and hung his head. "How do we fight so large an entrenched army?"

Dervla squeezed him. "Put on your war face. That will scare them."

He pulled her around in front of him and caressed her cheek. "And why is that, my darling? When I try it on you, you just dig your heels in harder." Lucius sighed, his eyes returning to the horizon. "I just wish I knew if Martinel is all right and if he got through with our messages."

Dervla smiled up at him, then twisted and gazed at the field with the sun lowering in the sky. Slowly, her smile faded. "Lucius, what's going on out there?"

He strained his eyes at a dusty haze in the distance. "I don't know."

An excited shout sounded from the bastion above them, followed by a runner bursting through the tower door.

Lucius held up his hand. "Hold, Legionary. What news?"

The soldier noted Lucius' rank and saluted. "Legate, it's our men. It appears to be about two legions. They're digging in opposite the Vandals."

Lucius nodded, and the soldier dashed down the battlement's flagstone steps. Lucius returned to his wife, and they watched the distant activity on the horizon until nightfall hid all from sight. Two customary legion fortifications rose during that time.

* * *

The next morning, both military personnel and civilians lined Rome's ramparts. Emperor Aetius, along with Lucius and Satewa, studied the field like a raptor. The Vandals repositioned troops to face the new threat.

After counting the banners, Satewa's face brightened as he called attention to some motion at the limit of his vision. "Two more full legions have arrived."

Aetius knitted his eyebrows. "What troops can those be? Maximus shifted all the mobile legions to Iberia."

His eyes swerved from the two new legion fortifications being built to the sudden swarm of activity from the Vandals to confront the expanding danger. The two sides spent the day staring at each other in silence over mounded dirt walls.

The morning of the third day brought thunderous cheers from the walls of Rome. Two more legions slogged in with their eagle standards glistening in the sunrise.

"Six legions!" Satewa roared. "We can sweep the Vandals into the sea."

Thoughtful, Aetius looked at the busy construction on both sides of the widening front. "True, but something seems very odd about this."

* * *

Inside the Vandal pavilion, a fuming Genseric pounded the table. "We can't maintain our siege. Their host grows every day, and we're stagnant. They're already too large for us to assault. We must return home with the treasure already won. At the rate the Romans are pouring in troops, we'll be overrun in a week." He sighed to clear his thoughts. "Our army is in intact, and our fleet rules the seas. Aetius is just one man, and he can't be everywhere. We'll wait for another opportunity and then strike hard."

The king stood under the wide pavilion holding back the late summer sun and looked at his frustrated commanders. Frowns abounded across all their faces, and the king cringed at how they'd react to his next order. "Start the evacuation."

* * *

The emperor reviewed a detailed map of the Tiber River area from Rome to Ostia. "It looks like they're definitely leaving. Our spies confirm the Vandals are loading their ships."

The militia commander rocked back on his bench. "Sire, your Red Fist legions are legendary fighters, but those other troops must be frontier guards from the Rhine. Your commanders must have stripped the border bare. They're not true soldiers. On open ground, they'll be cut to pieces."

The naval marine legate thumped the table. "The Red Fist won't be alone. Those were my ships they sank. I want to strike back."

Snarling, Satewa gave a knowing nod. "My Praetorians will be at the forefront."

Aetius held up his hands. "This will have to be done with care. We'll hit them hard when they're half evacuated. It will be the point when the Vandals will be most vulnerable."

Satewa scratched his head. "This will be tough, even for you."

Aetius sighed and collapsed on his throne. "I know, but I have no other options. Despite our grand history, we're a weak country surrounded by powerful neighbors. If the Vandals escape with their full army, they can hit us again at any time or place of their choosing. While we have our greatest strength marshalled, we have to find a way to hurt them. They must suffer so they won't even think of trying again."

Aetius glanced around the table. "Albinus and Justinian are experienced commanders. They'll be ready. When they see us make our move, six legions will fall on the Vandal flank. We attack with everything: the naval marines, the Praetorians, and the Second Legion. Rome has not been able to marshal such a force in over one hundred years."

* * *

On the morning of the second day after the war council meeting, Lucius and Dervla stood at their familiar place on the city's ramparts. Nervous, Lucius paced back and forth. He had nothing to do until he received the order to attack, but at least his legion stood ready. He studied the men in the tramped gardens below, where his Frankish lancers charged at one of his cohorts with blunted spears.

"This is good practice for them," Lucius observed. "The infantry will be facing Vandal cavalry soon, and they need to know what to expect."

Dervla looked up at him with strained eyes. "But why do you have to go? Your wounds are still not close to being healed yet. You'll be killed, and our baby will grow up never knowing his father."

Lucius pressed his hand on Dervla's flat belly. "I'll be very safe, my love. I'm a legate. My job is to direct the legion."

"I know you, Lucius Bernius. If you see a problem, you'll jump in and try to solve it yourself. One of these times, it's going to get you killed."

"I'll be careful."

"And in case you're not, I cornered Decurion Gentilius. I made him promise to drag you out of any fight you stick that big nose of yours into."

"Dervla, you can't go ordering my men about. It will—"

Motion caught Lucius' eye out in the no man's land between the two armies. A single rider wearing a colorful silk cape that billowed out behind him galloped toward the city. In hot pursuit and closing the distance were about twenty Vandal horse archers.

There's only one man who would try a stupid stunt like this. Lucius hollered down to his legionaries practicing below. "Ho, cavalry, I need you to run a sortie, now! Lord Martinel is in trouble!"

Seconds later, a couple hundred lancers barreled out of the opened gate. Lucius turned his eyes to the field as the two forces raced toward each other.

* * *

Martinel clung to his horse's neck as the ground flew by beneath his steed's hooves. Ahead of him, the walls of Rome still appeared far away.

Maybe this wasn't such a great idea after all. An arrow bumped into his armored back, perhaps the third one to do so, and he squeezed his eyes shut for a second. *Thank you, Master Takumi.*

The old swordmaster had told once of a story about his homeland. *"Our riders wore silk capes into combat because, if forced to flee, the silk would stop the arrows."* Martinel remembered having laughed at the tale back then, but the old boy proved himself right from beyond the grave. Martinel doubted the cape would stop a spear, however, and his pursuers drew closer by the second.

A moment later, he heard the sound of cheering from the city's battlement and felt the rush of air as a Roman cavalry unit swept past him. When he looked back, the Vandal horsemen beat a hasty retreat to their own bulwarks. Martinel slowed his horse to a canter and was soon joined by an escort of lancers.

Riding next to him was his old Frankish captain, Victorux, whose laugh caught the nobleman's attention. "Well, sir, I guess the Vandals weren't as bad of shots as we first thought."

Martinel glanced over his shoulder and sighed. Six arrows lay entangled in his cape.

He forgot the sight in short order when he led his procession through the wide-open city gates. Many had watched his flight from the city's walls, and a crowd had gathered at the portal. They broke into an uproarious cheer when the daring rider entered.

Martinel waved to his admirers until he spotted a very angry Legate Bernius approaching him. "You damn idiot! You could've gotten yourself killed."

"I missed you, too, Lucius." Martinel patted him on the back, but his joyful face soon turned somber. "You better join me. I have news for the emperor that you should hear."

* * *

"What? You're not serious!"

"I am afraid so, Your Majesty. We have but two legions."

Aetius slumped onto his throne.

"How can that be?" asked the city militia commander. "We saw six legions march in."

Martinel gave a wan smile. "No, you didn't. At night, most of the Red Fist marched out, and by morning, they marched back in again."

"But we counted them. They were full legions."

The Frank smiled but remained sheepish. "Did you? It was Prefect Carloman's idea. The standards were there for every cohort and century, but there wasn't near that many men. Oh, we trussed up some of the auxiliaries to look like legionaries, but there were only half the men you thought you saw. I can tell you that after three days of marching and fort building, the men can't stand much longer."

Aetius rubbed his jaw. "The ruse most definitely worked. It fooled us, and it fooled Genseric." Downcast, he stared at the map and shook his head in denial. "Unfortunately, it also means we can't end this. The fighting will continue. The Vandals will have time to regroup and attack wherever they will. All I'll be able to do is react, but it will always be too late."

The emperor clasped his hands behind his back and stared forlornly at the marbled floor. "Go prepare your men. When their rear guard is thin enough, I intend to hit them as brutally as we can. I want Genseric to have at least one sour memory of this venture."

CHAPTER XXXVII

GREEK FIRE

Clarions blared across the walls of Rome, and its great gates blew wide open. Horns in the distant Roman forts echoed the sound.

The men in the Second Red Fist Legion stayed calm as they waited for the orders to march, double-checking their equipment. They were all veterans now and had triumphed over every foe they had faced over the last four years. They were confident today would be no different.

Lucius' stomach twisted in a knot as he watched his soldiers. We're not strong enough to destroy our enemies. We beat them; they retreat and come back later in a different place. Each time we win, we lose a few more of our legionaries, and I lose a few more of the men who trust me. They're good men. Their lives shouldn't be wasted. They deserve a chance at a final victory.

The horns sounded again, and Lucius led his legion out of Rome and streamed toward the port town of Ostia. During the night, the marine legionaries slipped down the Tiber River on barges behind the enemy rear guard. The few thousand Vandals who thought were secure behind their palisades found themselves assaulted from the rear as they attempted to meet the oncoming Roman war machine.

The defenders remained unaware of the marine legionnaires until they heard loud shouts of, "Board them!" Resistance collapsed, and the surviving Vandals fled to their waiting ships. Many didn't make it.

As the remnants of the Vandal rear guard fell during the savage fight on the piers, Emperor Aetius and his commanders moved to the top of the lighthouse at the point of the harbor. The light of the rising sun enabled them to watch the enemy horde slip out to sea. Lucius stared with a sense of helpless impotence. Hundreds of Vandal ships bobbed in the water far outside the emperor's grasp.

Lucius spotted something and pointed to the south. "Look at that!"

On the southern sea, a small fleet of warships displaying Byzantine banners sailed right at the immense Vandal armada. The Byzantine ships sailed with such incredible speed, Lucius had to do a double-take to believe what his eyes beheld. Beside him, the emperor and the other officers gasped in bewilderment.

Fear flashed across Aetius' face. "Are they insane? That's a suicide mission!"

For those who watched, what occurred next would stay with them for the rest of their lives. The Byzantine ships spat streams of fire at any enemy warship that came within twenty yards of them. Rather than the casks of flaming oil the Romans used in their catapults, however, it was torrents of unquenchable flames that continued to burn even on the surface of the water. The screams of the afflicted carried all the way to the lighthouse where the Romans stood.

The Vandals gave up all pretense of fighting the hellish vessels and fled toward the African coast. The Byzantine fleet pursued on the light winds. The flames devoured the Vandal ships that could not keep ahead.

As the chaos subsided, one Byzantine ship broke away and sailed into the Roman port. Lucius gaped when he recognized his old friend Phokas, covered in soot, standing at its prow.

* * *

For the entire next day, Rome went wild with celebration, and Aetius hosted his first banquet as emperor. Braziers burned all around the imperial garden as the nobility arrived dressed in their finest togas.

Initially, most looked with disdain at the small, ragged group gathered in a corner. They looked out of place at an imperial function and made no attempt to mingle with the city's aristocracy. They kept to themselves, talking and laughing, content in each other's company.

But when the emperor interrupted the feasting to recognize and reward each of them, they became the center of interest. The guests saw a new center of power forming in Rome, and the self-serving courtiers attempted to join that circle. None stayed long. Petty flattery could not compete with bonds forged in fire and blood.

During the celebrations earlier, Emperor Aetius had presented each of the heroes with extravagant gifts inside well-crafted chests made of a dark lacquered wood. Even young Seamus was awarded one of those prized trophies for saving the day at the Porta Salaria.

In the midst of discussing the battle in the sea, Doctor Phokas arched an eyebrow at Marcus Carloman. "We call it Greek fire. You've seen it before. In fact, you carried a jar of it four years ago, when we first met."

Marcus stared at him, disbelieving at first, but then a glint of recognition dotted his eyes as he fell back in his seat.

The doctor basked in a few more praises and the food at the celebration feast before he poked Lucius in the ribs. "A bit different than our last visit to this place."

A young man in regal dress sat down to join them. Phokas bowed his head and handed him a silver goblet filled with wine. "I don't believe any of you have been introduced yet. This is Zeno, the son-in-law of the Byzantine Emperor Marcian." He waved a chicken bone in the general direction of the port. "He's also, fortuitously, the admiral of that fleet out there."

Phokas gestured to Lucius next. "Lord Zeno, this is Lucius Bernius, Legate of the Red Fist Second Legion; Satewa, Legate of the Praetorian Guard; and Marcus Carloman, Prefect of the Red Fist First Legion." The doctor smirked and almost contained a laugh. "You'll have to forgive Marcus' lowly rank. He wasn't even in the army the last time we spoke."

The three men bowed to the prince, and Lucius declared, "I pray that someday, we can find a way to repay you for what you've done. You saved Rome. If it takes us a thousand years, we will honor this great debt."

Zeno smiled in turn. "I pray my country will never need such aid. I'm just pleased the siphons worked so well. The pressurized liquid delivery system had never been tested in a combat situation until yesterday. If they had failed, I think my father-in-law would've been rather angry with me for losing his ships."

Satewa leaned across the table, drawing everyone's attention. "So how is it that you happened upon us at our hour of need?"

Phokas glanced at Zeno, who nodded back, so the former said, "I'll answer that one. I'm not much of a believer in divine intervention, but if there is such a thing, then this was it. I was on my way to Constantinople, as you all know, when my ship pulled in at Corinth for fresh water and supplies. My brother and his family live there, so I took the opportunity to visit." A wistful look crossed his eyes, and he nodded toward the prince. "By happenstance, my brother had another guest."

"I have been charged with finding some of the pirates plaguing the islands off the Greek coast," Zeno added. "We wanted to experiment with our new weapon on their ships, but the pirates all disappeared whenever we showed up. We pulled into port at Corinth to see the good doctor's brother, Ionnes. He's a successful trader and collector of ancient maps, so I was hoping he could point us toward some useful trouble spots and hidden ports. When Phokas told me of your plans to over-throw Valentinian, I got an idea. Marcian hated the man and has great respect for Aetius, so I thought a little show of force in support of the revolt would please my wife's father. Besides, he didn't give me any specific directions as to *where* to look for pirates."

Phokas laughed quietly. "As we came up the Italian coast, we learned of the Vandal invasion and decided to lend a hand."

Zeno shared in the laugh, but then his tone turned serious. "We Byzantines knew we would have to face the Vandals sooner or later. I just decided that it would be sooner." With a bitter sigh, he added, "It's a savage world. Where would our two countries end up if we didn't look after each other?"

Lucius swirled the wine in his cup, content. The threat from Africa was gone. Rome could now focus its remaining strength on its northern borders.

* * *

At the Carthaginian Harbor, Genseric sat alone looking at the reports with increasing horror. All of his commanders were out in the Great Hall; he'd dismissed them himself. He didn't want any of them to see him distraught and disconcerted.

Half my fleet sunk. Much of my army and treasure lost at sea with those ships. He looked out his window toward the port. The fleet at rest there was but a skeleton of what he held just a few weeks earlier.

The parchments slipped from his hands and floated to the floor, but he didn't notice.

CHAPTER XXXVIII

PARTING OF FRIENDS

The summer waned, and the brutal heat broke in Rome. A round Dervla stroked her stomach and lifted her head to glance around the expansive room and the gathering it hosted with moist eyes.

Lucius gave her a reassuring hug, as if he could read her thoughts. It was the first time either of them had entered the Aetius Manor since Dervla's parents died, and now they were about to say more farewells. Even if they spoke with people who still lived, the inevitability of their departure hung heavy nonetheless.

He reminded himself that the manor no longer belonged to Aetius. The emperor refused to set foot in it now that the manor held too many painful memories of his wife and son. Thus, he'd passed ownership to Satewa. The giant man had changed nothing about the house, however, as a tribute to his late wife, Brenda.

Lucius smiled sadly as Satewa entered the dining room carrying a full tray of figs, cheese, and fresh bread. He watched the emotions play across his wife's face as she reached across the table and clutched her brother's hands. Lucius had known this day would come, but the foreknowledge hadn't blunted the impact of the moment. *Not now. Not so soon.*

Dervla looked straight into her brother's eyes. "You're my only family. Stay with us. You don't have to go."

Seamus smiled at her thickened waist. "Sister, Lucius is your family now. Your life is full." The young man turned away, and his face clouded over. "There's nothing for me here. Rome holds too many bitter memories. You've found a way to forget them, but I can't."

Tears glistened in Dervla's eyes. "No, brother, those horrors will always be there. But I found love, and it's a great healer."

"I'm truly happy for you, sister, but it's not for me. When Father Patricius told me of his plans for a mission in Hibernia,

I knew I had to go. It's the land of our ancestors. Perhaps there, I'll feel at home and find peace."

Dervla eyes flashed at Father Patricius, who sat beside two large backpacks. "Look after my brother. I don't know why you have to go traipsing off beyond the reaches of civilization."

Father Patricius returned the look to her and Lucius with a peaceful expression. "I have grown very tired of civilization. I leave the intrigue and defending of empires to younger men." He turned a content gaze to the crucifix atop the rough wooden staff he held. "The Hibernians are a rough people, but fair. They'll hear me out. If they don't like what I say, they'll let me know right to my face in no uncertain terms. But from my time among them as a youth, I think I'll succeed. I believe they'll be open to the Word of God."

Nearby, Marcus sliced a chunk of yellow cheese and added, "Don't worry, Dervla. They'll travel with me as far as Avenio, and from there, I'll be sure they have a proper escort through Gaul. But it's time for us to go. I've been away from Julia far too long."

Lucius sighed, downcast. "Are you sure, Marcus? The legions desperately need you."

"I'm very sure, brother. You were always the soldier. You're the one who worries about saving the world. I was always content to stand beside you and help you fight for your vision, but I can't go through life with my heart torn in two. No, my friend, I'll be content tending my vineyards and leaving the empire to you." A whimsical grin crossed his face. "Besides, you have Martinel to keep you humble."

Martinel smeared some honey on a piece of bread and gave Marcus a sidelong look. "You leave me an impossible task. The man's dreams have no bounds."

"You know the offer still holds. If you tire of the army, I could help you get established around Avenio."

"A farmer. That would be almost as bad as herding swine on my brother's estate. No, I'll stay here. Life around Lucius always finds a way to be exciting."

Dervla turned next to a glum Satewa and Doctor Phokas, who watched the good-byes from the corner. "And you two? What decisions have you made?"

Satewa gazed with longing in the direction of the sea and lowered his head. "For me, there is no choice. The family I have left sits on the throne in the imperial palace. I will stay by his side until I am called from this world and rejoin my Brenda."

Doctor Phokas went to Dervla and brushed his finger along her cheek. "I'm going home to my brother in Corinth. I'm a foolish old man, and I've missed much of what's important in life by my own choosing. I mean to rectify that in the time still allotted to me. I'm going to spend however many days the Good Lord grants me to be with my family."

Tears welled in Lucius' eyes as he memorized the familiar faces around the table. "Then this is it, isn't it? We'll never be together again."

Marcus walked up to Lucius and wrapped him in a fierce hug. "A thousand years could pass, and I'll still call you my brother. Besides, stranger things have happened. Perhaps we'll be together again, or our children, or our children's children." Though he pushed back and wiped tears from his own eyes, his throat tightened as he faced Seamus and Father Patricius. "Come on. The sun won't hold in the sky, and we have a long way to travel."

The priest and the young man hefted their packs and followed. Seamus spun around and ran to his sister, hugging her. "I swear by all that is holy that, when I have a family, my children will always know you. I'll tell them every day." He dashed out the door before she could answer.

"I love you, Seamus," Dervla whispered as silent tears trickled down her face. As her brother disappeared along the street, she leaned on her husband and watched.

Lucius encircled her with his arm. "Let's go home, darling."

EPILOGUE

The highwaymen pounced on the group of monks without warning or mercy. Only Father Patricius fought his way out, dashing through the thick vegetation to the river. All the missionaries who followed him from Rome two months earlier lay dead. He cradled Seamus in his arms as he hid in the reeds on the banks of the Great Stour River. The cleric needed help; the boy was losing blood.

It felt like an eternity, but the thieves finished stripping the dead in time. The leader slit the throats of any who still breathed. Father Patricius heard the bandit he wounded in his escape plea for mercy. Another called out, "Hey, Beck, one of these monks had a pouch of coins."

Someone gasped. "Boys, there's enough gold here to set us up for life! C'mon, let's get outta here!"

The cleric listened to the fading steps of the gang until the woodland noises remained. He waited another fifteen minutes before crawling back onto shore and pulled off both of their waterlogged packs. He ripped open the boy's shirt and felt sick to the pit of his stomach upon seeing the severity of the wound.

Seamus looked at him through blurry eyes. "Am I going to die, Father?"

The priest dug through his bag and pulled out a poultice wrapped in an oilskin. "No. As God is my witness, you'll live."

As he finished tying down the bandages on the ugly gash, the cleric sniffed the air and smelled smoke. Charcoal smoke. A village had to be close. Seamus groaned as Father Patricius lifted him onto a hastily constructed litter. From there, Patricius didn't stop moving until they reached the small settlement of crude huts. By then, Seamus had fallen still and silent.

The suspicious eyes of the villagers stared at the priest as he fell to his knees in utter exhaustion. "Help me. Please, in the name of God, help me."

A young woman with dark eyes walked up and examined Seamus, then called over the gathered villagers. "Carry him to my house," she ordered. The others jumped to comply.

As they walked to a rough stone hut, she studied the monk's robe that Father Patricius wore. "So you're a follower of this Jesus?"

"I am," he answered proudly, "and you're a druid healer."

"I am," she responded with a cautious voice.

"Good. Seamus needs decent care."

Her brows lifted in surprise. "You're familiar with us."

"Aye. I was a druid myself until I found a greater truth. I am called Father Patricius."

The young woman nodded in return and replied, "Allis."

She pulled back the deer skin hanging over the entrance to her hut, and they followed the litter bearers inside.

* * *

Seamus returned to consciousness as he felt the warmth of a smoky peat fire. He watched a young woman by Father Patricius arrange her ointments and herbs and gave her a weak smile. The father called the woman Allis amid their quiet trade of words.

"Be careful around him," said Seamus. "Father Patricius could convert the devil himself."

Allis smiled back. "Oh, I will." She leaned over and removed the blood-soaked linen. Her raven-colored hair cascaded around her head.

"You're beautiful," Seamus whispered.

"I thought you said the monk was the one with the golden tongue. It appears you're the one I need to be wary of." She probed the wound with deft fingers, and her brows furrowed as she reached for her ointments. Allis smiled at him with reassurance. "I've seen worse. You'll live." She smeared the poultice over the wound. "You folks aren't from around here. Where do you call home?"

Seamus gritted his teeth at the pain but kept his head clear. "I have no home. Until two months ago, I lived my entire life in Rome, but it was never home. We journey to Hibernia."

Allis rocked back on her heels. "Rome... I've heard of that place. Is it as magical as the legends say?"

Seamus looked toward the thatched ceiling, his thoughts wandering through his memories of Rome. "It's no different from any other place. There are good people there, as well as evil—just a lot more of both."

Allis pressed the back of her hand on his forehead and nodded. "And where is this Hibernia? I've never heard of it."

"Oh, it's quite real, I assure you," Patricius chimed in. "I herded sheep there for two years as a slave. Your people may know of it as Eire."

She cocked an eye at him. "Traveling from a place of magic to the home of brutish savages doesn't speak well for your sanity."

"You mistake them. They can be gentle and thoughtful." The priest bobbed his head toward Seamus. "Some are even heroes. Did you know this man here personally saved the Roman Empire?"

Allis giggled and shook her head. "It looks like this will be a winter full of interesting tales. With the wound Seamus has, you won't be going anywhere until spring."

* * *

Every Sunday thereafter, the villagers gathered to hear the wondrous stories Father Patricius told. The priest found it a pleasant time. When Seamus grew hale again, he often accompanied Allis on long walks through the snow-covered fields. The village had never known a more pleasant winter.

As the days grew longer, it warmed the priest's heart to see the two young people go on those strolls hand in hand with their heads close together. Allis and Seamus never wandered far apart. It also pleased him that, one by one and then by families, the villagers came to him for baptism. As the spring flowers blossomed and the trails began to dry, even the druid healer became just the village healer.

One morning, Seamus despaired upon catching Father Patricius packing his bag. He gazed long at Allis and placed his fancy, lacquered box into his sack.

The priest turned his head at the sound, then met Seamus' eyes. "What do you think you're doing?"

"I'm packing," Seamus replied, confused that he'd heard the question at all.

"And why would you do that?" A small smile crept onto the priest's face.

"Because we're leaving?"

"Don't be absurd. I'm leaving and you're staying."

"But I promised to go with you to Hibernia."

"And I promised your sister to bring you home and help you find peace. You have found both here." Father Patricius looked fondly at Allis, who blushed a crimson red. "I have but one more task, if the two of you are agreeable."

Understanding, the two young people consented with nods of their heads.

* * *

A short while later, the first marriage of the year was held before the entire village population. The festivities lasted until sunset. The spring planting would start the next day, so the people all retired early. When most of the villagers had turned in, Seamus and Father Patricius sat alone by the dying embers of the bonfire.

"You'll have a good life here," said the priest. "Look to the future, but remember the past. I will live out my life by the Celtic version of my name—Patrick. It was the name I was known by as a slave in Eire."

Patricius pushed a charred branch deeper into the glowing coals. "My young friend, you've seen a lot of the world. Tell your stories to your children and grandchildren. Don't ever lose the gift of wonder." Chuckling, he threw the stick into the fire pit. "Perhaps someday, one of them will save the Roman Empire the way you did."

Seamus scoffed at the absurd notion, but he gave a serious look around the thatched huts of the simple village. He could never dream of anyone wanting to leave a place like this. Here, he could be who he chose without a king or nobleman to tell him otherwise. As much as he would miss the priest, he knew the village had become his home.

The next morning, Seamus rose and looked about and noticed Father Patricius—Patrick, rather—was gone. The priest's backpack and bedroll were missing. Seamus leaned on the door post and hung his head. *My last thin connection to Rome vanished in the night.*

The somber thoughts left him when two slim arms wrapped themselves around his waist. He turned and kissed Allis full on the lips. Her warm breath enveloped him as his hands slipped down her slim back.

Allis leaned her head against his chest. "Your friend has left?"

"Yes, and I expect we'll never see him again. I'll miss him. He was like another father to me."

"I believe you. He has an aura about him. He's a person of destiny."

"The man's a saint."

"So he's really going to that savage land?"

Seamus turned melancholy and looked down the empty lane. "Aye, the land of my ancestors, Hibernia."

Allis gave him a curious look and poked him in the ribs. "Then I pity the poor Celts who live there. They won't know what hit them. C'mon, darling. Breakfast is cooling."

Seamus stepped inside and paused as he spied the rich black lacquered box. He pulled out his knife, placed it inside his gift from the emperor, and put the box on a crude shelf by the fire pit. They would remain there as the last pieces of evidence of the life he once had.

He felt two arms wrap around him a second time, and a warm smile creased the young man's face. Seamus spun Allis around and kissed her again. "I love you."

They fell together laughing on the straw bed. Seamus had a late start planting the spring crops that day.

* * *

Little had changed in Rome since the Vandals' attempted invasion two years ago. Since then, the work to protect the empire hadn't ceased. Heading to meetings, as Lucius and Satewa did now, had become routine.

"Doesn't the man ever rest?" Lucius whispered to Satewa. "Ever since he ascended to the imperial throne, I've never seen him when he's not working."

Satewa furrowed his brows. "The man dreams of restoring Rome to what it once was and believes time is as much his enemy as the Vandals and Goths. Besides, we have yet to rest, either."

"Don't forget the Franks," Martinel growled from the other side of Lucius, nudging him with an arm. "I may be disowned for serving you decadent Romans too well, but they're also a force to be reckoned with."

Satewa let out a resigned sighed. "Very true, but the Franks and Goths aren't the immediate problem. The Vandals are."

Aetius rose from his chair and leaned on the table. "Gentlemen, we need to do more than react. Genseric has rebuilt his fleet, and it sails the Mediterranean with impunity. Wherever he strikes, we are always late to respond. It emboldens our enemies and costs us many good men that we can ill afford to lose, and we are too weak to assail him in Carthage." He pounded the table and leveled a look at each of the generals present. "We must draw his army away from their strongholds and hit them with our full might. I need ideas."

Bernius turned to Martinel and chuckled. "We could just ask King Genseric where his next attack will be so we could be ready for him."

Martinel sniffed and stifled a laugh, then paused as he mulled over a thought. After a few moments, he whispered, "Perhaps there *is* a way to ask him."

* * *

Six months later on a rainy spring evening, Lucius stomped past the guards outside the imperial throne room. In a slurred voice, he held a loud argument with an equally enraged Satewa. One of his hands carried a sealed jug of wine while the other jabbed the Praetorian legate.

As the guards opened the bronze doors for them, Satewa turned to the two guards. "We're not to be disturbed." He glanced at Aetius, who sat alone by a large table inside and gave him a pensive stare. "My prefect, Vivarius, will be joining us in about two hours. Admit him."

"Yes, sir," the two Praetorians replied in unison.

The two generals entered and strode to the table. They stood in silence until they heard the heavy door slam shut behind them. They both relaxed and saluted the emperor, then seated themselves at the table without waiting for permission.

Lucius thought Aetius looked more haggard than he did two and a half years ago. The Vandals had a chance to rebuild since those days, and their threat loomed large just like before. As Aetius predicted, the fighting had continued. Only a decisive blow would end the conflict and bring true peace to Rome. Lucius knew this, and he would not let himself rest until he fulfilled his duty to his country. Hopefully, their plan would lead them to the blow that they needed now more than ever.

Lucius nodded to Satewa before facing the emperor. "Your Majesty, everything is set." He pointed to the sealed jug that he deposited on the table and pulled a slim glass vial from inside his tunic.

Aetius rubbed his temples, now more gray than black. "Given everything you have done for me and Rome, you should be enjoying your just rewards, not doing this." Sighing, a deep concern etched onto his face. "We can still call this off. It's dangerous."

Lucius bit his lower lip. "The plan will work. Marcus' trading company is a legitimate enterprise, and Martinel is already there."

"Marcus is a Gaul; Martinel is a Frank; and your wife, Dervla, is a Celt. They can move there without drawing undo suspicion, but you are a Roman noble."

"A soon-to-be disgraced, treasonous legate who was once part of your inner circle, and one who knows all of your secrets." Lucius met Aetius' look with serious eyes. "I will be welcomed there."

"I love you like a son, Lucius. Be careful." The emperor stood, walked to the younger man, and clasped his arms. "These are desperate times, and Genseric is a crafty foe."

"I will be careful, but we need to learn their plans. This is the best way," Lucius said as he hugged Aetius.

"Then the die is cast. May you fare well in Carthage." The emperor returned to his chair and sagged into it, regarding the jug. "This is the poison?"

"Yes." Lucius unsealed the wax stopper on the small vial. "The jug contains a very toxic extract from a nightshade plant." He poured the contents of the small flask into two goblets. "And this is a sleep potion with death-like symptoms that will wear off in a day."

Satewa lifted his cup and swirled it. "Are you sure about this elixir?"

Lucius answered with a nod. "Dervla received meticulous and detailed instructions on how to brew the formula from Doctor Phokas. I insisted she try it on me when she made the first batch. I assure you it works as it's supposed to." His face turned hard. "Your Majesty, I haven't seen my legion for two months, but I know them. They'll remain loyal to me and fight to defend my honor."

Aetius rose, unsealed the jug of poisoned wine, and poured some of the contents into the goblets on the table. "Your legion has been transferred to Sicily. They're fairly isolated from other Roman units." A wry grin crossed his face. "They're also as close to you as we can place them in case you need help quickly."

Lucius bowed his head. "Thank you, sir."

"Three months is all you have," said Satewa. "Remember, I spent a year in Genseric's court. He is clever and will have his agents prying into every aspect of your story. They'll uncover the ruse eventually."

Lucius tapped his chest. "The reward of what I know is too great a temptation for someone that ambitious to ignore. He'll take the bait to use me against Rome." He regarded the goblets. "When your unconscious bodies are discovered, your imperial physicians will treat you for nightshade poisoning. It won't do any harm, but it will make you very nauseous."

Aetius lifted his cup and glanced at Lucius. "Leave through the secret passage behind my throne. It will take you near the spot where I told you to tether your horse." The emperor nodded to Satewa. "Let's drink. The traitors' attempted poisoning has been thwarted by my inept doctors. Lucius Bernius will be declared an enemy of the state within a few hours." He looked back at his young friend. "You better hurry and make the tide. The Praetorians and city guard will hunt you, and if you're caught, you'll be executed on the spot." Aetius embraced Lucius in a fierce hug. "For the sake of Rome."

Lucius hugged him back. "For the beauty of Rome that you have rekindled."

Satewa drained his cup. "To the success of our spy."

"And to the success of a truly noble Roman," added Aetius.

PRINCIPAL CHARACTERS

ROMANS

Valentinian III—Western Roman Emperor

Marcian—Eastern Roman Emperor

Zeno—Byzantine fleet commander, Marcian's son-in-law

Leo I—Pope

Flavius Aetius—Imperator (Commanding General) of Roman Forces in Gaul

Caecina Albinus—Legate (general) 1st Gallic Legion

Publius Heraclius—Imperial Chamberlain

Phokas—Imperial Physician

Verius Bernius—Roman Senator, resident of Mediolanum

Lucius Bernius—Son of Senator Bernius, Roman Tribune, new infantry

Julia Bernius—Daughter of Senator Bernius, resident of Mediolanum

Takumi Saegusa—Senator Bernius' bodyguard, from a distant island in the East

Marcus Carloman—Gallic Noble, Roman Tribune, new engineering officer

Satewa—Centurion, Aide to Imperator Aetius from a mystic island

Brenda—Aetius' housekeeper and wife to Satewa

Cilla—Decurion in roman Gallic Frontier Guard

Gentilius—Legionary recruit assigned to Gallic Frontier Guard

Vidin—Legionary recruit assigned to Gallic Frontier Guard

Petronius Maximus—Commander, Praetorian Guard

Seamus Conall—Celtic slave belonging to Publius Heraclius

Dervla Conall—Celtic slave belonging to Publius Heraclius

Unis Conall—Celtic slave belonging to Publius Heraclius

HUNS AND GERMANIC TRIBES

Attila—King of the Huns, scourge of Rome

Optila—Hun Captain

Valamir—King of the Ostrogoths

Genseric—Vandal King

Axise—Vandal war chief, cousin to Genseric

Merovech—King of the Franks

Martinel—Frankish Nobleman

Patricius—Frankish priest

Theodoric—Visigoth King

Thorismond—Visigoth prince, son of Theodoric

Braun—Visigoth swordmaster, friend of Thorismond

Sangiban—King of the Alans

AUTHOR'S NOTES

In our world, the Western Roman Empire came to an end in the year 476 when Odoacer proclaimed himself King of Italy. Flavius Aetius was successfully assassinated by Roman Emperor Valentinian on September 21, 454. The Vandals did sack Rome in the spring of 455. The Vandal fleet of captured Roman galleys went unchallenged in Ostia harbor. The Byzantines didn't have Greek fire as a weapon until the sixth century. The Vikings didn't have any recorded impact on Europe and North America until the eighth century. Father Patricius (St. Patrick) did work to convert the Celts in Hibernia (modern day Ireland) from following the Druids to Christianity in the mid-fifth century.

You've finished.

Please review this book on your favorite sites!

One of the ways for independent authors and small publishers to get exposure for their books is to receive as many honest, thoughtful reviews as possible.

Thanks in advance!

About the Author

John Caligiuri is a novelist with Guardian Tree Publishing, who has a lifelong passion for literature and pens primarily science fiction and fantasy. He blends his fascination with history and his professional background in software engineering to come up with some unusual story twists. His stories emerged from his curiosity about historical watershed events and asking, "what if."

Originally from Buffalo, New York, John lives in Rochester, New York with his wife, Linda. She's been married to him for over forty years and has supported his writing from the beginning. His children and grandchildren are scattered around the USA, which gives him and his wife an excellent excuse for their many road trips. For relaxation John enjoys gardening (which stretches his intellect, attempting to outwit the rabbits and deer) and distance running. He is a member of the Lilac City Rochester Writers, Greece Writers, and B&N (Greece) writing group.

John is an award-winning author who has published the Cocytus science fiction series: *Sanctuary in Hell, Planet of the Damned, Deal with the Devil and Face Ones Demons,* the alternative history novels, *The Red Fist of Rome,* and *The Last Roman's Prayer,* and numerous short stories. He can be contacted at

johndcaligiuri@gmail.com

For more information visit his website:

www.guardiantreepublishing.com

For new projects, John is working on a sequel to *Perdition's Angel* for the Novaroma science fiction series, and an anthology collection of his favorite short stories.